# KNIGHT AND DAY

### Gentlemen of Knights
### Book Three

# Elizabeth Johns

## ARE YOU SIGNED UP FOR DRAGONBLADE'S BLOG?

You'll get the latest news and information on exclusive giveaways, exclusive excerpts, coming releases, sales, free books, cover reveals and more.

Check out our complete list of authors, too!

No spam, no junk. That's a promise!

### Sign Up Here

www.dragonbladepublishing.com

*Dearest Reader;*

*Thank you for your support of a small press. At Dragonblade Publishing, we strive to bring you the highest quality Historical Romance from the some of the best authors in the business. Without your support, there is no 'us', so we sincerely hope you adore these stories and find some new favorite authors along the way.*

*Happy Reading!*

*CEO, Dragonblade Publishing*

# Additional Dragonblade books by Author Elizabeth Johns

## Gentlemen of Knights Series
Duke of Knight (Book 1)
Black Knight (Book 2)
Knight and Day (Book 3)

# PROLOGUE

E DMUND CLOSED THE door to the church after evensong, but did not lock it. He never locked it. He was proud of the reputation Saint Michael's had as a place of refuge, even if it was exhausting at times.

He had not even walked five feet from the entrance when there was a vicious pounding on the door. Edmund opened it to reveal a small urchin, who stood there panting.

"Are you Victor Knight?"

Edmund tried hard not to smile. "I am."

"Good, cause I 'ave a message fer ye from yer brother."

Edmund frowned. Only one brother was likely to deliver a message in such a fashion.

"Very well. Come in and have some food, and tell me all about it."

The little waif followed him inside, looking around as though something would jump out of the shadows and grab him. He clung close to Edmund as they walked through the now dark, Gothic nave to the vicarage.

Mrs. Lowe was in the kitchen and gave Edmund her usual look of dismay whenever he brought in a child or one of his "doves".

"What is your name, child?" Edmund asked as he indicated for him to take a seat at the table in the kitchen.

"Johnny."

Edmund nodded and took the seat next to him while Mrs. Lowe placed bowls of stew and slices of fresh bread in front of both of them.

"Can I tell ye my message now? I'm afraid I'll forget." The boy looked worried. He must be between eight and ten years old, Edmund thought. Street children were often malnourished and older than they looked.

"Of course."

The boy furrowed his dirty brow and thought for a moment, as though he had to recall every word perfectly. "'E said as there is a virgin auction at Madame Celeste's. 'E thought ye would want to know there is a lady there against 'er will."

Who *wasn't* there against their will? Edmund wanted to shout the words as he worked to control his temper. He had made it his life's work to help rescue women who were forced into prostitution unwillingly. But a lady?

"You are sure he said a lady?"

The boy nodded as he wiped his mouth with the back of his hand.

"Eat quickly and then you can take me to this place. Do you have a home, Johnny?"

The boy gave a little shrug as if he were embarrassed to answer.

Edmund did not press any further. After he had spent some time with the boy, he would bring the topic up again and discover if Johnny needed help. While he ate, Edmund went to shed his vestments for more suitable clothing and Mrs. Lowe packed a little sack of food for Johnny to take with him. A few minutes later, they headed out into the damp, cold night.

Edmund hailed a hackney and they both climbed in. "Did you walk all the way here, Johnny?"

He shook his head. "The toff put me in a hack like this. Said ye would feed me if I gave ye the message."

Heath knew him well. "You did well, lad." He tossed him a coin. "If you ever need help, you can always find it at Saint Michael's." The

2

boy was gone in a flash.

Edmund stood before the nondescript three-story wooden house that looked much like the others on the street. He had been here before, and a feeling of evil washed over him. Saying a quick prayer for strength and protection, Edmund climbed the steps and knocked on the door. Two large ruffians were guarding the entrance. He handed one of them his card—the one which proclaimed him Lord Edmund Knight. They looked him over and, clearly seeing just a well-dressed, arrogant young lord, nodded their approval. They stood aside for him to pass, and he followed the noise to the main drawing room.

The room was overheated and smelled of sweat, smoke, and spirits. It was dark except for the chandelier above a center dais, where a beautiful young woman stood. She was garbed like a harem girl, in nothing more than a tiny bandeau covering her chest and a nearly transparent skirt with slits up either side revealing long legs. Wavy russet locks flowed down her back, drawing attention to her shape. The girl wore a mask, but it did nothing to hide her beauty—or her fear. Edmund's blood boiled with anger. Was this the lady?

The auction was already in progress, as shouts of otherworldly amounts of money sailed through the room.

"Five thousand guineas!" someone shouted across the crowd.

"Eight!" another countered.

Was he too late? Edmund's heart sank. Spying his brother, Heath, across the crowded room, Edmund began pushing his way through the engrossed men.

"It took you long enough," Heath said into Edmund's ear when he reached his brother's side.

Edmund did not bother to reply to that. "Is this the one?"

Heath nodded. "There have been others, but she is the main attraction."

Edmund wanted to retch. "It appears we are too late, then."

"Ten thousand guineas." The bidding war was still going.

"I will distract the winner," Heath said. "They will take her to a room at the back of the house, where there is a door to the alley. If you can get to her before they do…"

Edmund nodded as he looked around the room. Lord Emerson was near Madame Celeste, smiling greedily as the amounts reached exorbitant proportions. Someone was going to be very, very angry if Edmund was successful. Who was this girl?

Lord Wethersby shouted, "Twenty-five thousand guineas!" and the room fell to silence. No one else spoke as Wethersby walked forward and ran his hand down the girl's arm. Edmund wanted to retch again when he saw her flinch. Wethersby cackled with laughter.

"Going once, going twice? Sold to Wethersby for twenty-five thousand guineas!" Madame Celeste shouted.

The men patted Wethersby on the back with congratulations as the madam led the girl away. Edmund looked at Heath and nodded.

Crossing the likes of Emerson and Wethersby was as good as a death sentence.

"If you are going, do it now," Heath warned.

Edmund slipped out with a group of men who were leaving since the auction was over. They were heavily intoxicated, so it was not difficult for him to sneak, unobserved, behind the house to the alley.

What Edmund was not fully prepared for was the guard standing at the back door. Falsehoods had never been easy for Edmund, but this was for a good cause. He put on his most bored face and hoped the guard was unaware of the identity of the man who had won the final auction.

He strolled up to the guard with as much hauteur as he could muster. "I am here to fetch my winnings," he drawled.

"Where is your carriage?" the guard asked, narrowing his eyes.

"My driver is bringing it around. I wanted to get my hands on my prize as soon as possible," Edmund said with a knowing wink to the guard. He pulled out a few gold coins.

The guard grunted appreciatively and then turned to unlock the door.

Edmund hoped his luck would continue when he saw the frightened girl sitting in the corner, shaking. She watched him warily as he quickly removed his coat.

"Who are you?"

He held his finger to his mouth. "I am here to rescue you. Hurry," he whispered with urgency.

She took his hand and he wrapped his coat around her before ushering her from the holding room and on down the dark alley. He prayed silently that he could hail a hackney cab quickly before anyone noticed the girl was gone. Instead, his brother's carriage was waiting for them. "Hurry, my lord," the driver said, indicating that Heath had indeed intended him to use it.

Edmund wished his profligate brother would show this side of himself to the rest of the world instead of maintaining an image as a complete wastrel. He bundled the girl inside and closed the door and the carriage set off immediately.

"Are you unharmed?" he asked the shivering girl.

"Wh-who are you?" she asked through chattering teeth.

"My name is Edmund Knight. I am a vicar and I try to help girls like you."

"This happens often?"

"More often than I would like to recount," he answered softly.

"Where are you taking me? If my father finds me, he will kill me."

"If Lord Wethersby realizes what I have done, he will kill *me*," Edmund countered. "What is your name?"

"Isabella."

"I do not think you understand. My f-f-father sold me."

To Lord Wethersby, one of Lord Emerson's cronies, Edmund thought with disgust. Of late, his brother Heath had been frequently associated with the same disreputable lord. Hoping his reflections were not revealed in his face, Edmund nodded. He understood perfectly.

"My father lost his fortune in a card game," she spat angrily, her teeth no longer chattering at least. "He thought to recover some of it by selling me for one night and then marrying me off with no one the wiser."

The hairs on the back of Edmund's neck were beginning to rise. He had a feeling that this girl was no mere lady.

"I appreciate what you were trying to do for me, but if you do not take me back, my father will do something terrible to us both."

Edmund shook his head vehemently. "Do you mean to tell me you are willing?" He wondered if the girl had been used in such a way before.

"Of course not! But you do not understand my father."

"It does not matter. My brother is a powerful man. He will help me protect you."

"You would take me to the ends of the earth?" she asked doubtfully.

Edmund had a feeling he might be willing to do just that, but for now he would do the next best thing.

"No, but I will take you to the ends of England."

The carriage pulled up at the back door of the vicarage and they went inside.

Mrs. Lowe was waiting for them. "Where to with this one, sir?"

"We must leave with haste. I will be gone for some time." Edmund cast a quick look at the girl. "I think it is time to visit the family seat."

A small whistle escaped Mrs. Lowe's lips before she nodded. "You will be needing lots of blankets and food, then. Come with me, I will find you some clothes. You cannot be wearin' that where you're going, dearie," she said as she led the terrified girl away.

Edmund shook his head, then set about packing and arranging for a post-chaise for the long journey to Devon. His brother, the Duke of Knighton, would take this girl in and shelter her—even if reluctantly. Knighton wore a hard outer shell, but would always help when Edmund asked. There was nowhere else Edmund could take her where she might be protected from the dangerous web she was entangled in.

When she came downstairs, Edmund was hard-pressed not to stare. Even dressed in a servant's garb of drab grey, a mobcap covering her hair, she was stunning. Her eyes were of varying shades of blue that made him think of a stormy sky. Despite her demure appearance, it would be hard not to imagine Isabella as he had seen her only a short time ago.

Thankfully, most people would see her as a governess or the sister of a vicar. It would probably be the best way to hide her.

Soon, they were packed into a traveling coach and on their way. Isabella slept for most of the journey, and they only stopped to change horses and tend to the necessities. Edmund could not imagine what she had been through while fearing what was going to happen to her. Even when she was awake, she spoke little and stared out of the window.

"I think it would be best if you did not use your real name or any name that your father might recognize."

She nodded her head and looked as though she was thinking. "My family calls me Bella."

"I think the easiest way to hide you would be to find you a position in my brother's household. I know it is unlikely, but do you have any talent for sewing, cooking, or cleaning?"

"I can do embroidery, but I do not know if that would be helpful." She twisted her mouth and thought. "Cook used to let me help her when I was small and left at the house alone. I used to sneak down to the kitchens when my nurse was napping." She smiled a little sheepishly.

By God, she was beautiful. It was no wonder Wethersby had paid several fortunes to have her. Even if Wethersby's intentions had been honorable, Edmund did not know if he could bear to let him have her. As it was, Wethersby was a lecher and already married, even if his wife was reported to be an invalid.

"Perhaps the kitchen would be the safest place for you." Most other positions would be visible to any guests, though Rowley did not host large house parties often due to the distance from London and his dislike of them in general.

"Miss Thatcher. I think that is what I would like to be called."

"Very well. You know best."

Once the eternal trip to Devonshire ended and they arrived at his family's estate, he alighted and showed Miss Thatcher to the kitchen to wait while he went to speak with his brother, the duke. He hated asking his brother for favors, but in this, he had no choice.

"Rowley!" Edmund said as he stopped, midway though pacing across the carpet when he realized his brother had come in the room.

"Edmund, to what do I owe the pleasure? Something tells me it is not a brotherly visit?"

Rarely did Edmund leave his parish unless it was to assist one of his "doves". "I need your help."

"What, or should I say who, is it this time?" Rowley drawled in that arrogant manner he had when he felt put upon. "You know I will help as best I can, but for practical purposes you are like to find more success by appealing to Cummins."

"Normally, yes." Edmund was frequently asking his brother's secretary for help. Rowley had a way of making them all feel like small children. He leaned back against his desk and crossed his arms and one leg over the other simultaneously. He did not bother to speak. "This particular person might be looked for. I was hoping there might be a place for her here at the Grange."

"Doing what, precisely?"

Edmund almost sighed. Rowley was softening.

"She is not afraid to work, Rowley, but she is deathly afraid of being found. I would not feel comfortable leaving her elsewhere, but I cannot keep her in London." He *hoped* she was not afraid to work. Edmund would not mention she had no experience.

"Who, pray tell, is she running from? And will I be expected to provide a nursery in the next few months?" Rowley asked.

"Unless she has greatly deceived me, I believe I saved her before she was defiled."

"Good Lord, Edmund! You speak as though she is a lady."

She was.

"If I had it my way, all females would be treated as such. Simply look to how God protected Rahab in the book of Joshua, for example."

"Yes, yes." Rowley held up his hands. "I am certain there is somewhere we can hide your latest dove."

"Thank you, Row," Edmund said, and embraced him heartily.

"Where is the girl?"

"I left her in the kitchen with Cook. She was too afraid to go elsewhere."

"Will you stay awhile?"

"I think I will stay a few days to make certain Miss Thatcher is situated in her new position."

"Find Mrs. Haynes and tell her to prepare a room for your girl. Once she has had some time to recover from her fright we can discuss what to do with her."

"You are the best of brothers, Row. I knew you would help." Edmund cast him a grateful smile and left the study to inform the girl of the good news. She should be safe here as long as she never left the estate.

# CHAPTER ONE

*Eighteen months later...*

EDMUND FELT AS though a weight had been eased from his chest as the family bid farewell to the newly wedded couple. Being able to marry his brother Heath and Cecilia in the proper way, after their rocky beginning, had lifted the burden on his soul considerably. Performing the ceremony for them, and witnessing their undisguised affection for each other, had been solace to his soul.

"Be happy," he said to Cecilia, dropping a goodbye kiss on her cheek.

"I intend to. Thank you, Edmund."

Heath shook his elder brother's hand, but it was obvious he was impatient to be gone. The family waved as the carriage departed; once it was out of sight, they returned, laughing merrily, to finish the small feast.

It gladdened his heart to be sitting around the table, all together again. In one year, Rowley and Heath had both found love matches. Edmund had once thought that would not be possible for either of them. They even appeared to be mending their differences. Heath had taken Rowley to see the Dower House and tenant farm which Heath had renovated as a safe place for Edmund's rescued men, women, and children. Could a man of the cloth be happier?

Even little George, Rowley's son, had been present for the ceremony and the breakfast, but he was now beginning to fuss.

Suddenly, Eugenia let out a shriek.

"Mouse!"

Soon the mouse was being chased by a hound—who knew Heath even had a dog?—followed by Jeremy and then Doris, wielding a broom.

"Come here, you little rat!" the servant girl cried, batting the air as she ran.

"Heel, Jasper! Heel!" The footman, Jeremy, commanded the dog with apologetic glances at the gathering, who watched with stunned amusement. Rowley, never one *not* to be obeyed and noticing his son's cries, immediately told the dog to sit. It obeyed, and looked at him with a foolish expression of hero-worship. Jeremy took the hound away, and Doris, one of the maids, chased the mouse from the room, but Edmund was further distracted by something else.

George's nurse came quietly into the room as if she had been waiting by the door. Felix was laughing at something their grandmother had said—she grew more outrageous every year—but something familiar struck Edmund. He looked up to see his intuition was not wrong. It was *her*. Despite her servant's costume and her mobcap, he would know those eyes and high cheekbones anywhere.

"Why the devil is she here?" Edmund said, in an uncharacteristic display of humanness.

Felix laughed. "How it warms my soul to hear you speak thus, Edmund."

"It is warranted in this case. It is when you throw oaths around like pennies at a fair that they lose their effect. Will you excuse me?"

"Of course," Felix said, looking rather amused.

Edmund began to hurry from the room, trying not to draw attention to his quarry, but following her nonetheless up to the nursery.

He watched as she patted the baby's back and bounced it lightly on her shoulder to put him to sleep. She had a natural way with children that immediately touched Edmund's heart, but how could she risk being seen like this? Granted, they were miles from anywhere here in the Kent countryside, he tried to reason, but if she were found, the consequences were unthinkable.

He continued to watch as the nurse hummed and rocked little George. Eventually, the baby was sufficiently asleep for him to be placed in the cradle. Edmund stepped into the room and quietly said her name. He did not wish to frighten her.

"Miss Thatcher?"

She jumped anyway, but muffled her exclamation. "Vicar, what are you doing up here?"

"I could ask the same of you. You should not have left the Grange."

She pointed to an adjoining sitting room. "His lordship is a light sleeper during the day," she whispered.

Edmund followed Miss Thatcher, hoping there was a good explanation. How could he help people if they would not help themselves?

"I thought you were to work in the kitchens. I explained to you how dangerous it would be if you were found."

"I do not need you to tell me," she said with a hint of defiance. "However, Their Graces needed my help and reassured me that they could keep me safe. My duties never take me away from the house or grounds."

"There is no one else who can be a nursemaid?" he asked in disbelief.

"I can settle him better than anyone except His Grace." She raised her chin, daring him to contradict her.

Edmund ran his hand through his hair. "Perhaps I am overreacting."

"I promise I am being careful. If I go out with the duchess in the carriage, I will keep my bonnet down low. People only see what they expect to see," she said.

"But I recognized you immediately," he argued. "I could not live with myself if I allowed something to happen to you."

"As long as my father never finds me, I should be safe," she remarked derisively.

"Lord Wethersby is also still a threat," he warned. "I had hoped he would move on to new pastures when you went missing, but he seems to have a hold over your father."

"Yes, I fear he does. Me."

Edmund narrowed his gaze. "I think it is time I found out the rest of your story—or are you content to live the remainder of your life in hiding?" He was still amazed that no uproar had been made over the missing girl from the auction or the fact that Lady Isabella Hartmere had disappeared. He had soon discovered who she was. A cup of coffee and a few minutes with his Debrett's Peerage, plus a little deduction, and he was quite certain that she was the daughter of the Duke of Frompton. It was no secret that he and Wethersby had become estranged.

"I think anything would be preferable to being sold. The duke and duchess are very good to me. And little George is an angel."

Edmund smiled at that. He was rather fond of his nephew, too. Nevertheless, he thought, something did not quite fit with Miss Thatcher's story.

"Did Wethersby know it was you he was bidding for?"

"I do not know how he could have known. But my father owed him a very large sum of money, so it was rather ironic that it was he who bid a fortune for me."

Edmund felt his jaw clench when he remembered that dreadful night. "I wish I knew how to make it safe for you to be yourself again."

She shook her head, a resigned look on her face. "I do not think it is possible as long as my father lives."

"What is the feud between your father and Wethersby?" Edmund asked, hoping to find the root of the evil and perhaps an idea of how to help this girl.

"My mother. A tale as old as time, I am afraid. She was promised to Wethersby and then married my father."

"He was betrayed."

"He felt that he was. And then the feud spilled into every aspect of their lives—especially politics."

"Their arguments in the Lords are infamous."

"Yes. So you see why I have little hope of returning to my old life. Father's behavior became untenable after he lost that vast sum to Wethersby. Why he agreed to play against him, I cannot fathom."

Edmund was quite sure it had to do with taunting and male pride. "Why keep your disappearance a secret? There has been no gossip about your absence."

"Pride, I have no doubt. However, it will not be long until it becomes known."

Edmund looked at her curiously.

"If Father does not repay Wethersby by my twenty-first birthday, he owes him me."

Edmund was trying to assimilate this level of depravity. "So that was why he decided to sell your virtue. Forgive my frank speaking."

"Of course. If he had to give me to Wethersby, at least I would be soiled goods."

"But Wethersby would have had the last laugh. It is almost as if he knew, except that such immoral conduct is nothing out of the common way for some."

"So you see, I cannot go back to my old way of life. Even if I could, I would rather die than be given to Wethersby or see my father again!"

Edmund could hardly blame her. "How long is it until your birthday?"

"One month."

"That gives us one month to come up with a fortune or find you another husband."

"Or hope that my father and Wethersby die."

"I pray we may find a better solution, but do be careful. I fear your situation just became eminently more dangerous."

THE NEXT DAY, everyone removed to London. There was a bill the duke wished to vote on in Parliament, so naturally, Isabella went along with the family too. She had not returned to London since that fateful night her father had thought to bargain with the devil. How naive she had been when he had finally invited her to go to London! She had always dreamed of what the big city would be like, but how quickly those dreams had been destroyed. Once upon a time, he had been kind to her. Then he fell deep into debt and his obsession with destroying Wethersby consumed him. What kind of man would sell his own daughter in order to best his enemy? It did not bear thinking of.

While on the way to the auction, she had thought she was going to the theater. Dreams of London Seasons and a good marriage had filled her head. Yet when her father had handed her out of the carriage that night, in a dark alley, reality would have been welcome when compared to what she had faced.

Her father had not even apologized. Madame Celeste had met them inside the back room of the brothel, where her father had explained brusquely, "This is how it has to be, Bella. It is only one time and then you will be able to marry as you wish."

Isabella had not even understood what he meant. He had walked out of the door and left her there with Madame, an older woman who looked as though she had been beautiful at one time. Now, she was weathered and painted and reeked of perfume.

"What is happening?" Isabella turned to ask Madame Celeste, who was eyeing her as though she were buying a horse.

"All you have to do is stand there. Try not to look like a frightened puppy. If you fetch a high enough price, it will only take the once."

"The once?" Isabella whispered, though she thought she under-stood.

"When it is over, the winner will come to fetch you and take you upstairs. That will not take long, either," the older woman cackled. "Then I will send you home with no one the wiser, and your pater and I a whole lot richer."

"I do not understand!" Isabella protested.

"Understanding is not necessary. Your father is under the hatches and this is the only way to come about."

"No! How could he?" she cried.

"Easily. It happens all the time. Now, we must get you changed. You are on in a few minutes." Madame Celeste began to unbutton the back of Isabella's gown and she clung tight to the bodice in protest.

"Do not make me force you. I have my ways, you know. This is not my first time." She laughed at her pun as though she was enjoying Isabella's pain. "Most girls have to stay here and don't have the option to go home. You should consider yourself lucky."

Tears streamed down Isabella's face as the woman near ripped the sleeves from her gown. "People might recognize me later."

"Not with a mask on, they won't. Now, stop that caterwauling. A blotched face will not help your price."

Isabella hoped no one would want her. That would serve her fa-ther right.

She continued to fight, but the older and larger woman simply ripped Isabella's shift from her body, wrapped a small, transparent confection around her chest and tied an equally immodest skirt over her lower half. Celeste pulled the pins from Isabella's hair and brushed out her long curls before tying a mask over the upper half of her face.

She had then been led like a cow to slaughter and been made to stand before a crowd of leering men. She would never forget the faces or names of those who had ogled her and bid on her as if she were a slave. When the vicar had arrived, it had almost been too late!

Thankfully, young George awoke from his nap, babbling sweetly and playing with his toes, before she could revisit her humiliation and anger with her father. She wished for his death daily, and feared that if she saw him again, she would kill him with her own hands. Not a night went by that when she was free from that dreadful event in her sleep. Whenever she allowed herself thoughts of retribution, she would always stop herself as she held a knife to her father's throat. She could not go through with it even in her subconscious.

Walking over to the baby's cot, she bent over to pick him up. He smiled at the sight of her and reached his hands up to her.

"Sweet Master George," she cooed. "Are you ready to visit Papa and Mama?"

In answer he blew some bubbles in a gurgling noise.

Isabella put fresh clothes on the little earl and then took him downstairs for his afternoon playtime with his parents.

However, when Isabella reached the bottom step, she heard a familiar voice. She halted, as though turned instantly to a block of ice.

"We must pass this bill. Can I be assured of your vote, Knighton?" Her father's voice boomed from the duke's study, sending tremors of fear up her spine. Isabella would have to walk by the study in order to reach the drawing room. She did not know if she could do it. The chances of being seen and recognized were next to nothing, but any chance was too much. What would he do to her? Would the duke and duchess even believe her if she told them? They would be bound, by law, to turn her over to her father. Then where would she be?

George pulled at her cap and made another gurgling noise. The duke appeared in the doorway, looking out into the hall.

"Ah, there is my son. Bring him in here to meet my guest, Miss Thatcher."

Presumably hearing, the duchess then came out of the drawing room. Isabella tried not to panic but she shook her head and handed the baby to the duchess.

Her Grace must have sensed something was wrong. "Go," she whispered. Isabella turned and fled back to the nursery.

Where was she to go now? The duke and duchess would not want her to stay here, and she could hardly ask them to hide her any longer. She paced about and fretted while watching out of the window for a glimpse of her father leaving. It was another hour of agony before she finally saw him climb into his carriage. It was a startling sight. Only a quick glimpse was enough to show her he looked haggard. The hair she could see under his beaver hat was now completely silver, and his face was wearied with wrinkles and worry. *It serves him right*, she thought bitterly.

There was only one month left until her birthday. What would happen to her father then? Had he even looked for her? Or had he found an alternative way to pay Wethersby off?

A light knock on the door brought the duchess and the baby. Isabella knew her escape and place of refuge was coming to an end.

The duchess picked up George's favorite teething coral with a silver ring and sat down with him in her lap. Isabella watched warily, but saw no signs of judgement in the lady's face.

"Will you sit with me?"

Isabella nodded and sat nervously on the edge of the chair opposite the duchess.

"I think you had better tell me who you are now, or else we will not be able to help you. I confess I had forgotten about your past and why you came to us in the first place. It was apparent you were unsuited to be a servant when you arrived, timid and frightened, but you soon took to George and now you feel like a part of the family. But you are a lady, are you not?"

Isabella could only nod again as she tried to blink back the moisture in her eyes.

"Would you please tell me about it?" the duchess asked kindly.

"I am afraid you will be obliged to send me back. What happened is unfathomable."

The beautiful duchess made a face. "Oh, I think not. If Edmund felt it necessary to hide you, I imagine you had just cause for running away. But you would be wise to tell me the whole so Knighton and I are prepared, come what may."

Isabella looked into the duchess' earnest, moss-colored eyes and sighed. "Very well, but burdening you with the knowledge was never my intent. From the beginning, I swore to myself I would leave if my situation ever became known. I had not realized the duke was acquainted with my father, but I should have known."

"Frompton is your father?"

Isabella nodded and felt her composure slip. The duchess reached over and took one of her hands, but waited for Isabella to speak.

"He tried to sell me at an auction, to pay his debts."

The duchess let out an unexpected oath under her breath. "We will return to the Grange in two days. I will warn Knighton not to invite your father here again, but you must keep to the house and garden. Your father's house is just across the square."

Isabella was astonished; just like that, the duchess believed her? "Do you not want to know the rest of the story?"

"It will all come out in time, I have no doubt. For now, we must keep you safe until we can think of how to handle the situation. You cannot hide forever."

"If I can hide for one more month, at least, I will be grateful."

The duchess gave her a curious look, but nodded.

# CHAPTER TWO

EDMUND COULD NOT stop thinking about Isabella on his way back
to London. He could not think of her as Miss Thatcher, even
though it was dangerous not to. When in London, he began to make
discreet inquiries. Rowley had mentioned he was returning to London
in order to vote on a controversial bill, and it was likely Frompton and
Wethersby would be there as well.

He argued with himself frequently over whether or not to tell his
brother about his nursemaid. Matters were bound to come to a head
between Frompton and Wethersby over the matter of Isabella. As a
duke, Rowley was more likely to hear gossip in his clubs if he put forth
the effort to attend one. Heath had been Edmund's eyes and ears in
the underworld as Rowley was in the fashionable one. But would it be
a betrayal of Isabella's trust to inform His Grace? It had been one thing
to keep the secret when she was in the wilds of Devon, but quite
another if she was to be in London.

Now he was back at Saint Michael's, Edmund had many duties to
catch up on. In a poor parish there was always more to do than write
sermons. In fact, sermons were typically written in haste the night
before services. He had always felt he could do more good by his
actions than his words. Parishioners who attended services were not
the ones he needed to convince of God's grace and mercy. In the
slums, a hot meal and shelter spoke to souls faster than did any

recitation of scripture.

He opened the back door to the vicarage to be greeted with the smell of fresh baked bread and a warm smile from Mrs. Lowe.

"Welcome home, Vicar," she greeted him. "There's a visitor waiting for you in the drawing room. I was about to take some tea to him."

Edmund smiled and gave his longtime housekeeper a kiss on the cheek, which always made her blush. The last thing he wanted to do was greet a visitor, but it was his duty and so he shook off his travel dirt and washed his hands and face before going to the drawing room.

A ruddy-faced gentleman with frizzled grey hair turned when Edmund entered the room.

"I am the vicar, how may I assist you?"

"I am Ned Smallbone, sir, from the Bow Street Runners."

Edmund raised his brows as if in surprise. This was not the first visit he had had from an investigator, nor, he suspected, would it be the last. There were rumors that he was the one who helped prostitutes and orphans escape, but his poor parishioners protected him. No one would dare speak his name aloud as long as they benefited from his generosity.

"Will you have a seat?" Edmund invited his visitor as Mrs. Lowe brought in the tea tray.

"Don't mind if I do," the older man said, and sighed in relief as he sat on the edge of an armchair. "It is a lot of long hours on me feet, chasin' after people," he added.

Mrs. Lowe poured the tea and handed each of them a plate of sandwiches.

"Thank you, ma'am," the runner said to the housekeeper with a wink.

Edmund watched with interest until Mrs. Lowe left the room. "What may I do for you, Mr. Smallbone?"

"I can be assured of yer discretion, sir? You being a vicar an' all?"

"Of course," Edmund agreed. Almost every person asked him that question.

The man nodded, as if it was just as he had expected. "I am investigating a missing girl. Unfortunately, she has been gone for more than a year, but her family thought to hush it up. Now they are becomin' desperate."

"Why the urgency after so long? I assume the trail will be quite cold?" Edmund asked, though he knew exactly who the man was looking for. His sandwich suddenly felt like a brick in his stomach.

"Indeed it will be difficult, although not impossible. I have yet to solve such a case in all me years," the man stated.

That was what Edmund was afraid of.

"Ye see…" The man leaned forward as if to impart a great secret. "… I have heard as how ye help rescue unfortunates."

"I do what I can to serve the needy," Edmund answered carefully.

"But ye do more than that, and we both know it." The man winked at him. That was becoming an annoying habit of his.

"Who is the girl? I will need to know as much as you can tell me if I am to help you."

"The father doesn't wish for me to divulge names if possible. It is likely she would not tell ye her real name anyhow."

"Perhaps not," Edmund agreed. "A description, then?"

"A real beauty," the man said as he pulled out a sketch of Isabella.

Edmund kept his face impassive. "I would remember a face like that had I seen it," he answered cautiously, trying not to lie. "What were the circumstances of her disappearance?"

Edmund could tell that the investigator was debating how much to divulge. It was obvious he knew exactly what had happened.

"The girl 'ad been taken, by mistake, to an auction at Madame Celeste's. Ye were there that night with yer brother, Lord Heath."

Of course, Edmund had left his card. "I was at one some time ago."

"Ye don't seem like the type, but I 'ave heard of stranger things." The man shrugged.

"I was not there looking for services. My brother thought some of the girls were being forced to participate against their will."

"And were they?" the man asked with a keen gaze.

Edmund frowned. "I was too late. The auction ended moments after I arrived."

"This girl was the last one. 'Appen you might look again? Jog your memory?"

The man slid the sketch back in front of him—as if Edmund did not have every detail of Isabella's face memorized.

Edmund shook his head. "Her face was covered, though I doubt many noticed, with her lack of clothing—if you catch my meaning. I do recall Lord Wethersby won the bidding with an exorbitant sum. After that, I left."

The runner snatched back the sketch and stuffed it into his coat pocket.

"Have you questioned Wethersby? I would assume he was the last one to see her," Edmund suggested.

The man snorted. "He claims 'e never touched the girl. Says she was taken 'fore he could get his paws on her." The man stood to leave, but handed Edmund his dog-eared card. "If ye 'appen to remember anything else, please send for me. Sometimes details you think 'nsignificant can be jus' the clue I need to solve the mystery."

"I will give it due thought," Edmund assured the man. "After all this time I hope she is alive and well. I see a lot of bad things happen to young women in my line of work."

The man took his hat and coat from the side-table near the front door. "Don't think I'm not mindful of the work ye do, Vicar. Most of us are aware ye an' your brothers brought down Lord Emerson."

Edmund gave a tiny nod of acknowledgment. That was best kept quiet.

"The word at Bow Street is that someun' powerful like Wethersby has taken over where Emerson left off, though." The man shook his head. "It would not surprise me to know he 'ad done somethin' with the girl, but I say too much. A thorough investigation will get to the truth," he said, as if to reassure himself.

"Indeed. I assure you I will let you know if I hear anything at all."

"I need not remind ye, coming from the family ye do, that the utmost discretion is required?"

"Completely unnecessary," Edmund said placatingly.

Edmund waved the man on his way before closing the door and leaning against it. He banged his head on it once for good measure, but the pain did not clear his head. Isabella was in more danger than he had thought if her father had enlisted the help of the Runners.

"Is aught amiss?" Mrs. Lowe asked as she walked back along the hall to fetch the tea tray.

"I am afraid so," he said with a heavy sigh. "Do you remember the girl I took to the Grange?"

"How could I forget, the poor soul," Mrs. Lowe replied. "What kind of trouble could she be in, out in Devonshire?"

"That is the problem. She is here in London, at my brother's house. And her father is looking for her."

Mrs. Lowe scowled. "That good-for-nothing scoundrel is just now looking for her, what, over a year later?"

"I am sure he *has* been looking for her, but now he is desperate and that means she is in danger. There is only one thing I can do. I must tell Knighton the whole. He may be the only one who can help."

"Then away with you, sir." Mrs. Lowe made a shooing motion. "The new curate is doing an admirable job and will keep on doing, I am sure."

"Yes, madam," Edmund made his beloved housekeeper a royal bow and then left to seek the duke's help.

ISABELLA HAD BEEN unable to sleep except in short, distressful spurts. Knowing her father was so close and that her birthday was less than a month away made her eager to leave London. Grateful though she was that the duchess had supported her without a full explanation, she did not wish to cause any harm to her wonderful employers. They had treated her as more than a servant and she loved little George with all her heart.

She threw back the covers to her bed and gave up on sleep, knowing it was useless. She tidied her hair and pinched her cheeks, but was aware nothing would take away the dark circles under her eyes until this was resolved. Isabella was no coward, and she was willing to confront her father if only she knew it would have a good resolution. But she had little money at the moment and she did not believe the amount left for her in trust by her grandmother would be enough to settle her father's debts. Their name would soon be ruined, and of course, it was not her fault. Why, then, did she feel so much guilt?

There was a knock on her door. Isabella frowned. No one ever knocked. She placed her cap on her head before she opened the door to see one of the footmen.

"His Grace requests your presence in his study, miss."

Had the duchess been unable to convince the duke to help her? Isabella's heart sank. She walked down the stairs with a deep sense of foreboding. Surely he would tell her before he informed her father. Would he be there? She began to shake with fear as she followed the servant.

"Do you know if he is alone?" she asked.

"I could not say, miss." He put his hand out as if to open the door.

"Wait!" She shook her head. "I need a minute. You may go."

She was a coward, but she needed to know if her father was in there. Nervously she waited, hoping to hear voices. The front door was nearby, but where would she go if she ran away?

"Miss Thatcher?" Isabella jumped. "I did not mean to frighten you," the duchess said. "Did His Grace also ask you to come down? Edmund is here and wishes to speak with you."

Isabella felt herself relax.

The duchess took her hand. "We will not betray you, you have my word. That was your fear, was it not? You thought your father was here?"

Isabella nodded. "I am sorry. I did not know if His Grace felt as you do."

"Come. You may see for yourself." She opened the door and Isabella followed her inside. Both brothers rose to their feet.

Isabella was tempted to run into the vicar's arms. He was her refuge and comfort, even if he did not know it. A truer hero there could never be, in her eyes. Before, when he had rescued her, she had barely registered his physical beauty so numb was she from her pain. Now, not only was she aware of his kindness, but his almost indecent handsomeness for a man of the cloth. She wondered devilishly how many of his parishioners were there to ogle instead of worship. At times when he would visit, she would steal glimpses at every opportunity. When lonely, she would spend her time daydreaming of him and what their life might be like together if things had been different.

"Lady Isabella." He made a bow. "I am pleased to see you looking well."

She looked back and forth nervously, but made a curtsy to the vicar and the duke. "And I you, sir."

"Please have a seat," the duke said. "My wife has brought your situation to my attention. I understand why you kept your identity a secret. In fact, I avoided asking because I did not want to know. It does put me in a difficult situation, as you know; your father is one of my colleagues."

Isabella swallowed hard and inclined her head.

"However, I have become apprised of the circumstances surrounding your departure from London and I will not give you away."

"Thank you, Your Grace," she said barely above a whisper.

"I am astonished and, frankly, disgusted," he continued. "I do not come to London often, but even so I am aware of the animosity between your father and Wethersby."

"You mentioned you were promised to Wethersby if your father had not repaid his debt by your twenty-first birthday," Edmund stated.

"Yes, my lord."

"I had a visit from a Bow Street Runner earlier today. He had traced my presence back to Madame Celeste's on the night you disappeared. He suspects me of having come to your aid. Due to my reputation, he said."

Isabella gasped. "Then I must leave! I could not live with myself if any harm came to you for helping me."

"It is too late for that, Lady Isabella," the duke interrupted. "You are under my protection and we will not abandon you to your fate. We will leave for Devonshire as soon as I have voted tomorrow."

Isabella did not know how to express her gratitude. It was no small thing they were doing for her—now in full knowledge of her circumstances.

"Thank you, Your Grace. If I can attain my birthday, then perhaps the situation will resolve itself." She no more believed her words then they did.

"I will try to discover more about the details of what is owed to Wethersby, but for now I believe distance will be the best protection. And though I am loth to continue treating you as a servant, I feel it would be best to keep your identity unknown to the household as well."

"I agree wholeheartedly, Your Grace. I am more than happy to be George's nurse."

The stern duke smiled one of his rare smiles. He turned to his brother. "Will you join me for dinner at White's? Perhaps together we can uncover some of the pieces to this mystery."

"Please be careful, both of you. I could never forgive myself if something happened to you."

Edmund smiled at her and she had to avert her eyes to keep from blushing. This was no silly matter, but she could not help but be warmed by his presence.

"Will you take a turn about the garden with me, Lady Isabella? I think it should be safe there."

"As long as you remember to call me Miss Thatcher," she warned with a smile.

"Of course." He opened the door and followed her to the walled gardens behind the house.

"I have given a great deal of thought to your situation," he said as he walked, with his hands behind his back, alongside her. The stone path, lined by a manicured hedge, led to a fountain surrounded by lush plants full of blooms in pinks, yellows and purples. Bees flitted from flower to flower as the fragrance wafted through the air. It would be easy to forget her problems in such a setting. Wandering around the garden was one thing she missed about her old home. It had been a fairy-tale life, up until the moment it ended. Or so she had always thought. Looking back, perhaps there were small details she had missed because she was not looking for them. She *had* been left alone in the country, and her parents rarely visited.

"Is there anything at all that you can remember about your family which might help? Anything about the feud? Do you have any siblings?"

They stopped in front of a white stone bench and sat down.

"I do not know what would help. I have spent the last eighteen months trying to think of a way in which I might be myself again...yet I always come back to the question: would I want to go back? My father betrayed me, yet I have to hide."

"What about the rest of your family? Do you not miss them?"

"Of course I do, but no one will stand up to my father. My brothers have their own families and rarely visit. My mother stays in Town with father. He dare not let her out of his sight."

She could see Edmund was having difficulty understanding. She had seen the love his family had for one another. She had not been unhappy with her solitary life at Hartmere, but she was equally happy as George's maid. Isabella realized now that she was simply a commodity to her father. Her two older brothers were already married, and they had never been particularly close due to their age disparity. It would surprise her if they even knew she was missing. Father had always kept her in the country, and no one would question otherwise.

"There has to be something we can do," he said.

"I appreciate that you care and that you wish to help me, but there is nothing to be done, I fear. After my birthday, I will try to look into the trust my grandmother left for me. For all I know, my father has found a way to get his hands on that, too. I hold no illusions that anyone would wish to marry me in these circumstances, either—not once they know who I am, anyway."

"Isabella."

She looked up into the dark, kind eyes and his handsome face and knew what unpleasant sacrifice he was contemplating. How she wished things were different, but their lives were as different as night and day. She was touched that his honor compelled him to even consider her, but a vicar could not afford to marry a ruined woman, no matter how powerful his brother might be.

"Please, Lord Edmund. Do not offer for me out of pity. I could not bear it." She rose and walked away before she agreed to something they would both regret.

# CHAPTER THREE

EDMUND WAS SULKING in the house when he heard his brother, Felix, and sister, Eugenia, return from an outing in the park. It would be childish to withdraw now. He glanced at Rowley, who gave a brief shake of his head.

"Edmund!" Eugenia exclaimed as she strode into the room while unlacing an extraordinarily gaudy scarlet bonnet topped with flowers, plumes and a bird, that was not apparently designed to match any dress he had ever seen. "I did not know you were here or we would have returned sooner. The park was a dead bore today."

"And why was that?"

Their brother Felix answered. He looked decidedly handsome and tidy in his uniform, a sharp contrast to their little sister.

"Because, everyone was gossiping about the Frompton-Wethersby tangle and no one paid her any mind."

Eugenia hit him with her reticule which she had yet to put down. "That is not true."

Felix sat and crossed one leg over the other in a casual manner, refusing to be drawn. He had matured an astonishing amount in his time away, Edmund reflected, and must be a formidable foe indeed to the French.

"What were they saying about Wethersby and Frompton?" Edmund asked.

"Oh, not you, too!" Eugenia threw herself on the nearby sofa in evident exasperation.

Felix waved his hand. "Mostly, people are beginning to wager on how it will end. Some were speculating on the mysterious Lady Isabella who will be sacrificed if Frompton loses."

"Why mysterious?" Edmund enquired, feigning ignorance.

"Because no one has ever seen her and the duke refuses to bring her up from the country," Felix explained.

"Have you seen her?" Eugenia asked Rowley, who cast a look at Edmund.

"I have had the pleasure," he answered.

"Is she as beautiful as they say?" Felix asked with a mischievous smile and Edmund wanted to throw something at his brother.

"I suppose she is," Rowley said.

"I think they are both hateful wretches to have made an innocent lady the pawn in their wagering!" Eugenia cried.

"Indeed, a highly unusual wager," Edmund agreed. "It is a very serious matter to play with a young lady's reputation and future, if not to say quite immoral."

"What will happen to her?" Eugenia asked. "I do not know her; the poor soul has all my sympathy, nonetheless."

"Nothing pleasant," Felix remarked. "She will either be lost to Wethersby and become a notorious mistress, or she will be ruined and unmarriageable. Frompton must be up the River Tick or he would have paid the debt by now."

"I think there is more to it than him repaying the debt," Rowley remarked with a thoughtful look on his face. "It is not an insurmountable sum for him if he chose to find it."

"Too bad she cannot escape and run away to Gretna with someone. If she were already married it would solve her problems, at least, and it would serve him right," said Eugenia stoutly.

Edmund had to bite his tongue. He would take her to Gretna immediately, would she but agree to it.

"If I did not have to return to the Continent, I would be tempted to go and rescue her myself," Felix added with a grin.

Edmund covered his snort with a cough, which caused Rowley to eye him suspiciously.

"So soon?" Eugenia asked, looking distraught. "You have only just returned!"

"It was only ever a temporary reprieve, my dear. I am still on orders."

"I do not have to like it," she retorted.

"When do you ship out?" Rowley asked. Edmund knew his brother hated sending Felix off, but the military was in his blood and Rowley tried to allow him to spread his wings. Nevertheless, that it worried him was clear, at least to Edmund.

"As soon as some documents are ready. Any day now."

The room fell silent. No one wished to speak of what might happen, but Rowley chose to say nothing because it made Felix happy to serve his country.

"Were there no admiring beaux in the park, Genie?" Edmund teased, to lighten the cloud which had descended. "Surely there had to be some conversation other than Frompton and Wethersby and the elusive daughter?"

"I tell you, it was so!" she bemoaned.

"It did not help matters that Wethersby and the duchess were both present," Felix remarked.

It took Edmund some strength of will not to look at Rowley again. Calm as you please, the duke remained silent. Eugenia or Felix would indulge them, Edmund was certain. They did not wait long.

"Wethersby approached the duchess, as bold as could be, and they strolled away to speak together for a time. I do not see what all the fuss is about." Eugenia waved her hand dismissively.

"Have you listened not at all?" Felix looked heavenward. The two younger siblings were closest in age and therefore were more inclined to brangle with each other.

"Of course I listened," she snapped, "but I do not see why everyone cares so much. They were betrothed, she chose a better title, and then the two men gambled and the duke lost. He refuses to pay the debt and they will duel. The end. 'Tis naught but a penny novel."

"I trust these conjectures will stay in this room," Rowley said, in a deceptively quiet voice.

Eugenia fell just short of glaring at her eldest brother.

"Would you like to visit Devonshire? We would be delighted for you to join us," Rowley remarked, after the merest pause, in a manner that indicated anything but delight was in store for her.

"Of course not, you wretch. I would not be so vulgar in public!"

Felix snorted.

"I merely pointed out," she went on, ignoring him, "that I am bored with it, not professing vulgar interest in it. If it keeps the gossips from speaking about me, for once, for that I should be grateful, I suppose."

"The situation is a very serious matter, Eugenia, and someone may die. I am acquainted with both parties and have a vested interest in seeing this settled amicably." The reproof in Rowley's voice was unmistakable.

"Did anything else occur? Wethersby did not threaten or harm the duchess?" Edmund could not help but ask.

"Apparently, the duchess is furious with the duke for wagering Lady Isabella," Felix reported. "She was seen to be pleading with Wethersby about something, but no one quite heard what was said."

"Not for lack of trying, though," Eugenia added.

"They conducted this conversation in the park?" Edmund asked.

"She could hardly call at his house," Felix countered.

"Perhaps, in public displays she thought to achieve more success?" Rowley suggested.

"Pray that is the case," Edmund muttered.

"Not so easily done, I am afraid," Felix said, continuing in his calm repose. "Frompton rode up and accosted both Wethersby and the duchess."

"That is all? No skirmish?" Rowley was stirred enough to ask.

"I told you it was a bore," Eugenia replied. "There was some shouting, Frompton's face turned purple and then he led the duchess away. No one would speak of anything else, so we left."

"It is not every day one sees a farce between a duke and an earl on such a public stage," Felix drawled.

"I do not see what the attraction is. Even I do not behave in such a fashion!" she grumbled, causing her brothers to laugh.

"And you shall not," Rowley commanded, even though he was smiling.

"Must you return to the country so soon?" she asked. "It is much more fun having you and Emma here than Aunt Hambridge. Although she is a dear, *of course*, she tires too easily."

"We must. I have business to attend to and I cannot abide London in the summer."

"I adore it at all times," Eugenia stated.

"Then you must adore it without us," Rowley retorted.

"Why do you look so glum, Edmund?" Eugenia asked, catching him off guard.

"I, glum?" he protested, though he was shocked to have had his feelings noticed. Was he wearing them on his sleeve for all to see? All his siblings turned to stare with consideration. It was disconcerting. Rarely was he the object of any of their particular notice, being the calm, mild one of the five.

"You do look a little peaked," Felix remarked.

"What can I say? I am human on occasion?"

"No." Eugenia puckered her lips and shook her head.

Felix frowned. "She is correct, you never look harassed."

Edmund threw up his hands and looked to the eldest of them for help. "Where is Heath when I need him? No one ever pays me any mind when he is about."

"I would guess our devout brother has had his first proposal rejected," Rowley tattled.

Edmund stared openly at Rowley. How could he know his intentions? And Edmund could not believe he had been betrayed by the one who valued privacy above all else!

Rowley simply shrugged. "Tit for tat. You are an open book."

"You cannot mean you think I interfered with you and Emma?" Edmund could not believe what he was hearing. "I am a man of the cloth!"

"But you did, and all for the good."

"I see; so telling our two younger siblings my embarrassment, that they might meddle is for my own good?"

Both of said siblings were watching them with open astonishment.

"Who is she?" Eugenia asked when she could apparently no longer contain her curiosity.

"No one you would know," Edmund tried to remark calmly. "Besides, she did not give me the opportunity and there is nothing else to say."

"I would like to know, all the same." She pouted. "It is not every day that the brother who has proclaimed marriage to the church changes his mind."

"I had excellent reasons for doing so. Perhaps it is not God's will that I marry, after all," Edmund answered—except his heart did not want to accept his well-rehearsed words. He had never before felt so disappointed in his life.

ISABELLA WATCHED EDMUND leave the garden and desperately wanted to go outside these walls. She felt enclosed. Would it really be so dangerous to go beyond the gardens if she was well disguised? It was time for Lord George's nap, and it was the wet nurse's turn to watch over him.

She looked out across to the park and was sorely tempted. If she wore her most obscuring bonnet with her plain gray worsted and kept her head down, how would anyone know who she was, dressed as a servant? People saw what they expected to see.

Giving into temptation, Isabella decided to escape. She tied on the massive bonnet and hurried down the back stairs. The park was a very big place, and no one seeking Lady Isabella would expect to find her in a servant's guise. There were numerous secluded paths that the fashionable stayed away from, where she had, on many a morning, taken Lord George for an airing.

If she did not have some time away to think, she would surely run mad. Lord Edmund had offered her marriage!

If only she could have accepted, it would have solved many of her problems. Even if she never spoke to her family again, she knew the Knights would welcome her if they knew the whole truth.

The park was unexpectedly crowded and Isabella did not know which way to go at first. She decided to go away from Rotten Row towards the Serpentine and keep her head down as she went.

It was not so simple a matter to accomplish. Gentlemen, and ladies in their finest gowns, simpered and preened at each other from their horses or open carriages. Several times she found herself dodging to the side to avoid being hit. These people and their lives were so different from her own simple existence as a nurse—and even when she had occupied her rightful position as Lady Isabella. If these were the manners of the *ton*, she had never learned them and was certain she would not wish to.

No one paid her any attention, as she expected, but the crowd seemed to be very interested in one particular couple. No matter which direction she seemed to go, it felt as though they were following close behind.

She could even overhear some of their conversation and it sounded like a lovers' quarrel. Isabella had almost forgotten her need for inconspicuousness when she had heard the familiar voice. Fearing she was openly staring, she moved on a little, stepping behind a large oak tree, but not far enough that she could not see.

"Why must you pursue this, Oliver?"

"You know very well why, Rosamund."

"You harm no one but my daughter and make a fool of yourself!"

"You would not allow me to have her otherwise."

"Now I am to blame? Why must you hurt me like this? You know very well why you could not have her, so you now try by malicious means? Hurt me any other way but through an innocent child."

Her mother truly cared? So often Isabella had wondered if her mother remembered her existence. She was never deliberately cruel, but neither was she overtly affectionate. Was there a deeper reason for that?

Her mother was still a great beauty at close to fifty years of age. Isabella had inherited her features but not her vanity. Her Grace of Frompton was speaking with Wethersby just a short distance away from a crowd of onlookers. They seemed to be relishing it as they might an act of a play, and almost seemed to be leaning forward as one, straining to hear.

Why was her mother speaking thus to Lord Wethersby? Isabella could not help but remember him that night at the auction. Had he known who she was? She resembled her mother very closely, and they were obviously still well acquainted. The thought made Isabella's stomach churn. They had now drawn closer, and Isabella strained to eavesdrop. Somehow she was certain they spoke of her. Afraid of what she might hear, she yet could not seem to stop herself from listening.

"There must be another way!" her mother insisted.

"You know my terms, Rosa."

"You know I cannot. It is impossible."

"Is it?" he taunted.

Isabella could see the worry on her mother's face. Did she love this man? How could she when she knew the treachery he was capable of? Isabella wanted to reach out to her mother and warn her away, but it was impossible. She had to save herself, now, for no one else could.

*That is not true,* her conscience corrected. *Edmund.*

Oh Edmund! If only he could have offered for her with love! Yet, she feared such a luxury of emotion was not in her future.

"Where is the Lady Isabella, Duchess?" someone called from the crowd, causing Isabella's heart to pound.

"Yes, we want to see the object of Wethersby's desires!" The crowd laughed and her face burned with embarrassment. How could her father and this beast have done this to her? And why did her mother not put a stop to this horrid scene?

That lady was waving her fan. "My daughter will remain in the country until I can persuade Wethersby to drop this ridiculous wager!" She seemed to force herself to laughter. "How could I subject my sweet, innocent girl to such villainy?"

The crowd murmured a bit, but some young bucks were not so easily deterred.

"Is she as beautiful as her mother?" a young fop called.

"More so, I believe." Her mother, at least, was attempting to preserve her reputation.

"You are too modest, Duchess, but I will gladly relieve you of the burden of her instead of such a one as Wethersby!" His crowd of friends slapped him on the back and cheered him on.

"Hear, hear!" another of the gathering called.

Why? Why? Why was this happening? Isabella silently bemoaned what appeared to be her fate. Would she ever be able to be herself again without shame falling upon her? There was no way to escape notoriety, even if her father and Wethersby could be persuaded to settle their differences. She could take no more of the humiliation and had already turned to escape back to Knighton House when the crowd parted and she saw her father trotting wildly towards her mother and Wethersby, his horse suffused in sweat and his face purple with rage.

He only just pulled up his mount in time before dismounting.

"Rosa, come!" he ordered, as though she were a naughty dog expected to obey her master.

Her mother raised her chin. "I wish you would not do this. Please settle your differences without involving Isabella," she pleaded.

"It is too late for that." Frompton glared at Wethersby and Isabella flinched. She had never before seen such pure hatred in anyone's eyes. It was as though the man who had brought her up had become a different person.

*Possessed,* she thought, a little afraid.

In that instant, she lost all hope of a peaceful end to her situation.

The duke pulled the duchess away and led her with him like a lamb to the slaughter, his horse plodding tiredly behind. A tear ran down Isabella's face as her parents left; both now seemed complete strangers to her. Even if she survived this ordeal unscathed, would she ever feel welcome in their company again?

Perhaps with her mother there was some small reason for hope, she thought as she began to walk away from the disquieting scene. Thankfully, they were to leave for Devonshire on the morrow, where she would wait out the days until her birthday and then, once she was of age, she would find a way to make a new life without her family.

Her throat constricted as she walked away, and then she became blinded by tears. She had thought the old wounds could not hurt any more, but they were still painfully raw.

Had her parents even looked for her before now? Was she simply a tool for them to hurt each other with? She wanted no part of it. Life as a maid was superior to being a pawn of hate.

# CHAPTER FOUR

E DMUND DID NOT like going to gentlemen's clubs. Some days he
felt as though he led a double life and he never felt like more of a
fraud than when he entered the hallowed walls of an exclusive
establishment. Compared to the squalor he worked desperately to
combat, it was difficult to be a part of such luxury, even if he had been
born and raised to it.

However, this time it was for a good cause, as Rowley believed
both Wethersby and Frompton were likely to be present. Both were
trying to gain favor for a vote, and of course, they were on opposite
sides of the fence, as usual. Edmund wondered if they only disagreed
with each other out of principle.

"I imagine there will be a good show tonight," Rowley said sardonically.

"Of the sort you abhor," Edmund pointed out.

"Yes, but it is for a good cause. My son is an excellent judge of
character, and if he approves of Miss Thatcher, who am I to question
it?"

The carriage pulled to a stop in St. James', in front of the tasteful
Palladian structure made of white Portland stone with the single bow
window at its front.

Rain was falling lightly and the porter rushed out with an umbrella
to shield them to the door. The club was crowded as they made their

way into the hall; the smell of smoke, spirits, and warm males filled the air.

Edmund and Rowley walked through to the billiards room and greeted a few acquaintances. Slowly they made their way upstairs, where some gentlemen were playing cards, but there were groups filling the coffee room and already having lively discussions.

"This is what I expected." Rowley motioned towards the gathering. "When there is a controversial bill up for a vote, everyone is trying to persuade, control and even bribe people to their side."

"Have I mentioned how glad I am that *you* are the duke?" Edmund teased.

"Once or twice," Rowley muttered. "There is Frompton, sitting at the center of that group." He inclined his head to the right side of the room. "He thinks as I do that it will harm our poor if we stop importation of grain."

"Wethersby is on the other side, I see," Edmund replied. "I assume he is against importation?"

"Yes. In theory, it would be ideal if we could grow our own grain at an affordable price and keep profits at home, but it is not reality. One bad storm and an entire nation's crops can be ruined. I am in favor of making it more desirable to use our own crops, of course. I am a land owner, after all, but profit at the expense of our poor is inhumane."

"I could not agree more. Why not lower the taxes on domestic corn and increase it on imported?"

Rowley raised a sardonic brow at his brother. "Are you certain you do not wish to be the MP for my district?" Edmund ignored the question. He loathed politics. "Wethersby is fear mongering." Rowley and Edmund stood at the edge of a group of those willing to listen to him giving a speech.

"Hear, hear!" someone shouted at Wethersby's proclamation that this was for the good of England.

"Would that someone would convince our radical friend across the room. Perhaps he should switch parties!" Wethersby shouted so the other half of the room could hear. Indeed they did, for everyone grew quiet. Frompton stood and the crowd parted so he could step towards Wethersby's side of the room.

Silence reigned as those assembled eagerly awaited a confrontation. "Trying to gather votes by instilling fear rather than common sense, I see," Frompton said. "If you care more about your pocketbooks than your people going hungry, then by all means vote his way." Frompton turned to leave.

"If we do our duty as landlords, no one will go hungry," Wethersby said to the crowd.

"If only it worked in that way," the duke replied with a few pointed looks towards some of the men in the room who were notorious wastrels.

"Speaking of duty, dare I hope you are prepared to fulfill your debt in a month's time?"

Glaring at Wethersby, the duke suddenly looked old and tired. Edmund could not feel sorry for the man, only anger and pity. Perhaps he had not been so wrong to marry for love in the beginning, if that was what it was. But he had certainly gone beyond all decency when he attempted to sell his daughter to both spite and repay his debt to Wethersby. Frompton's jaw clenched. "I have a month, as you say."

"Perhaps if you would consider voting differently, your fortunes might turn," Wethersby taunted, to chuckles from a few of the crowd and the rising choler of Frompton's angry face.

Frompton left abruptly without uttering another word. The crowd dispersed into smaller groups and began debating in murmurs, no doubt disappointed that there had not been more argument.

Rowley and Edmund went over to join a group of acquaintances as a waiter brought them all drinks.

"What is this debt that Wethersby refers to?" Rowley asked casually as he and Edmund took a seat at a table with Petersham and Lord Perth.

"Have you been living under a rock for the past decade, Knighton?" Petersham asked.

Rowley gave him one of his infamous annoyed looks. "You know I prefer the country, and that gossip bores me."

"Then why the interest now?" Lord Perth, the duchess' cousin, asked.

Rowley shrugged one of his shoulders and waved a hand. "It appears to be affecting the vote."

"They used to be the best of friends at Cambridge, then Wethersby's betrothed jilted him in favor of becoming a duchess."

"Perhaps it was a love match," Edmund suggested. Four pairs of eyes looked at him as though he had windmills in his head.

"Two or so years ago, they were playing cards together..." Perth began.

"Playing with enemies never has a good outcome," Petersham interjected.

"Frompton lost a fortune he did not have to lose and Wethersby said, if he could not repay him with money he would take his daughter on her twenty-first birthday. Apparently, that date is quickly approaching."

"Frompton declared he would rot in Hell before he let Wethersby touch his daughter, but he has not repaid the debt otherwise," Petersham finished.

That was ironic, because Edmund was thinking there was a special place in Hell for people who sold their daughters.

"Mayhap he is holding out until the last minute, simply to toy with Wethersby," Rowley suggested.

"Quite possibly," Petersham agreed, "but I do not think his estates are as solvent as he would like the world to think."

"It is a shame. Wethersby is a snake."

Edmund agreed, but he did wonder what would happen to Frompton if he did not find Isabella, and Edmund knew he himself would do everything in his power to keep that from happening.

"I heard Ruskington returned from Lower Canada to try to prevent Frompton from selling off parts of the estate," Perth remarked.

"I do not know how he could prevent it unless they trade the daughter," Petersham argued.

"Word has it that Ruskington made a fortune in the colony," Perth added.

"Maybe he will bail the duke out and save the daughter, then," Petersham pondered.

"At least she would be a Countess," Perth offered.

"You forget; he is married," Petersham countered.

"The wife is an invalid and not expected to live, though it does not make the situation better now."

Edmund listened to this banter until he was ready to commit murder when they took their leave.

Once back in the carriage, Rowley spoke.

"The situation is worse than I thought. I had hoped the animosity might be less from time, but it appears to be worse."

"Frompton did not look good."

"Who would with a missing daughter and massive debt about to be called in?" Rowley shook his head.

"You forget he tried to sell that daughter," Edmund growled.

"Quite inexcusable," Rowley agreed. "However, no one else seems to know about it, which is fortunate for Lady Isabella. I have a small acquaintance with Ruskington. Perhaps he might be willing to help."

"I wondered the same thing," Edmund remarked, "but you must be careful not to give Isabella away until you are sure of him."

"Do give me some measure of credit, Brother."

"Forgive me, but I worry. You did not see that night at the auction."

"No, but I must tread carefully. It is no small thing to accuse another duke of such villainy. I believe Isabella's word, but who else would? Bringing it out into the open will only do her harm."

Edmund could not reply for a moment through his suffocating anger. His throat was clogged with acrid emotion.

"How will he explain her disappearance? He will not be able to hide it much longer. What will happen when he cannot repay the debt?" Edmund asked.

"Frompton will be ruined despite the fact that Wethersby means to dishonor Lady Isabella."

"Over my dead body."

Rowley looked curiously at his brother. "What do you mean to do, Edmund?"

"Keep her safe, even if it means marrying her first. Her father cannot give away what does not belong to him."

"It is a dangerous game you play. I have said that many times. However, I will support you in whatever you think is best."

"I wish I knew what was best, but even my situation in life would be better than that she would face with Wethersby. If she would even have me, of course."

The carriage pulled to a stop and the brothers alighted. Rowley turned to Edmund. "I will call on Ruskington in the morning before we depart for Devonshire."

≫≫⊁≪≪

THE HOUSE WAS in a frenzy, the servants hurrying to pack in order to leave for Knighton Grange. Trunks were being stacked and carried down the stairs, food was being baked for the journey, and maids were scurrying around making certain no necessary items were left behind. The duke wanted to leave as soon as he returned from a morning call.

Isabella was walking around in her Brunswick brown traveling dress, carrying George to keep him out of the way, and hearing Edmund's voice, she hurried down to wish him farewell.

"Good morning, Vicar," Isabella said as she entered the drawing room holding baby George on her hip. He gurgled with pleasure and held his hands out for his uncle.

"Come here, George," Edmund cooed in a way that warmed Isabella's heart. He was the kindest man she knew and he would be a wonderful father. Isabella watched as he cuddled the boy in his long clothes to him and wished the vicar did not know of her shame. At least he was willing to help her.

"I am glad you came. I wished to thank you for helping me," she said.

Edmund looked at her and the earnestness in his eyes made her heart yearn. If only she were not ruined for a gentleman like him... but the fates had conspired against her. The rich chocolate of his coat reflected in his eyes and warmed her more than a cup of the delicious drink.

"I wish I could do more," he said. "Wethersby is more determined than ever to ruin your father, I fear." He leaned forward speaking quietly. "Last night, he publicly reminded your father of his debt."

"And what did my father say?" she asked warily.

"Only that he still had time."

Isabella closed her eyes. She did not want to see the pity on the vicar's face. He laid a hand on her arm in comfort and she might have thrown herself into his arms, had it not been for George.

"My brother has gone to see Ruskington. He has returned from Canada."

She opened her eyes. "Alexander is here?"

"One of our friends mentioned it last night. I think he is perhaps here to help. Are you close?"

"My brother is much older than I, but he and father had a falling out after the card game. I wonder what made him return?"

"I suspect the matter of your birthday—or perhaps the wars have driven him home."

"You are probably correct. How I wish I could see him!" she said longingly.

"He is unaware of your absence?"

"He will be aware soon. Poor Alex."

"But you believe he would be willing to help you?"

She nodded. "If he could, but unless he has made a fortune in Canada, I do not know what he could do. He can hardly overrule my father."

George began to wriggle, so Edmund put him down on the floor where he began to rock back and forth on all fours, trying to crawl. Neither of them could resist a smile at the darling child.

"Miss Thatcher—Isabella—I wanted to offer a solution..." he began as the sound of the front door opening indicated the duke's return.

Edmund went to the door. "Rowley. Why don't you come in?" He inclined his head, probably so the duke would not misunderstand that he wanted to speak with him.

"Of course."

Edmund closed the door behind the duke and Isabella dropped into a curtsy. "Your Grace."

"Miss Thatcher."

George smiled with pleasure when he noticed his father.

"Forgive me, Your Grace, but I was told you went to speak with my brother. Is it true he is here?"

The duke cast a subtle look at Edmund. "He is, but I was unable to speak with him privately."

Isabella felt her heart sink. Her hopes had been lifted, if only for a moment. "Did he appear well?"

"Indeed. Tired, but well. Unfortunately, his wife and child were killed in one of the Indian raids." He scooped up George and drew him near, as if to assure himself his own son was well.

"How horrid! Poor Alex!" Isabella gasped, putting a hand over her mouth.

"How confident are you in your brother, Miss Thatcher?" Edmund asked.

"Unless he is greatly changed, he will support me. He left because of his disappointment in my father's dealings with Wethersby."

"Perhaps a note, then, inviting him here for dinner?" the duke suggested. "But it would delay leaving for Devonshire and I should not wish to jeopardize your safety, Miss Thatcher."

"It would be worth the wait if I knew I had his support."

"We must be certain," Edmund interjected.

"In that case, perhaps you should stay out of sight until we can be confident?" the duke further suggested.

Isabella nodded her head in agreement. "He might not agree with Father, but he might not see matters from my point of view. I cannot tell you how much it means to me that you are willing to help me. I promise that, after my birthday, I will try to find another situation so you will no longer have to involve yourself with me."

"Do not be ridiculous, Miss Thatcher. You have become a part of our family and what has happened to you is unconscionable." Baby George had unraveled the duke's normally pristine neckcloth and was sucking it. "If you are certain you wish me to speak further with your brother, I will tell the servants we are delaying our departure for another day. I will send a note to Ruskington to invite him to dine."

"Thank you, Your Grace. Do you wish for me to take George?"

The duke looked fondly at his son and kissed him on the forehead. "I suppose that would be best or it will take me two hours to write the note," he said with a wry smirk.

The duke left the room and his son babbled after him as his lean frame disappeared from sight.

"I should probably take the baby back to his wet nurse."

"I had wanted to speak to you," Edmund said, "but I expect it can wait a little longer, since you are not leaving today."

Isabella paused in the middle of picking up George. "He is not fussing yet, if you wish to speak now."

Edmund inclined his head and suddenly looked very serious.

"Is something else troubling you?" she asked.

Edmund clasped his hands behind his back and walked over to the window. "I have given a great deal of thought to your predicament," he began.

Isabella stared after him.

"I cannot abide the thought of Wethersby ruining you. He has nothing honorable to offer."

"My father has already ruined me."

"No one but my brothers and I know your identity."

"I believe that is a rather optimistic view, sir. It seems too coincidental that Wethersby was the person to win the auction," she countered. "Nevertheless, regardless of that, my father's actions, and Society knowing I am owed to Wethersby, is ruination enough. I cannot hope to make the match my birthright should have secured for me."

"Perhaps not, but you can still make an honorable one."

George laid his head down on her shoulder as if he knew she needed his support. She cradled him to her.

"How?" she whispered in disbelief. "Who would want me if they knew the truth?"

"What about me?" he asked, turning to face her.

She had thought before in the garden he had been making a hasty effort to rescue her again and had not expected this. She walked over to him and took his hand. "You are the best of men, Vicar. I am deeply honored that you would even consider such a thing, but I cannot permit you to do this."

Oh, how she would regret those words later, she knew! However, she could not allow him to sacrifice his happiness when he had already done so much for her. How she wished they had met under different circumstances, she reflected sadly.

"I know I am no bargain, and I certainly cannot offer a duke's daughter the life to which she is entitled..."

"How could you think I care about that now?"

"I would hope your good name could still be preserved," he answered.

She shook her head. "I deeply appreciate your kind offer, but no man should have to martyr or sacrifice themselves for me." She attempted a smile and left the room, trying not to scare the baby as she hurried back to the nursery, and not stopping when Edmund called after her. He would offer pretty, reassuring words that she would not be able to resist. Marrying and having her own children seemed the distant dream of a different person.

The sad reality was that Edmund was her knight in shining armor, she thought ruefully. There could never be another man to fill her heart as he did—but she would not become another act of mercy for him. Her soul could not bear that on its conscience.

# CHAPTER FIVE

EDMUND WAS STUNNED as he watched Isabella leave. He should feel relief, but all he felt was hurt and disappointment. Why? He had never thought to marry. His life of service was hardly conducive to a family. The case of Isabella was a prime example – he had rescued her in the middle of the night and taken her to Devonshire. Now there was a home at his brother Heath's estate in Kent for the doves, so only the special cases would require such extreme measures. While Edmund was far from being poor, he was not a wealthy man. He had chosen the living in Shoreditch in order to help more people. If he married, he would be forced to take a more lucrative living.

There was something about Isabella which made him not even hesitate to offer. She had dealt with her situation with grace and dignity. Perhaps she would rather remain a maid than marry him. He shook his head. It had hardly been a proposal of the romantic sort, which she deserved, and he had not couched it as well as he might. He could hardly blame her, but how else could he help her?

Since it was time for dinner, he dressed in the chamber kept for him there and began to make his way down to the drawing room to greet their guest. Edmund was not acquainted with Isabella's brother, and he was hopeful if somewhat cautious about Ruskington's willingness to help. He hoped Rowley knew how to direct this, because Edmund would have no compunction in helping Isabella to escape again if necessary. He decided to call in at the nursery on his way to dinner.

"Good evening," he said, as he looked at his quarry. She was sitting in a chair looking out of the window.

"I am glad you are here. I wanted to apologize for running away during our conversation this afternoon."

He shook his head. "That was badly done of me."

"I think it is the kindest thing anyone has ever offered to do for me. I already owe you so much."

"Nonsense! Your situation was not of your doing."

"Still, there are not many people like you who help others so self-lessly."

"I truly enjoy helping those less fortunate," he said softly.

"One day, if I am ever again in a position of comfort, I hope to do the same."

"If I have anything to say about it, you will be. I wanted you to know that I have not offered for anyone before. I know it was not the proposal of your dreams, but I meant it. I think we would deal well together."

She opened her mouth to respond, but he held his hand up. "Please do not decide now. Think about it and if you change your mind, have Rowley send word to me."

"Thank you," she answered quietly.

"I came to offer you reassurance that if things do not go well with your brother, I will continue to help. Is there anything you wish for me to know about him?"

"I have not seen him in years; he is nine years older than I. How-ever he is very mindful of his duty and what is right and wrong. He was always very kind to me."

"That is reassuring," Edmund said. "Will you be nearby?"

"Yes, I intend to listen from the other side of the door. I hope I can be disciplined enough to remain there."

"It is your choice, of course."

"Vicar..." she began.

"Edmund, please."

"Edmund, I cannot say how grateful I am to you. I am very flattered by your offer. If circumstances were different..." She reached out and boldly caressed his face with her hand. Turning his head, he kissed her palm and gave her a swift nod.

"Everything will be well, Isabella."

He left before he could say something he might regret. The touch of her hand had awakened feelings in him he had suppressed long ago when he had chosen his calling.

Rowley and Emma were already in the drawing room.

"Good evening. Have you thought about how to approach Ruskington?" he asked.

"We were just discussing it," Rowley admitted. "I knew him well at school, many years ago, so I have it in mind to be as forthright as possible. Games are not my way."

"No," Edmund agreed. "I reassured Isabella that I would help her."

"Did she accept your offer?" Rowley asked with piercing look.

"She did not, though I made a mull of it," he answered sheepishly.

Emma came over and kissed him on the cheek. "You are the best of men, Brother. Perhaps Isabella will change her mind when she knows you did not offer out of mercy."

"I did not," he admitted. "I like her very much. Perhaps she does not wish to be a vicar's wife. Who could blame her? It is not always a simple life. She deserves much better."

"The living at the Grange is still available for you. Just say the word."

"Thank you, Rowley. It might become necessary."

The butler entered. "Lord Ruskington, Your Grace."

Pausing just inside the doorway, Ruskington bowed.

"Welcome, Alex. This is my wife, Emma, and my brother Edmund." Rowley went over and shook his old friend's hand.

"A pleasure," he said as he bowed over Emma's hand. Edmund instantly saw the similarities between Alex and Isabella. They were both tall and slim, with russet hair and stormy blue eyes, but the brother wore a thick beard and a wary look—as though he were not quite tame.

"I confess I was surprised by your invitation, but I have been gone from England so long that I have not known where to begin with renewing acquaintances."

"And I will confess I am not often in Town, but it is good to see you again."

Banks, the longtime butler, appeared at the door, indicating the meal was ready. "Shall we go into dinner and we can continue to renew our friendship?" Rowley proposed.

After they were seated in the elegant dining room with its classical plasterwork, Rowley spoke again. "I asked the servants to bring all of the food at once so we may speak freely while we dine."

"Of course." Ruskington looked a little suspicious. "I do not suppose this has to do with my father and Wethersby, does it?"

"It does. Edmund and I were at White's two nights ago and there was mention of a debt."

Ruskington picked up his claret and took a slow sip before staring into the glass. "I had hoped it would not become common knowledge, but yes. I desperately hoped that Father would have managed to settle the debt by the time I returned, but that is not the case."

Rowley inclined his head.

"It was not the only reason for my return. The war took the lives of my wife and child and it was no longer safe to remain."

"My condolences. I am not pleased we are choosing to fight that battle, especially when we are fighting Napoleon."

Ruskington gave a curt nod. "If you were at White's, then you will have also heard that my father is to give my sister to Wethersby on her twenty-first birthday if he cannot settle the debt. Not in an honorable way either, I am sorry to say." His jaw clenched and he held his glass so tightly, Edmund thought it would break. He was inclined to like the man.

"Your father and I are not close, but we have always agreed on politics. Will he be able to meet the debt?"

Ruskington shook his head. "I do not see how, but Father will not speak of it. I have offered to help, but he insists Wethersby cheated him."

Edmund and Rowley cast questioning glances at each other. "That is the first I have heard of it," Rowley said.

"And my enquiries of those present at the game indicated no obvious cheating occurred. I fear Father is delusional when it comes to Wethersby."

"Do you know the extent of the debt?" Rowley asked.

"It was some thirty thousand pounds. Father and I had a great row over it. 'Twas why I left."

"And there is no unentailed property to be sold?"

"Not of that great a value. If it comes to a duel, I fear Father will commit murder. Wethersby is a lecher, to be sure, but not a criminal."

Edmund wanted to scream the truth, but it was Isabella's story to tell, not his.

"And what of your sister? Does he intend to surrender her on her birthday?"

Ruskington slammed his fist on the table. "Over my dead body," he growled.

"How will you keep her safe, then?" Emma asked.

He hesitated. "I wish I knew. I would take her somewhere safe until I knew she was no longer at risk."

"Why not do it, then?" Emma asked.

Again he hesitated for a moment. "Because Father does not know where she is. She has been missing for over a year." The man's face wrinkled in anguish.

"How could that be? Why has there been no suggestion of it about Town?"

"Father is ashamed. He says his actions caused her to run away, but it has been so long without news he fears she is dead. He hired a Runner to look for her, but there has been no trace of her. Mother carries on as though they simply left Isabella in the country." He ran his hand over his face. "Forgive me. This is none of your concern." Ruskington stared unseeingly across the room as though fighting for composure.

Wondering what was keeping Isabella from bursting through the door, Edmund looked from Rowley to Emma. The duchess was biting her lip.

"Tell us how we may help," she said.

"Alex?" Into a sudden silence, Isabella's voice sounded from the doorway.

⇢⇢⇥⇤⇠⇠

"BELLA?" ALEX ROSE and came to her, enfolding her in a hug.

"Alex!" she cried into his shoulder. The family rose to leave. "No, wait!" she delayed them. "We can go elsewhere. Please finish your meal." She led her brother into the adjoining parlor.

She closed the door behind them and leaned against it. Her brother was looking at her in disbelief.

"What happened, Bella?"

Isabella was so relieved to see her brother that she could not speak for a moment. She was close to crying with emotion. She thought she had composed herself. It was why it had taken her some minutes to make her appearance, but it had been so long since she had seen anyone from her family, or been hugged for that matter, she was overcome.

"It was horrible, Alex. Father tried to s-sell me and the vicar helped me escape. The duke and duchess have been hiding me at their estate in Devonshire, as a nursemaid to their son."

Alex let out a blaspheme that made her blush. "Why did you not write to me? I would have returned immediately!"

"I did not know how. To be fair, Knighton did not know who I was until two days ago. They have been so supportive, I can never repay them for their kindnesses to me."

"But—a servant, Isabella?"

"It was an excellent way to hide," she pointed out.

Isabella sat down and her brother joined her on the sofa. He raked his hand through his long hair. He looked as though he had come from a wilderness.

"Tell me all of it, please. Spare no details, for I must decide what is best to be done."

"I will not go to Wethersby, no matter how desperate Father is!" she said angrily.

"Never!" Alex agreed. "There will be no good outcome for Father, either way."

"I know," she whispered. She told him everything that had happened that fateful night when the duke had tried to force her into prostitution, including how Edmund had saved her.

"We are indebted to him," Alex remarked.

"Indeed. He even offered to marry me." Isabella tried not to blush as she said the words, but she felt her brother's gaze on her. "I refused, of course."

"Why 'of course'? It could be the solution to everything, for you at least. Only if you are willing, that is."

"I cannot bear to force him into a marriage, Alex. He has been so good to me."

"Then what will you do? My solution had been to find you a husband."

She swallowed hard. "I suppose it would be the easiest way, but I had hoped..." She shook her head. "It is foolish to hope for anything."

"It is not foolish to hope for happiness. What Father did is unforgivable."

"Then what do you advise? Shall I return to Devonshire with the family?"

"It would be the easiest answer for now," he admitted. "It will buy us time. Father is unlikely to find you there if he has not done thus far."

Isabella was almost sad that her brother had not pushed her harder to marry Edmund. Why was she being contrary about her feelings? Edmund was whom she wanted to marry, but she wanted him to love her in return. Oh, he would love her in his own way, she knew, but he deserved every happiness and she would not take it from him.

"Then I shall go with them and await news from you."

"I do not know how to return to Father's house without murdering him for what he did to you."

"How is he?" Isabella asked, disgusted that she still cared after everything he had done.

"He has aged a great deal, although having this on his conscience explains much. Mother is vaporish and keeps to her apartments most of the time."

"Little has changed, then." Somehow she wanted them to care – to have looked for her –but it seemed her father only cared with regards to paying his debts.

"I am sorry I ran away, Isabella. Can you forgive me?" her brother asked, a look of torment on his face.

She bit her lower lip. "It was not your fault. A parent should know better than to sell their child merely for spite and pride! It is difficult to describe what it feels like, to know you are dispensable. And I know you are grieving. Neither one of us has had an easy time of it, have we?"

"Once this is over, we can start again, I hope. This will be over soon, I promise you."

"I have been telling myself, if I can only reach my birthday, I may win free."

He pulled her into another tight hug.

"I am so grateful you came back, Alex."

"I am too, Sister. I cannot regret running away, for I learned a great deal. However, there was a high price to pay."

"And I cannot regret having escaped. I did not once suspect what was coming. How naïve I was!"

"All we can do is get on with our lives."

"What will happen to Father? He cannot pay, can he?"

"He refuses to speak of it. It was only when I said I was going to visit you that he confessed you were gone. The coward did not explain the whole of his sins to me, however."

"Shall we tell the duke and duchess I intend to remain with them?"

Alex held her hand as though he did not wish to stop touching her. She felt the same way.

"Bella, are you certain you cannot marry the vicar? Even I consider him to be a good match for you, and if he wants you, knowing everything as he does...?"

"No, I am not sure," she confessed, "but it is not fair to force him."

He looked at her long and hard. "Very well. I will not try to change your mind. Only you know what is best for you."

"Do I?" she whispered as they went back into the dining room. Edmund and the duke stood up at her entrance.

"Will you not please join us and finish your meal? You too, Miss Thatcher."

"Miss Thatcher?" Alex asked. "She was our old nursemaid," he explained to the others.

"She was more of a mother to me than our own. I knew no one besides you and James would recognize the name."

Edmund held a chair for her and she hesitated. It felt strange to be amongst her peers again.

"Will one of the servants see?" she asked.

"They have been excused," the duke answered.

"Very well, thank you. I confess I could not eat today for the worry."

"We will not abandon you, Isabella." The duchess repeated what the others had already said.

"My sister has been fortunate in her friends indeed. When I think what could have happened to her…" Alex paused to compose himself and had to look away. "I can never repay you."

"There is no price on innocence," Edmund said carefully. "You owe me nothing. Would that I could save more than I do."

"Nevertheless, I humbly thank you for doing what I should have been here to do."

Edmund inclined his head and looked Isabella in the eye. "I would do more if she would allow it."

"For now, I think it will be for the best if I return to the Grange, if you will allow it, Your Grace," Isabella put in quickly, not looking at Edmund for fear she would betray her true feelings.

"Of course. Emma and I would be delighted, as well as George."

"Thank you." Isabella and Alex ate quickly to catch up with the others, who were finishing their meal.

Rather than linger, Alex decided to depart. The duke and duchess repaired upstairs to see George before he went to sleep.

"I will send word as soon as I know something," her brother said as he kissed Isabella goodbye. "You will remain in Town?" he asked Edmund.

"Yes. I will help in any way I can. I am at Saint Michael's." He extended a hand to Alex.

"I pray I can find a solution. If she will not marry, then I must try to find a way whereby she may live as she chooses. I pray it will also serve to restore her good name—our good name."

Isabella watched Edmund closely for any sign of returned affection, but he was too much of a gentleman to behave in so vulgar a fashion. Especially after she kept refusing him.

Alex took his leave and then somehow the two of them were left alone again.

"I imagine this is farewell," she said.

"I will see you soon, when this is over and then I hope circumstances will be different."

Dare she hope? She looked up into his dark eyes, searching them for some hint to the feelings he hid behind a mask of propriety.

He caressed her cheek and took her hand. So many thoughts flitted through her mind. Had she been wrong or was he trying to convince her he cared for her sake? He kissed her hand before she heard footsteps coming towards the dining room. They jumped apart like naughty children caught stealing from the biscuit jar.

Edmund smiled kindly as he placed his hat on his head. Isabella could not smile, but only stare after him as he left, doing her best not to call to him that she had changed her mind.

# CHAPTER SIX

F OR A MAN who was often praised for his way with words, he had
utterly failed when it had come to the first female who had really
held his interest. If Edmund was being honest, he probably would not
have noticed her had it not been for the predicament in which he had
found her. Gazing upon her in vulnerable state, he had been tempted.
Normally, he was excellent at controlling his desires, because it only
required thinking of those less fortunate souls he helped in order to
quell any wayward thoughts.

However, since then Isabella had often been on his mind. Flashes
of that dreadful night often came to him and he checked himself for
remembering her beauty when she had been in distress.

A third son *could* make a respectable marriage, but not, in usual
circumstances, with the only daughter of a duke.

It was foolish to think further upon it, but he could not help it.
Isabella had said no. In hindsight, there were many things he should
have done differently, but now she was leaving and his chance was
lost. Isabella was Ruskington's responsibility now.

Edmund climbed down from the hackney and paid the driver. It
was late and he was tired, but the hairs on the back of his neck
prickled. He looked around, but everything looked the same as always.
People were sleeping in doorways, a group of rowdy youths was
taunting each other about something or other, and one of the ladies of

the night blew him a kiss.

"Good evening, Edith," he called.

"Evenin' Vicar!" she replied jovially.

Edith was one of the ones that did not care to be reformed.

Edmund could not decide what was making him uneasy, so he went on to the door of the vicarage. There was a note nailed to the front. Written in a crude hand it read:

*I am watching you*

Edmund took the note down, then turned around and saluted to the night. Whoever had done it was likely to be watching. Then he calmly went inside, even though he had an uneasy feeling in the pit of his stomach. This was not the first time he had made an abbess or bawd angry, but it had been some time since he had made any rescues. Was it too big a coincidence that Isabella's father was becoming desperate enough to hire a Runner? Although he did not think the note was the work of Ned Smallbone. The runner was too forthright for this type of behavior.

Edmund frowned. He was always very careful, but perhaps Wethersby had someone following the runner?

He would need to send word to Rowley to be on the lookout. The only place Edmund had gone was to Knighton House. He would wait until first thing in the morning, though, because whoever had placed that note would no doubt be expecting him to react tonight.

Edmund was not certain how to proceed. Rescuing Isabella had not been as simple as stealing her from a furious brothel owner. A powerful duke and earl were involved, not to mention the stumbling-block of a decades' old feud.

He was weary, so he went to bed, sleeping fitfully as concern for Isabella preyed on his mind. When he awoke, he sent a note to Knighton House and also one to Lord Ruskington. Hopefully, Frompton did not read his son's mail but Edmund worded the note very carefully in case.

He was just sitting down to break his fast when there was a pounding on the door.

"Now, who would be calling at this hour?" Mrs. Lowe asked in a scolding tone.

"You have lived here long enough not to ask such questions," Edmund teased.

She returned with a letter. "It was delivered post."

Edmund furrowed his brow as he split open the seal and read the note in haste. It was from Heath.

*The Dower House was broken into during the night. The four new doves there have been taken and it looks as if there was quite a struggle. The others were at the main house when it happened and are safe for now. We will place guards there from now on, but I am terribly sorry, Edmund. Cecilia is devastated.*

Edmund's worst fears were being realized. Someone must have been trailing him for some time if they knew about the safehouse at Woodcrest. It was well-hidden, though word would spread quickly enough that there was such a place. He had hoped it would be kept mum amongst those who needed it most. Now Heath and Cecilia would need to guard the place or abandon the idea altogether. Had they been looking for Isabella? The thought chilled him to the bone. Frompton was getting desperate, but did he have a hand in this? Somehow Edmund did not think so.

Perhaps he should pay a visit to Mr. Smallbone, he reflected. First, however, he sent a reply back to Heath and related some of what was happening to him. Heath had been the one to tell him of Isabella's plight in the first place, after all. Then he set out to find the runner and see if he had any inkling of who might be following either Edmund or the investigator himself.

On his way to number four, Bow Street, Edmund could not shake the feeling that he was again being watched. Yet when he stopped and looked around, there was nothing out of the ordinary to be seen. It was a pleasant, sunny summer's morning in the city, with flower sellers, newspaper boys, and meat pie vendors hawking their wares on the crowded streets.

Edmund looked closely at everyone in case he might recognize someone again later, but folk seemed to be minding their own business, down to the street-sweeper.

Never one to ignore instinct, Edmund filed away everything he could, then proceeded into the building. A clerk sat behind a desk to the rear of the entrance hall.

"May I help you, Reverend?" the bald, slightly heavy man asked.

Edmund pulled out a card and handed it to the clerk. "I am looking for Mr. Smallbone."

The clerk gave a nod. "Let me see if he is here."

Edmund was in luck. "Vicar," the runner greeted him, coming into the lobby after a short delay.

"May I have a few minutes of your time?"

"Of course. Will you walk with me? I was about to set out on business when I was told of your visit."

The man donned a coat and hat and they stepped outside.

"To forewarn you, Mr. Smallbone, I believe we are both being followed."

The man eyed him sideways and with considerable suspicion. "That would be a new experience for me, Vicar."

"Perhaps," Edmund replied. "I cannot say it is the first occasion for me. You yourself said you knew of my reputation, and while I have never been blatantly accused, people suspect, I am sure. I have helped girls and they have been found and murdered or punished severely."

"'Twas bound to happen," the runner agreed.

They reached a corner of Covent Garden and stopped. Edmund pulled both notes from his pocket and handed them to the runner.

"The first was nailed to my door last evening. The second I received from my brother, Heath, this morning."

"Where did this happen?"

"Lord Heath converted an old dower house on his property in Kent. We were to use it as a safe haven for women who had been forced into brothels against their will. Those he refers to were the first women we had sent there." Edmund's voice cracked with sadness.

"There is nothing I can do 'bout it, unfortunately," Smallbone said as he handed the notes back to Edmund.

"I know. I wanted you to be aware that someone may be following you. I suspect Wethersby's man. The discord between Wethersby and Frompton goes back three decades, you should know, if you were unaware."

"His Grace did mention Wethersby was angry about the duchess havin' chosen him."

"The duchess had been Wethersby's betrothed," Edmund replied dryly. "Then the duke was sufficiently lacking in judgment as to be coaxed into cards with Wethersby."

"I had heard of that."

"Did you also hear that, if Frompton cannot repay the debt, Wethersby demands Lady Isabella instead? And Wethersby is a married man."

The Bow Street Runner gave a shake of his head.

"There is a great deal at stake in protecting Lady Isabella, and I know you are a man of honor," Edmund said softly. "Watch your step, Mr. Smallbone." Edmund stuffed his hat on his head and walked away.

ISABELLA FOUND IT hard to be content once she had returned to Devon with the duke and duchess. It was a constant source of self-deprecation, for she knew she was fortunate indeed to be safe. Why, oh why, did she have to have principles which forbade her from marrying Edmund for convenience? She sighed. Whatever the whys and wherefores, she did possess those moralities, and she wanted him to care for her in the way she cared for him. It was madness that her heart could have been captured almost instantly, despite being virtual strangers. Yet it had. He deserved happiness more than anyone she knew. Hopefully, it would be possible when all of this was over.

Little George kept her from completely succumbing to a fit of the dismals, but it felt like as though it took months to receive a letter from Alex. When it did come, the duke hand-delivered it himself when Isabella was out with George and the duchess, relaxing on a blanket under a tree by the lake.

"Good afternoon," he greeted them. They looked up from where they were watching the baby rock back and forth on all fours. He babbled excitedly when he saw his papa.

"To what do we owe the pleasure?" the duchess asked.

"Must there be a reason?" he asked coyly.

Isabella wanted to laugh as the duchess eyed him.

"I just happened to have a letter to deliver." He handed it over to Isabella. "Your brother sent it through me."

"Go and read it in privacy," the duchess encouraged with a smile. Isabella rose from the blanket and walked down towards the lake, where she perched on a rock before unfolding the letter from Alex.

*Dearest Bella,*

*I hope you are well. By the time this reaches you, we should be one week closer to your birthday and hopefully your freedom. I consulted with Father's solicitor, and he informed me that your inheritance from your grandmother appears to be safe. I had to be careful how I asked because he might be aware of your absence.*

*Father seems to be deteriorating with worry by the day. He has hired a Bow Street Runner to look for you, Bella. Please do be careful. Lord Edmund has been visited by the same Runner and says the man is suspicious of him. 'Twas why I sent the letter through the auspices of the duke.*

*I believe Father could meet the debt if he sold the unentailed properties and jewels, but he seems adamant that he will not pay.*

"He would rather give me to the scoundrel?" Isabella demanded of the paper.

*I do not know what the conclusion will be, Sister. I can only hope you will be safe until it is over. Please express my eternal gratitude to Knighton and his duchess.*

*Ever your loving brother,*
*Alex*

Isabella thrust the paper down into her lap and stared, unseeing, over the water. It still hurt as if it had happened yesterday, that her father could have betrayed her in such a way. She should have accepted it by now.

Would the runner come looking for her? She should probably warn the duke, although Alex had probably written to him as well. Would there be trouble for the duke and duchess? That gave Isabella pause. She would do anything not to bring harm to this family after they had been so good to her.

Yet where would she go if someone found her here? It gave her a sickening feeling to think about leaving the Grange. It was easy to be complacent about her safety this far from London, but if her father had hired a Runner then her time was doubtless running out.

"Isabella?"

She looked up to see the duchess approaching. "Is something amiss? I heard you raise your voice."

"No, ma'am, I am merely angry." Isabella slid down from the rock and began walking back with the duchess. "Did His Grace tell you my father has hired an investigator?"

"He did mention it. It seems he has suspicions about a connection between you and Edmund."

The thought of something happening to Edmund because of her was more than she could bear.

"What will they do to him, Your Grace?"

"Try not to worry. Edmund has been doing this for years and understands the risks."

Isabella shook her head. "I would rather die than have something happen to him."

The duchess reached over and took her hand. "He feels the same way about you."

Isabella did not think it was the same. What Edmund did was out of his love for God. "I should leave."

"I beg your pardon? That is the last thing you should do!" The duchess looked affronted.

"He would not be in danger now if it were not for me."

"You cannot know that," the duchess said reasonably, but Isabella knew it was true. It was one thing to anger an abbess, and quite another to thwart a duke and an earl. Her father might be in some trouble, but he still had friends in high places and a great deal of power.

"Will you help me think of somewhere to go? No," Isabella contradicted herself, in that instant changing her mind. It would be safer if no one knew.

"Isabella, what are you considering? Promise me you will not do something rash."

"I do not believe it to be rash to protect people I care about."

"Think of how we would feel if you ran away. We care what happens to you and would be compelled to search for you. Would that not draw more attention to yourself that you do not seek?"

"No one searched for me last time, and I beg of you not to."

"You must not make a quick decision. At least sleep on it. Promise me?"

"I will sleep on it, but if there is any hint of danger or of them discovering my presence here, I cannot swear I will not leave to protect those I love."

"Perhaps..." the duchess began and then stopped.

"What is on your mind?" Isabella asked as they neared the duke, who was playing with the baby. Isabella watched longingly, thinking her own motherhood was unlikely to happen.

"For a moment I thought that perhaps we might give you a few ideas of where to go, but Rowley would never approve. He will think he can protect you best under his own roof. No one would dare try to harm you here... and I think perhaps he is correct."

"I need to think on it. It is difficult to know what is best!" Isabella wrung her hands.

"We do not speak of it now, but I was once in a predicament and I could have saved myself a great deal of trouble if I would have depended on those who cared about me. My father failed me, and I was too proud to ask others for help."

"If only my story could end as happily as yours," Isabella said wistfully.

"I believe it can, my dear, but you must trust us to help you."

"I do, it is just that I do not believe either party will behave honorably and if Edmund is in the way, he will come to harm."

"Rowley has long since fretted over his siblings. He is more like a father to them than a brother," Emma remarked.

"I also worry that Alex will be hurt in all of this."

"You must trust the men who love you to arrange matters. I fear what will happen to you alone, and once this is taken care of – and it *will* be taken care of – your reputation will be preserved the better by having been under our roof."

Isabella sighed. "I know you are correct, and I hope I may remain here without any ill to any of you." Isabella hoped it could be, but she could not preclude having to leave.

They had retraced their steps and were standing before the duke. He was leaning back against the tree, holding little George who had fallen asleep on his shoulder. Knighton raised his eyebrows in question.

"Please help me convince Isabella that she is safest under our protection. She fears, with the Runner now searching for her, that she is putting us at risk."

"And the vicar," Isabella added, trying not to blush.

"I will be frank, Lady Isabella, I cannot like my brother's involvement, although I applaud the cause. However, leaving the Grange is out of the question. We are close to a conclusion, and chasing after you would be dangerous and ineffective in achieving your aims. What could a Runner do to me? Even if your father discovered the truth and arrived here, he would not invade my house looking for you."

"I wish I could be certain of that," she replied.

"Your brother and mine are doing all they can to help. The gates here are guarded. Try your best not to fret."

"That is easier said than done, Your Grace." She offered a half-hearted smile.

She gathered up the blanket and they made their way back up the hill to the house. Many thoughts were going through her mind, but she could find no good solutions. It was difficult to leave everything in someone else's hands. It was her future at risk!

When they climbed the steps, the door was opened by Quincy. "There is a man here from London to see you, Your Grace. He says he is a Bow Street Runner," the butler almost whispered.

Isabella's heart all but stopped.

"Quickly, we will go to the garden entrance," the duchess said, pulling Isabella back through the door. The duke was still holding little George. Isabella hesitated. "Come! He can manage the baby."

Isabella obeyed and kept her head down, thankful for her large bonnet. The time had come to make a decision, and she no longer had the luxury of sleeping on it.

# CHAPTER SEVEN

EDMUND WAS APPARENTLY susceptible to the follies of most of the human race. He felt like a lovesick fool, and a helpless one at that. He wished there was something he could do to solve Isabella's difficulties, but it seemed as though there was bound to be a catastrophic ending.

Ruskington had invited him to dinner at Frompton House, so he was on his way there now. He did not know Isabella's brother nearly as well as Rowley did, and he was afraid they would somehow give her away.

Perhaps Ruskington was hoping Edmund could convince the duke to settle his debts and repent of his sins. If Edmund were to predict, nothing of the sort would occur.

Edmund paid his cab driver and walked up the steps to the grand mansion. The butler opened the door before he could knock. "Welcome, my lord," he said using Edmund's courtesy title. He took his hat and coat. "Lord Ruskington is waiting for you in the drawing room. Right this way."

Edmund had grown up in luxuries such as this. Still, it was a stark reminder of his current position as opposed to where Isabella's rightful place in society was. It was also a reminder of how appearances could be deceiving. Though Edmund suspected that the duke could come up with the debt if he truly wanted to.

Was his pride worth losing his daughter over? Edmund's blood was boiling with anger.

"Lord Edmund Knight, my lord," the butler announced before leaving the room.

"Welcome, Knight," Ruskington said as he held out his hand and shook Edmund's.

"I confess I was surprised by the invitation," Edmund said quietly.

"I thought it was worth a try. Perhaps you will succeed where I could not. Stubborn does not begin to describe my father's state of mind when it comes to Wethersby."

Edmund was afraid that was his intention. Did he expect him to read him a sermon over port?

"You do not think he will draw any conclusions? The runner is already suspicious of me."

"I do not think there is any harm in trying to help. I am at my wits end, Vicar. This will—this has ruined my family. I only hope not beyond repair."

"You put great faith in my reasoning skills. How forthright should I be?"

"I would be as truthful as possible without revealing your connection."

The door opened behind them and Frompton entered. "What's this? You did not mention we were having guests."

"Only one, Father. Lord Edmund Knight," he introduced him.

"Knighton's brother, then. That's all right. You are a man of the cloth?"

"I am, though my flock is not of the beau monde. I serve the poor in Shoreditch."

"Why ever for? Your brother could surely find you a better living?"

"Indeed. He frequently reminds me of that. Perhaps one day I will accept if I have others besides myself to consider." Why had he said that out loud?

"Come let us eat," the duke said. "We are informal these days," he remarked. They followed the duke into the dining room and the three of them were seated at one end. A footman began to serve them some leek and potato soup and poured them each a glass of claret.

"Father, Lord Edmund knows about Isabella. I have asked for his help."

The duke's spoon slammed down into his soup. "Why would you air our dirty linen?" he demanded of Ruskington.

"Only because our situation has become desperate. Regardless of what you owe Wethersby, my sister is missing!" Ruskington said, barely controlling his temper.

"I do not wish to make trouble, Your Grace. You can be assured of my discretion."

"Yes, of course," the duke muttered, somewhat mollified. "Our families have been friends for generations. But how can you help? I have a Runner looking for Isabella."

Edmund gave Ruskington a look. He was wondering the same thing himself. "Is there any chance I could mediate between you and Wethersby?"

"I have nothing to say to the man."

"But surely something can be done? The deadline fast approaches and he believes you owe him a vast sum of money."

Perhaps Edmund had been too frank, but apparently someone needed to be.

"He cheated me!" he shouted, appearing deranged.

"Then what shall you do when the twenty-first of June arrives?"

"I suspect he will call me out and one of us will be dead." Frompton stood. "Forgive me, I have lost my appetite." He stormed from the room and Edmund's heart sunk.

"Please do not feel guilty," Ruskington said. "This is how every day has been since I returned. I am afraid he has become unbalanced in my time away."

"Do you think it would be worth speaking to Wethersby?" Edmund asked.

"I am willing to try anything at this point," he answered.

The footman brought in a braised veal cheek and fillet of sole in butter and herbs. "If Father refuses to see reason or liquidate any of his assets to pay his debt, I do not know what else is to be done." Ruskington speared a fillet.

"Do you think he would give Isabella away?"

"I wish I knew what he was thinking. I would've sworn on my life he would not have tried to sell her. It seemed he was trying to pay the debt a couple of years ago, but perhaps it was just to make certain Wethersby did not have her virtue. And now, the sudden rush to find her? It all makes me so sick that I cannot believe it is anything but a nightmare."

Edmund agreed. However he had been privy to the dark world for years now, and nothing completely surprised him anymore. England decried slavery, yet children were bought and sold every day to fulfill the carnal sins of the rich.

"What could have made my father change so? The man that raised me never would have considered selling his daughter."

"Sin is like a tiny weed that takes over the garden. At first it looks innocent and then it chokes the life out of every other living thing."

"It still makes little sense to me. I know of course about the blood feud between father and Wethersby over mother. That was never a secret, but I cannot fathom father wagering the dukedom over it." He dabbed his mouth with his napkin and then tossed it on the table. "Shall we go and see if Wethersby is available? Time is running out and I'd rather have done."

Ruskington called for his carriage and they rode to White's in silence.

Once inside, they saw Wethersby was back where he had been the previous time proposing to a rapt audience.

The vote had been tabled until the next session because there was not a quorum, but it did not damper Wethersby's passion for his cause. He was still trying to convince people that importation of grain was unpatriotic.

The crowd was laughing at something Wethersby said when he looked up and saw Ruskington. He inclined his head to Wethersby's raised brows.

"A word, my lord, if you can spare the time?"

"Of course. Excuse me, gentlemen," he said and he followed Edmund and Ruskington to the quiet corner of the club.

"To what do I owe the pleasure?" Wethersby asked as they sat at a table.

"I have only recently returned to discover the situation between you and my father," Ruskington said somewhat carefully, Edmund thought.

"I will be frank, my lord, I would like to see how this may be resolved peacefully."

"The coward sent you as his second, did he?" Wethersby snarled.

"Indeed, no, he has no notion of my seeking you out."

"That is true, my lord," Edmund assured the man.

"The argument is between your father and myself, Ruskington."

"Except it involves my future and my sister, does it not?"

Wethersby clinched his jaw and waited for some moments before speaking. "Very well, Ruskington. I applaud your willingness to resolve this. An apology from your father and the debt is forgiven and your sister may be free."

Edmund knew there was no chance this side of Hell that did the duke would agree.

"That is generous of you, my lord, and I will speak with my father, but he is a stubborn man."

Wethersby laughed as though that was the funniest thing he had ever heard. When he finally stopped and wiped his eyes, he was still smiling. "That is the understatement of the century, Ruskington."

"Is there any way to resolve this with a lesser sum? I can meet most of the debt myself."

"But it is not your debt to settle, lad. This has been a long time coming and it is time to resolve it once and for all."

"You seem like a reasonable man, my lord," Edmund said wanting to try something even though it was not his fight. Can you remove the stipulation about Lady Isabella? You are a married man, sir."

"Pious ideology has no effect on me, Vicar. No, I will not leave Lady Isabella out of this. It is the best way to seek revenge."

➤➤➤⧫⧫⧫

ISABELLA COULD ONLY compare her state of panic to the night at the auction. Her fears had come to fruition much more quickly than she had anticipated. By the time they reached the back of the house, she was breathless as was the duchess.

"Should I hide somewhere on the estate?" Isabella asked.

"Perhaps. There is an old hunting lodge across the ridge," she seemed to consider, "but do you not want to hear what he has to say?"

"I do, but is it safer to have you listen for me?"

"What if he brought someone with him who is sneaking about the grounds?" she reasoned. "I think you should stay with us until we decide what to do. We can listen at the servant's door adjoining the study."

The duchess went in to the kitchens first to ensure the coast was clear and then she waved Isabella to follow.

They entered the intricate set of passages the servants used to move about the house. Isabella rarely used them herself, but the duchess was surprisingly aware of where she was going. As they neared the study, the duchess held up her hand to indicate they were on the other side of the door.

The runner's booming cockney voice carried well. "Here's the thing, Your Grace, I am looking for a high-born girl that is missing, and a few people think your nursemaid looks like her. They seen her in the park with the baby."

"Our nursemaid has been with us for a very long time," the duke said. Isabella almost laughed at the haughty tones in his voice.

"That's part of the problem, Your Grace, the girl has been missing nigh on eighteen months now.

"And her family is just now looking for her?" Knighton asked disapprovingly.

"They were trying to search on their own and became desperate enough to ask for help," the man admitted, not seemingly bothered that people did not care for the runners.

"Who is this high-born girl? Surely I would have heard of one of my peer's children gone missing?"

"The person in question was too proud to admit 'is daughter ran away." The runner added in a confiding tone.

"The odds of finding her now are very slim. Nothing good happens to runaways – especially young ladies."

"There is truth in what you say," the runner admitted, "however, we have not found any bodies matching her description." Isabella cringed at the man's crudeness. "I have a sketch of the young lady."

There was a few minutes pause while Isabella assumed the man was showing the duke a picture of her.

"This girl is very young. My son's nurse is considerably older, Mr. Smallbone."

"Ye would not mind if I spoke with her having come all this way now would ye?"

"I do not see what good it would do. And I do not know how you intend to keep Lady Isabella's disappearance a secret if you are flashing her picture all over England," the duke scolded.

"So ye know of Lady Isabella?"

"Her father and I have been acquaintances for years. There is a portrait of her as a child with her family hanging in Frompton's study."

Isabella looked at the duchess who held up her hands questioningly.

"Besides, she has the same eyes as her brother. I would have known her parentage anywhere. Her father has made no mention of his daughter's absence, though it is hardly something one would want to advertise."

"No, 'course not."

"I also think you must be desperate indeed to come such a distance."

"I had very strong witnesses and the connection with two of your brothers being near the night she disappeared. What with the vicar's history of helping unfortunates, it all seemed too much of a coincidence to ignore."

"I see."

The duchess motioned to Isabella to come close. "I am going to speak to the servants to warn them not to give you away," she whispered.

Isabella nodded with what she hoped was gratefulness. It would only take one person saying the wrong thing to expose her.

"If ye don't mind, Yer Grace, I'd like to speak to the servants. Mebbe they saw the girl with another household and can give me another lead."

Isabella's blood began to pump so hard it sounded like galloping horses in her head and stampeding on her chest. She had to get out of here if the man was going to search the house!

She turned and began searching for where to go, but she could not think straight. Why was this happening when things had been so good for over a year? "Stop it, Isabella," she chastised herself. "Now is not the time to panic." She considered hiding there under the stairwell, but if anyone searched very hard, they would find her easily.

If she left and went to the hunting lodge the duchess spoke about, would she be safe there?

It was worth a try, if only temporarily.

She pulled her bonnet down tight and headed for the side door. What would she do for food or cover? Thank goodness it was summer. The duchess should know where she went and should help.

Leaving the house, she tried to walk at a leisurely pace. It would draw more attention to her if she ran like she wanted to.

She made it past the garden to the woodland and breathed a sigh of relief. She turned back to look at the house and wondered if she would be able to return to it. She turned to face her destination not knowing precisely where it was. She had not been beyond the ridge before, and it was several miles across the estate. But she continued west for what must have been a couple of hours. Her feet ached and her half boots had rubbed blisters.

Thankfully some plums were ripe in the orchard, so she filled her pockets. As she progressed upwards to the ridge, she came upon a stream and followed it to the top.

"How much farther could it be?" she asked, feeling weary and beginning to grow more afraid by the minute.

She would never survive out here very long on her own, but where else could she go? She wandered for some time not finding anything resembling a dwelling of any sort. It took a great deal of reminding herself what her future would have been otherwise to keep her courage up.

The sun was in the far western sky by the time she found what she would describe as a small hut, not a lodge. The roof might have been thatched at one time, but now it almost looked as though it were a part of the woods that it inhabited.

Had someone lived here before? She felt compelled to knock even though it looked abandoned. No one answered and the latch gave way. Her eyes slowly adjusted to the darkness. There was a single room to the wooden structure, with a fireplace to one side, a small table, two chairs and a bed. It was surprisingly tidy and was certainly an excellent place to hide. Isabella pulled the fruit from her pockets then sat in a chair to remove the boots from her swollen, achy feet. A multi-colored, braided rug sat in front of the hearth and Isabella could almost imagine hobbits or fairies from childhood stories living in such a place.

After resting her feet a few minutes, she got up and began to explore. There were a few candles and dishes in the cupboard and a bit of wood by the hearth. If only she had food. A few plums would not satisfy hunger for long. How long would she need to stay in this place? Perhaps until her birthday, then she might ask the duke to send a message to Alex.

She took a pan and walked outside to fetch some water from the stream. It really was a beautiful, enchanting place and if she were not so afraid—or alone – she might have enjoyed being here. But as the sun begin to set, the magnitude of her situation began to fully sink in. What would the runner have done if he found her? Would the duke have allowed him to drag her away in shackles? She had not committed a crime, after all. However, she was underage and her father could not be trusted. There was still a chance he would give her to Wethersby. What had she ever done to deserve such a fate?

Darkness fell inside of the hut and Isabella began to tremble with fear. She was well and truly alone now and needed to find her own the way out of this. Closing her eyes, she tried to imagine happy thoughts like Miss Thatcher always used to tell her to do when she was scared. The only thing that seemed to calm her mind was thinking of Edmund with his kind eyes and handsome smile.

He was her true savior, and she prayed one day when this was over that she would have a chance to prove herself worthy of him.

# CHAPTER EIGHT

EDMUND RETURNED TO the vicarage again, feeling discouraged. It always frustrated him when people held on to feuds and grudges without listening to reason. How could people be so selfish? Did they not realize the effect it had on those around them? What father would sell his daughter for spite? Edmund was beginning to wonder if Frompton was of sound mind. He had not listened to any of Ruskington's reasoning.

Perhaps he had been right about one thing—taking a living in the country would certainly be more peaceful, but would it be fulfilling?

Edmund climbed down from the hackney and paid the driver before walking through the iron gates. He walked up the stone pathway to his home and heard something rustle in the bushes.

"Psst. Vicar!"

"Johnny?" Edmund asked quietly, falling in with the boy's furtive mien.

"Yes, sir. Some feller what looked mean nailed a note to yer door."

Edmund yanked the note from the door and pretended to fumble in his pocket for the key.

"After I have gone in, and you are certain no one is watching, go around and enter through the church."

He unlocked the door and entered. Edmund was growing weary. He was not really in the mood to go through a daring rescue that evening, but he would, because anything those girls or children were going through was much worse than his being tired.

He dropped his hat on the side-table and unraveled the note.

*This is your last warning*

Edmund frowned. He had not rescued anybody for some weeks. In fact, the four girls who had been taken from the Dower House had been the last. He should have done more to protect those girls, and it still weighed on his conscience. Walking through the vicarage to the church, he found all was quiet and dark in the house. Once inside the church, he saw the usual two lone candles burning where they would not cause a fire.

He walked through the transept into the nave, looking around cautiously for any sign of trouble. By the time he reached the opposite end, Johnny slipped through the door.

"Victor," he said, a little out of breath.

Edmund could not help but smile. "What can I do for you, Johnny?" *Besides give you a meal,* he thought. The boy was more skin and bone than he had been when he had helped Edmund rescue Isabella.

"I brought you them four girls."

"You brought four girls here?" Edmund blinked in disbelief.

Johnny lowered his eyes. "I'm sorry if it were wrong to do. I didn't think the cove would follow me all the way here."

*Oh dear.* Edmund crouched down so he would not tower over the boy.

"Where are they, Johnny?"

"They are hiding in that room." He pointed towards the vestry.

"How did you get them here, Johnny?"

"I asked a jarvey." He shrugged as though it were no great matter.

"Do you think the... ah... cove who followed you here is the pimp?"

"Nay, but I think he works for 'em. I'm right sorry, Vicar. But I had heard as you helped these girls afore and they was stolen back, so I thought you would want 'em. I didn't 'ave a chance to come an ask ye first."

"Take me to the girls and we shall see what we can do."

Edmund's mind worked furiously as he considered where he could make four women safe. He had thought the Dower House would be the answer to his prayers, but even that refuge had been discovered— and quickly too.

Devonshire? Rowley would want to strangle him, but he could no more turn away someone in need than Edmund could. He had to admit that he wished to be there with Isabella again and have a chance to convince her of his suitability as a husband. However, he pondered sardonically, bringing four doxies along might not recommend him.

Edmund lit a candle from the tallow tapers and followed as Johnny led the way to the vestry. He held up the light to see four girls huddled in a corner and trembling with fear. He did not blame them for being afraid. He had promised to help them the first time and they must have suffered greatly because of it.

"Martha, Susie, Bertha, Kitty," he greeted softly. "Are any of you harmed?"

Four pairs of eyes looked at him, but all shook their heads.

"Kitty's arm's still broke from when Old Ben took us from that house, but the rest of us got no more than a few cuts and bruises," Martha answered.

Edmund closed his eyes with disgust, mostly at himself.

"Will we be safe here?" she asked him.

"For a little while. I must think of somewhere else to take you, though. I fear Old Ben might have followed you."

"They wouldn't dare hurt us in a church, would they?"

"I do not know," he answered frankly. Most of those people had no soul, or respect for anyone who did.

"Come, let us find you a bed for the night and we will decide what is best in the morning."

He had never sheltered so many girls in his home at one time, but if the house was being watched it was dangerous to take them anywhere during the night. It would be easier to sneak them out one at a time during the day or under the cover of a church service.

The girls rose to follow him and he noticed Johnny was standing off to the side.

"Come along, Johnny." He motioned to the boy. "You will need to stay as well. It is not safe for you to leave either. Is there someone expecting you?"

"Not 'xactly." He shifted from foot to foot nervously.

"Who, then?" Edmund assumed the boy was an orphan and had probably been bought by one of the sweeps.

He muttered under his breath.

"You might as well tell me, Johnny." Forewarned was forearmed, he hoped.

"Old Ben," he admitted.

"You work for the man who took these girls?"

Johnny nodded and flinched as though expecting Edmund to hit him.

"I will not hurt you, Johnny. How long have you been working for him?"

"Since the last time I saw ye," he answered. "He found me outside Madame Celeste's and offered me a warm place to sleep 'iffen I did odd jobs fer 'im."

Edmund chastised himself for not helping Johnny sooner. "Have there been other girls?"

Johnny shook his head. "Not what I've seen. There are girls what live in the brothel, but no new uns that I've seen 'cept these."

Edmund did not doubt there had been other girls, but perhaps the madam had decided to be more careful after Isabella had escaped. The boy's loyalty to him was very touching.

"Did Old Ben pay anyone for you?"

"Nay. I was 'posed to live with me aunt when mam died, but she didn't want me.'

"How long has it been since your mama died, Johnny?"

"Not long afore I met ye the first time."

Edmund needed to think, but there was never much time for that when these things happened.

"Come along, now." Edmund took the five into the vicarage. Seating the girls in the kitchen with Johnny, he pulled out some cheese and bread for them to eat while he woke Mrs. Lowe. She might snap and moan about his rescues, but she had a heart of gold underneath. He wondered if he should tell her about the notes, which, it seemed safe to assume, were from Old Ben, but was the man liable to harm innocent servants? The thought of anyone else coming to harm for Edmund's decisions was unthinkable.

"Mrs. Lowe?" he called as he knocked on the door to her private rooms. She had a parlour and a small bedchamber. He heard rustling in the room before his disheveled housekeeper appeared, looking half-asleep.

"Yes, sir?" she asked hoarsely.

"I am sorry to disturb your slumber, but little Johnny has brought those four girls back here. I am going to put them upstairs for the night while I decide what to do with them."

At the news, she woke up quickly. Her eyes grew wide. "But sir! The bad people will know they are here."

He nodded his head. "Very likely, but I cannot see any other options tonight. Perhaps we can steal them away during service tomorrow."

"And where will you take them?" she asked, almost scolding.

"I suppose it will have to be the Grange. I cannot think there is anywhere else."

"Lord have mercy." She looked heavenward. She walked on into the kitchen, where the girls were finishing their meal. "Well, now! Let's be getting you all to bed." She motioned for the girls to follow, then looked back at Edmund and Johnny. "I will leave you to deal with him, sir. He needs a good scrubbing before he is fit to touch the sheets."

Edmund smiled and saluted. "Yes, ma'am."

He took Johnny over to the wash basin in the kitchen and handed him a bar of soap and a rag. The boy scowled at the offending objects, but took them and did his best, while Edmund racked his brains for what to do with these escapees. It would have to be the Grange. He would have the girls sneak into a carriage under cover of the parishioners the next day.

They went upstairs and he directed Johnny to a truckle bed in his dressing room. The boy was asleep before Edmund had pulled a sheet over him.

Edmund himself was nearly asleep before he collapsed into his own bed.

ISABELLA WOKE WITH a start, but she did not know if there had been a noise, or where she was for that matter. It took a little while to remember the horrible events of the day before. Why had she run away? She had not had time to consider, and the thoughts which had assailed her had not been exactly rational. She could not wait to see if the runners had come to take her!

What was she to do now? What if no one found her in this secluded hut? She would have to find food eventually. Would it be safe to go back to the house? A stream of light seemed to peek into the hut through an opening in the brown tatty curtain. Isabella stood and stretched. The mattress was surprisingly tolerable, but she was still sore from her long walk. The thought of putting her half-boots on her feet made her cringe. As she pulled her fingers through her knotted hair, trying to untangle it, she laughed a little. She had not been gone for even one day, and she was already resembling a wild creature in the woods.

Walking to the door, she stepped out and was amazed by the beauty of the morning. Sun was glistening from the tops of the grass and leaves, and the stream could be heard forging its way down through the ridge nearby to the sea. Tentatively, she stepped out in her bare feet and walked around. A baby rabbit hopped by in front of her and around the house, birds sang on a nearby branch, and a young deer watched her warily.

"Perhaps I am not completely alone," she said softly to it. "I am not sure who is more afraid, little one, you or I."

She sat down on a mossy rock, trying to think clearly. Was it safe to go back now? Surely the duchess would remember telling Isabella about the hut and send someone to find her when it was safe.

Maybe this was a sign it was *not* safe…

Isabella's imagination began to run wild. Although it was hard to imagine anything being worse than being sold to those horrid men at the auction, her flights of fancy were far from comfortable. She did not know what could happen, but she knew she had no rights until her birthday. Albeit, as a female, such rights would be limited even then.

She inhaled deeply of the fresh air and resolved to stay at the hut a few more days if need be. The orchard was possibly an option for food if she was very careful, but it was so very far.

Hopefully, the duchess would soon recall her words to Isabella and let her know how to go on.

She walked on down to the stream and washed as best she could in the cold water. How on earth was she to occupy herself in the small place with nothing to do? Never before had she felt more ill prepared for something – no, that was untrue. When she found herself at the auction, she was equally unprepared. Yet she had survived that, thanks to Edmund, and she would survive this. There was water, there was a little fruit, and she had shelter and a bed. Many were far worse off than she.

If only she had a book or two, this might be enjoyable!

Maybe she would write one when this was all over.

THE DUKE HAD finally rid himself of Mr. Smallbone. He had personally seen him out through the gates on pretense of running an errand, and instructed his gatekeeper to close them to further visitors except family. He had sent the grooms to ride around the house and farm to ensure there was no one else spying. Emma had gone to speak with the servants, and now, as he went to find Lady Isabella, he had a conundrum to face.

How much should he tell the servants? It had already been necessary to tell them to keep their mouths closed when the investigator wanted to look around and question them. In all likelihood she was back in the nursery by now.

He climbed upstairs to find the girl. As he approached the upper floor, he could hear the frantic screams of a child and at once hurried to reach the top.

"What is the matter?" he asked the older nurse, trying to keep the panic from his voice. Emma had arrived before him and was holding the baby in her arms.

"Master George seems to have a fever, Your Grace," the wet nurse replied as she watched the duchess trying to soothe the wailing babe.

Rowley walked over quietly and put one hand on his wife and one on the child. He was burning with fever. Emma looked up at him, half in anguish, half in despair. Mothers took their children's illnesses personally, and fathers tried to heal them.

"I will send for the doctor," he said calmly.

Emma nodded as she comforted George.

"I do not suppose you have seen Miss Thatcher?" he asked softly, trying not to alarm his wife. A quick glance had informed him the girl was not here.

She shook her head. "I left her hiding in the servants' hall, wondering if she should try to escape. I assured her that was a silly notion. I will take George to my rooms and wait for the doctor. Tell Miss Thatcher not to worry about him tonight."

There was no question of telling Emma about Isabella—that the girl no doubt knew something was amiss since she was absent. Nevertheless, Rowley had a duty to Isabella and she was unaware of George's fever. *Let it be something mild and short-lived,* he prayed as he hastened downstairs again. He remembered many times when his siblings had given him a scare, but the doctor had always said fevers were normal in children.

Rowley hurried down the wide mahogany staircase to find Quincy. "Send for Doctor Teague at once, please. Lord George has a fever."

"Yes, Your Grace." The butler turned to go but stopped again at Rowley's question.

"And Quincy, did you see Miss Thatcher go out?"

"I did not, Your Grace."

"Could you have someone look for her in the house and send her to me? I have just come from the nursery and she was not there."

"Of course, Your Grace."

Rowley gave a nod then turned back to his study. Where could the girl have gone? Not far in Devonshire by herself, at any rate. It would be dark soon and if she had gone out, hopefully she would think it safe to return shortly if she had not already done so.

He waited in his study until Quincy came back with the news he expected.

"Miss Thatcher is not in the house, Your Grace. However, her belongings are in her room, untouched. Perhaps she went out for a walk?"

"Thank you, Quincy. I believe I will alert the stables. Will you have the footmen search the gardens to make sure she has not turned an ankle?"

"Of course, sir." The butler bowed.

Rowley strode to the stables and saw one of the grooms ride off for the doctor. How far could a girl have walked on foot? She would not have gone to the main gate. Smallbone had been alone, and Rowley had personally seen him off the property.

Several of the grooms were about their duties, feeding, watering and removing dung. Two stable-boys were sweeping the yard. When he walked into the stables, the head groom came to greet him.

"Have all available men mount and search the property on this side of the ridge for Miss Thatcher," he directed. "I fear she may have gone for a walk and come to some harm."

"Yes, Your Grace."

Six men were mounted in short order, including Rowley, the head groom and an assortment of under grooms and stable-boys. They set out in a deliberate pattern from the house, but with evening coming on, Rowley knew they would only be able to safely search part of the estate. Having issued instructions to his servants to search the farm and tenants' houses, he headed at once for the only empty cottage he knew of.

Rowley understood perfectly why the girl had fled, but could she not have told one of them where she was going? He had made it clear to her he would protect her, so it was difficult to keep his temper in check when he was worried about his son.

When he reached the three-storeyed, five-bedroomed brick Primrose Cottage to which he had always hoped Edmund would one day bring his bride, it was in darkness. Not that he had expected her to light candles and start a fire, but the door was latched and as he searched from room to room, holland covers and dust greeted his every turn. He was quite certain this was not Lady Isabella's hiding place. He called her name in every room to no answer. He cursed as the light faded, knowing they would have to suspend their search for the night. Had she ventured over the ridge? Or had she chosen somewhere more primitive? There were thousands upon thousands of places on the estate where she could be. He had spent many a fond afternoon in his childhood, running wild with Heath and Tinsley amongst the woods and park.

He set the latch back on the cottage door and mounted his horse. Perhaps one of the other fellows had had more luck, but Isabella was a grown woman and he hoped she had sought shelter for the night. They would search again in the morning if she had not come to her senses and returned to the house by then. He would gladly sigh with relief if he were to discover she was tucked safely in her own bed.

# CHAPTER NINE

EDMUND HAD BARELY closed his eyes when he heard what distinctly sounded like the breaking of a window. He opened his eyes and listened, wondering if he should rise and investigate. Mrs. Lowe slept on the ground floor but would she be asleep yet?

The words of the warning note echoed through his head and hearing another crash of broken glass, he threw back the covers. The sound was definitely in the vicarage and someone intended foul play. He threw on his dressing gown. Dawn was already beginning to creep over the horizon. If ever there was a time he needed sleep, it was now, but he pulled on his boots and went downstairs, even though his mind was in a fog.

Another crash sounded. This was no warning, they were under attack! He awoke his housekeeper.

"Mrs. Lowe! Mrs. Lowe! You must get everyone out of the house!"

"What is happening?" she asked when she came to the door. She was rubbing her eyes and her cap was askew.

"I am not certain, but I have heard three windows being broken. Quickly, now, get everyone out of the house and into the church. Send the curate to find the watch while I try to discover what is happening."

The housekeeper nodded while Edmund turned to go and seek who was attacking the house—and with what. He opened the front door and began to shout, to bring as much attention upon the culprits as possible. Some of the neighbors shouted for him to quiet down from their open windows. He would beg forgiveness later. There was a little darkness left to hide them, so he hoped the worst was over; he looked all about but could see no one outside the vicarage, nor yet in the vicinity. Turning back to the house, he entered his study to find a rock covered in horse dung had been thrown through the window. Shards of glass littered the floorboards and a dirty stain marred the unfinished sermon on his desk in mute evidence of the stone's passage. The offending object lay on the floor in front of him. In the close confines of the room, the odour was none too pleasant and he covered his face in an attempt to mask the smell.

Walking on through to the drawing room, he found the same thing, and the same again in the dining room. Sinking on to the closest chair, he shook his head in disbelief. Perhaps he *had* gone too far and should not be surprised by such a petty attack on his home. But was he to sit feebly by while women were kidnapped and abused? He had hoped that the death of the Lord Emerson would have curtailed the trade, but it seemed there was always someone willing to take over.

Sounds of Mrs. Lowe upstairs, herding Johnny and the girls, made him cease pondering and move. They would have to hide in the church and leave as soon as the service was over. He stepped into the hall and met five terrified women and one boy standing wide-eyed at the bottom of the stairs.

"Find all of them bonnets and take them into the church," he instructed. "We will leave discreetly with the parishioners after the service. I will arrange for a carriage to be waiting outside the church and then I will meet you at an appointed place. We cannot be seen leaving together in a large group."

"Where will we go this time?" Martha asked.

"Far away—until this is resolved, at least. My brother has an estate in Devonshire."

"I want to go home!" Kitty cried.

"If you think you can, I would be more than willing to bring that about. For now, go."

Mrs. Lowe looked at him sadly. "This business has gone too far, sir," she pleaded.

"Perhaps it would be safer for you to leave for a time, as well," he said to her, but privately he agreed.

"Who would take care of the church and Mr. Wright?" she replied, as though insulted.

"Who indeed?" he asked. "If something happens, please keep yourself safe."

There was a knock on the door and he gave her a swift pat on the shoulder. "Go."

Edmund did not think Old Ben was one to knock on doors, and he opened it to find his curate with the watch.

"Thank you for coming," Edmund said, opening the door wider to admit them.

He led them into his drawing room, then the study and the dining room, to show them the damage.

Mr. Wright, his young curate, looked wide-eyed at the damage. "Who would want to do this, sir?" he asked. The man lived in rooms adjoining the vicarage, and was unaware of Edmund's doves.

Edmund quickly explained what had happened—omitting the part about the girls, of course—but telling them about Johnny and Old Ben.

"I have to leave London for my brother's estate in Devonshire. I want to make certain nothing else happens."

"Aye, sir, I'll keep an eye on the place. But I don't know of this Old Ben."

"I think he normally stays closer to Covent Garden. I have only previously met Johnny when I was in that area and he knew where to find me. Johnny assures me Old Ben does not own him, so I intend to find him a better situation."

"Aye, sir." The man left and Edmund was tempted to call on the runner. He decided to send a note instead. He knew there was little that could be done, but at least there would be more eyes upon the place while he was gone. It did not sit well to leave his old retainers vulnerable because of his crusading ways.

He shut the door on the watch and turned to the curate. The thin, young man with a babe's face looked frightened.

"I would like you to stay in the house with Mrs. Lowe and the other servants." He walked into his study and scrawled the address for Knighton House on a piece of paper. "If anything happens, you may find shelter here."

The young man frowned with concern. "Do you think this is all because of the boy?"

"And, I dare say, some of the prostitutes I have helped. I do not know how long I will be gone, Mr. Wright. However, I know you are more than capable of managing affairs here."

He nodded. "Thank you, Vicar."

"I need you to have the windows repaired while I am gone." The young man looked around at the mess. "And there is one other thing."

He turned back to Edmund. "Yes?"

"I need for you to arrange a post-chaise for me to be waiting down the street from the church immediately after service."

"Traveling on the Lord's Day?" He looked taken aback.

"Only because it is an emergency, Mr. Wright, and not until after the service."

Edmund reached into his desk and pulled out a purse, handing it to the man.

"I will see to it, sir."

Edmund left him and went upstairs to pack for the journey and to prepare for that morning's service. Never before had he felt less like delivering a sermon, but it was necessary, for he had little doubt someone was watching his movements. Sneaking five people out of the church undetected would require some skill.

His sermon was more heartfelt than anything scripted or straight from the Scriptures. Setting aside his half-written homily, he spoke of helping others in need as much as possible. Kindness did not have to mean the giving of money.

Then, somehow, he drifted off into sins of the flesh and gambling. It was what was on his mind and in his heart and he spoke with perhaps more passion than usual. As the service ended, he stood at the door and while bidding farewell to those of the congregation who paused either to thank him or comment, he gave subtle hints to Mrs. Lowe to take the girls one by one to the waiting carriage. Mr. Wright had been given the task of squiring Johnny so that he wasn't seen with Edmund. Thankful for the flattering size of the gathering, he went to shed his vestments and thence to change into traveling clothes. It was when he was leaving his bedroom that his nose began to twitch at a horrible smell. He lived in the slums, therefore the smell of the sewer was not unfamiliar, but this was very strong and very close.

Covering his nose with his handkerchief, he ran down the stairs… and immediately saw the reason for the foul stench. The ground floor of the house was flooded with sewage. With a deep, sinking feeling Edmund knew it had been deliberate. At least, he reflected thankfully, the carriage containing the girls and Johnny should be away from danger now, and at a safe place waiting for him to meet them.

Had the privy pipes somehow been diverted into the house?

He ran back up the stairs to find his oldest pair of boots to put on before he trudged through the muck. When he returned downstairs again, Mrs. Lowe was in the kitchen, trying to sweep the soil outside, all the while crying hysterically.

Edmund did not bother trying to offer his sympathies.

Running out into the street, he quickly saw that the privy flow had indeed been diverted, by a pipe, to flow straight into the vicarage. Needless to say, Edmund's mind was in anything but a holy or forgiving frame at that moment. Thoughts of revenge and hatred filled his heart as he worked to remove the pipe from the house. There seemed to be more waste than could be accounted for by one privy, but he only found the one pipe.

Some poor wretches lived in sewers, he knew. The reflection made him even more furious at the injustice of the world he lived in.

It was several hours later before all the sewage had been shoveled back out of the house. It would be weeks, if ever, before the smell was gone. Edmund went to Knighton House to bathe and change, taking Mrs. Lowe with him. Something might happen to the house while he was gone, and he would not allow anyone else to be harmed.

It was some time before Edmund was able to meet the chaise and Mr. Wright prior to setting out on the road to Devonshire. He sank with relief into the crowded carriage and realized he was beginning to question his own sanity—and profession.

⫸⫷

THE DUCHESS MUST have forgotten about her, Isabella mused worried-ly. It was the third day of being gone, she was fairly certain, although she was the beginning to feel weak and perhaps not concentrating as well as she should. She had slept a lot, and thought perhaps that might not be a good sign. Her hunger had overcome her good sense to ration her fruits and she had run out.

No one was going to come for her if they had not done by now, so Isabella made the decision to try to return to the manor house. It was a very long walk and she dreaded trying to find her way back. However, if she set out now, perhaps she could arrive before dark.

One way or the other, she had to find food. It was a testament to her state if she was willing to be captured for a piece of bread. Tying her hair into a knot, she looked around the small place that had been her shelter. She was grateful for it, but she was also glad to leave.

Reluctantly, she put on her half-boots and latched the door on her way out. She followed the stream as far as she could, thinking it was the best way back. It was a steep, downward climb and she struggled to walk and grew tired easily, stumbling from time to time. Pausing for a rest, she watched the river flowing around a bend, too far down the cliff at this point for a drink to quench her increasing thirst. She quickly began to lose heart.

What a silly goose she was! She had been certain the duchess would remember telling her about the hut. No matter, she told herself briskly, whatever had happened she needed to return soon and pray they would accept her back. Her steps were slow, but she moved steadily onward. The sun was two-thirds of the way across the sky and a gloomy haze was beginning to cover the sky. The air was damp and thick, which meant a storm was coming.

A large tree stood atop the ridge and Isabella stumbled towards the shelter. She had not gone far if she had only reached the ridge. It was a discouraging thought. There must be hours of walking yet to reach the house, she thought disparagingly. It would be at least an hour on a horse. She sat in the shade of the tree, hoping to recover her sense of direction. Never before had she gone beyond the wooded part of the estate. It was a wonder she had found the hut at all.

Feeling very sleepy, she closed her eyes, intending to rest for a moment.

The rumble of thunder and drops of rain falling on her face later awakened her. She had no idea how long she must have slept but the sky was dark with thick clouds. Isabella scrambled to her feet and began to hurry towards the forest bordering the river.

She found herself climbing again and close enough to the river to take a drink. She knelt down and lapped some much-needed water, feeling a little refreshed. Rain began to batter the earth in sheets and Isabella grew even more discouraged and frozen from the wet. She had no idea which way to go. Everything was beginning to look exactly the same and she would have sworn she had passed a particular chestnut tree, or a rock shaped like a face, hours before.

Growing weaker by the hour, she knew she had to continue. How long could a person live without food? At least she had water, she reflected, not really comforted by the thought. Her last bite had been of a juicy plum yesterday morning. How did people survive in the wild? At this moment, if she could find the orchard it would feel like Eden. What she would not trade for a bite of the forbidden fruit!

Was this what it felt like to become obsessed by something to the point of madness? She was beginning to understand her father a little better with regard to Wethersby, but it still did not excuse offering up her virtue to the highest bidder!

At the present time, she would certainly be willing to bargain for a little food.

Her body began to shake. The further she pushed herself, the worse it became. She even began to see things that were not there— like her old room back at Hartmere, and her nurse. Was she beginning to have hallucinations? Did that mean she was close to death? She didn't feel as though she were dying, but she was very tired, and very, very weak.

"Perhaps a little rest," she told herself again when she was certain she had passed the same place for a third time. Weeping took too much energy, but she was utterly desolate that no one had found her. "Surely they have looked for me?" She had also asked herself this thousands of times.

Closing her eyes, she drifted off to sleep quickly and began to dream. She was dressed in the scandalous costume and was back on the dais to be auctioned at Madame Celeste's. Men were leering and had grotesque expressions in their eyes. They drew closer and closer, as if about to pounce on their prey. She felt as though she would suffocate at any moment if they did not attack her first. Their eyes turned possessed shades of yellow and, suddenly, all of them began to bare their fangs as drips of saliva fell on her skin.

Frompton and Wethersby were there and began taunting each other, calling each other horrible names. Wethersby taunted the duke by describing what he was going to do to Isabella when he won her.

Isabella's entire body began to tremble and it was as if the pack sensed they were about to move in for the kill. Something sharp clawed at her leg and she retreated, only to come up against something hard. There was nowhere to go! She began to scratch and fight but there was nothing but arms and legs surrounding her. Her father and Wethersby unsheathed their swords and began to parry each other's blows, the clanging of steel upon steel sounding loudly yet not distracting the ravenous wolves now laughing at her feet.

Had she died and descended into Hell? She had to escape! Sinking down to her haunches, she looked around for a path to freedom. She took the form of a snake and began to slither through the crowd of beasts looking for their next victim.

She slithered on her belly to where her father and Frampton had both stabbed each other with swords. Both called out for them to save her, but she wanted nothing to do with either of them. At last, she found a hole to escape through the wall of snarling wolves and on the other side there was a beautiful meadow, bright with green grass and yellow and purple flowers. She laughed at her cleverness in escaping the den of Hell as she turned into a beautiful doe and began to prance through the meadow. Off in the distance she could see Edmund smiling and calling to her.

"I am coming!" she returned, but he seemed to grow farther and farther away. Two small children were holding his hand and waving.

She began to run faster and faster until her sides ached from the effort. Why could she not reach them? They turned to walk away from her.

"No!" she cried. "Wait for me!"

Bright white clouds rolled in and overtook them. They faded from her sight until she could no longer see them.

"No!" she wailed again, and she collapsed as her strength failed her. "Do not leave me here!" she begged, but no one could hear her. A pair of doors slammed shut in front of her and she opened her eyes. "I am not ready yet," she whispered to the sky above and slowly she began to crawl back to the hut where she had started from.

# CHAPTER TEN

AFTER SEVERAL LONG days of continuous traveling, Edmund was near bursting with pent up dreams, plans, and ideas of how to convince Isabella to be his wife. Never before had it mattered to him; he left those considerations to his brother and the various peers who needed wives. Yet, the more he thought about being married and having someone to share his life with, the more he liked the idea. There was still the nagging voice in the back of his mind that Isabella deserved someone more suited to Society, but she was essentially ruined in the eyes of the upper crust after her father's surfeit of pride. Where was Isabella's mother, the Duchess of Frompton, during all of this?

Edmund directed the carriage to the back of the Grange. He had also spent a great deal of time thinking of what to do with the four girls. Leaving them here would not do for long, so he hoped Rowley would agree to house them in the empty cottage he repeatedly used to entice Edmund, and allow them to learn sufficient skills for them to find positions in service. While the bawds preyed on young girls fresh to London from the country, he had not heard of them plucking said girls straight *from* the country.

Edmund helped the doves alight from the carriage. Johnny had already jumped down.

"Stretch your legs for a few minutes while I go in and speak with my brother," he told them.

"Cook!" Edmund exclaimed, pleased to find one of his favorite old retainers from his childhood.

"Master Edmund!" She put her hands on her hips after he bent over to kiss her cheek. "What brings you to Devonshire this time? Do you have some more help for me?"

"As a matter of fact, I do. I must go in and speak to His Grace. Will you take care of them? They have had a hard time, I am afraid."

"Oh, the poor dears! They? How many are there?"

"Four girls and a young boy. He will be as pleased as punch in the stables, and I thought to put the girls in the empty cottage."

"If His Grace agrees, that might be a possibility," she conceded as she dusted off her hands off on her apron.

"Once they have gained the necessary skills, we will find them suitable positions. They are all from the country, so I suspect they may well have some skills already."

She nodded and turned to take a batch of raspberry jam biscuits from the oven.

"My favorites. How did you know I was coming?" he teased.

"Is there a biscuit you do not like, Master Edmund?" she asked with a fond look.

He selected one and blew on it until he took a bite. "Perfection as always," he said as the biscuit melted on his tongue. "How is my family today?"

"Master George has had a dreadful fever for days," she answered, shaking her head. "The household was set by the ears."

"Is he out of danger now?" Edmund asked worriedly.

"His fever broke during the night. They've been up worrying, night and day, poor souls."

"My timing is poor indeed. In that case, I will take the liberty of putting the girls in the cottage and Johnny in the stables. I will not trouble Their Graces until necessary."

"Very well, Master Edmund. I will pack some food for them and send a couple of maids over to help them get situated. I know Mrs. Haynes will be happy to help."

Cook went to speak with the housekeeper while Edmund went out to tell the girls they were in good hands. He hoped they were somewhat able to fend for themselves, because he needed to make Isabella the center of his attention for now.

Dare he go to the nursery? He was near to bursting with excitement to see her.

Mrs. Haynes and Cook readily agreed to take the four doves under their respective wings. Once they had left for the cottage, Edmund found his own chamber, washed off several days of travel dust and shaved. Creeping by the duke and duchess's apartments, he made his way up to the nursery. There was a strong possibility that Isabella was also exhausted from caring for George, but if she was available, he wanted to speak with her.

When he reached the top floor, nostalgia hit him as it always did at the familiar sights and smells of his childhood. He smiled, for despite losing their parents while still young, they had been very blessed with each other. For the first time, he had a longing to see his own children and raise them in the way he had been. The children forced to survive on the streets and the prostitutes had always been his substitute, for he expended his energies on helping those who had no loving family. Perhaps he could have both?

Instead of knocking, Edmund opened the door quietly and looked around. The nursery appeared empty. It looked rather stark and white when empty, the toys placed neatly on the shelves. Moving from room to room, he soon saw his nephew was not there and neither were his nurses.

Maybe they had all moved to be near the duke and duchess. Disappointed, he went back down to the study to await the family. Eventually, they would come downstairs. He knocked lightly on the study door to be certain, and was surprised when he heard his brother's voice bid him enter.

"Edmund?" Rowley strayed from behind his desk and came to greet him, looking exhausted. His embrace felt as though he were trying to transfer some of the weight of the world from his shoulders.

"George is going to make a full recovery?"

Rowley stepped back and gave a nod. He looked exhausted. "It was a close-run thing for a few days."

"Did he have the measles or the influenza?"

"I could not say what he had. Dr. Teague says children often have fevers they cannot explain. I thank God you are arriving to good news rather than preparing for a funeral."

"As am I. I expect it matters not to you why I am here."

"More doves? Or Lady Isabella?"

Edmund gave a curt nod to both. "A great deal has happened in London, but now is not the time to assail your ears with it."

"No, I am all curiosity. I could do with a diversion, I assure you," Rowley said as he stood to pull the bell-rope. He ordered a tea tray from Quincy and then went and sat next to Edmund in one of the chairs by the fire.

"Well, the doves—all four of them—are on their way to the cottage. These four had been stolen from Woodcrest, and then found again. Mrs. Haynes and Cook are seeing to their needs. Once they have acquired some skills, I will try to place them in appropriate positions. There is also a young boy, and I gather he is beside himself with glee in the stables at this very moment."

"I am glad someone is happy," Rowley muttered. "I am certain there is more to that story. By the way, the runner visited here. He said he had also made your acquaintance."

"He came here?" Edmund sat forward in his chair.

"Indeed. Several days past. In fact, not long after we arrived. And Edmund, there is something I must tell you."

Edmund knew what it was before Rowley uttered the words.

"Lady Isabella ran away when she heard why he was here. I searched for her and my men are still out looking. There has been no sign of her since, and she did not take anything with her. No one other than the runner has passed through the village, so she has to have left on foot."

"How long has it been?" Edmund asked calmly, while feeling as if he was being eviscerated.

"Three or four days?" Rowley shook his head. "George has been so ill I have lost count. I do not know where else to have them search."

Edmund could hardly be angry with his brother. Isabella was a grown woman and had, it seemed, left on her own.

"You are certain the runner did not come back and take her?"

"Reports from the village are that he left alone. We have been guarding the gate and you know as well as I do the geography here makes it difficult to enter the estate elsewhere."

"There are thousands of places she could hide here," Edmund said, trying to reassure himself.

"I said the same thing. Now that George is better, I can go back out to search with you. We will speak with the grooms first and see what areas have already been searched."

"We must hurry. If she has been out as long as that without food or shelter..." Without conscious thought, Edmund was already on his feet and ready to leave, eyeing the dark clouds brewing outside the window.

"I do not understand why she did not come back," Rowley said as he also stood to leave.

"Isabella is missing?" Both brothers turned to see the exhausted duchess standing at the door. "The woodman's hut. Over the ridge. I-I think I mentioned it when she spoke of hiding... but I thought... oh, how dreadful. Please go and find her!"

"Isabella! Isabella! You must wake up!"

Was she dreaming again? Isabella reached out and tried to touch the man who had spoken. The figure felt like a person… but was she wishing for what could never be again? Was it too late?

"Yes, that's the ticket, wake up!" he commanded.

She felt as limp as a rag and hardly able to support her head when she was scooped up into strong, warm arms.

"It is I, Edmund."

"Edmund?" she rasped. Her mouth felt like cotton.

"Yes, my dear, I thought we would never find you!" A cup was placed against her lips. "Take a drink," he ordered gently.

She did, and the liquid was like nectar to her throat.

After a few minutes, she felt like opening her eyes. The sight of Edmund was the sweetest thing she could have imagined.

"Are you a dream?" she whispered, reaching up to touch his face.

"I am quite real." He turned his head to kiss her palm. "How many days have you been here? I cannot think what made you run away! But I am too happy to have found you to scold—very much."

"I was afraid. The runner was here, looking for me. He had my picture."

"I know. You should have trusted Rowley to protect you. I am sorry I was not here sooner."

"I am deeply thankful you have found me now."

"You are very pale—and weak. Did you bring naught to eat?"

"I ran out of food. I had some plums, but they were soon gone," she explained, feeling foolish.

"I have some victuals in my saddle-bag. Cook thought they might be necessary. I will be but a moment."

He returned with some bread and cheese. It was as good as a feast after having so little and then nothing; so much so, in fact, that she found it difficult not to gobble like a pig.

"I know it may be hard, but do go slowly," he urged.

"I know I must seem the most complete fool for leaving, but the duchess told me of this place and I stupidly thought she would remember and send for me when it was safe," she explained once she had a little more energy. "Then I tried to find my way back and became lost. By the time I found myself back where I started, I was too weak to go any further."

"The duchess was distracted, unfortunately. George took a fever and was ill for a few days. When she realized you were missing, she knew where to find you."

"That explains a great deal," Isabella answered. "Is Lord George better?"

"He is on the mend, I understand. His fever broke during the night."

"Thank God," she said, with much relief. Her heart could not bear the burden of also losing the baby.

"How very like you to worry about him when you are the one suffering now."

"Through my own stupidity!"

"Nonsense. You were hardly prepared for an investigator from London arriving to seek you out."

"He is gone?"

"He left that very day. Rowley escorted him from the property."

Could she have been more stupid? She could have died if no one had found her!

"It is safe to return to the house, and by the look of the clouds I think we should make haste."

"You mentioned you have a horse?"

"I do." He smiled. "But only one."

"Thank goodness, because I doubt not I have the energy to walk or sit my own mount... and I do not know the way either," she said sheepishly.

"How did you find your way here in the first place?"

"It was not so difficult, leaving from the house, but I had no land-marks to retrace my steps on the way back."

He took one of her hands and held it. "I thank God we found you in time. I have been thinking a great deal, you must know, since last we spoke."

"As have I," she confessed. "Indeed, I have done little else."

He chuckled.

Afraid of what he was going to say, she kept talking. "Has anything else happened since I left? I have had one letter from my brother but I received that just moments before the runner arrived."

"Very likely they were on the same mail coach," he conjectured. "There has been little progress, if that is what you are asking. I dined with your father and brother just last week and your father still did not wish to listen to reason."

Isabella's spirits sank at this news.

"We also tried speaking to Wethersby, and he agreed to cancel the debt in exchange for an apology."

Isabella gave an unladylike snort at the idea of her father apologiz-ing.

"Precisely. Unfortunately, he would not release his claim on you."

"I wish I could not care what happened to him. I want to hate Father!"

"No. You do not want to let hate control you. This will soon be over," Edmund said calmly.

"Will it?" she asked doubtfully. "My name has been bandied about the clubs as the prize in a wager. I cannot imagine I will be welcome in any drawing rooms again."

"While I cannot deny what you have said, I do not think your reputation to be beyond repair. You have done nothing wrong."

"So would say many a ruined damsel, I am sure. Such is the way of Society."

He did not respond to this. "We should be going if we are to beat the storm," he said instead, as he looked out at the darkening sky.

"Yes, of course," she agreed. Suddenly, however, she felt very shy about returning to the house after committing such folly. She attempted to stand and almost lost her balance when her knees buckled beneath her. Stepping swiftly forward, Edmund caught her. "I am weaker than I thought," she said, giving him an apologetic smile.

Suddenly, she found herself scooped into his arms and carried through the door, seemingly without effort. A beautiful bay gelding stood grazing nearby and did not demur when Edmund lifted her onto its back.

"I pray you can hold on for a moment," he teased before then mounting behind her.

The rush of feeling that swept over Isabella almost startled her into falling from the horse. She was weak as it was, and the new sensation caught her off guard. Had she ever been held thus by a man? No; at least, not since she was a child and then by her father or one of her brothers. Even in her fuddled state she knew it was highly irregular, if not improper, and yet his strength made her feel secure.

Edmund was so tender and kind, it was easy to be captivated by him. She wanted to stay with him and forget the rest of the world existed.

"Are you awake?" he asked softly into her ear.

"Of course," she mumbled, her words receiving another low chuckle. The rhythm of the horse swaying back and forth, along with the staccato throb of his heartbeat against her ear, was soothing in a wholesome, safe way she had not experienced before.

"Sleep, if you wish," he said, pulling his thick woolen cloak around her, thus encompassing her in a comforting cocoon.

"I have done nothing but sleep for days," she whispered. "I wish I were not so tired."

"A few days of rest and nourishment and you will feel quite the thing again," he assured her.

"A few days and this dreadful situation will be over. I have lost count, but it cannot be much longer until I become of age."

A fat raindrop fell on her cheek and she looked up towards the sky. "Could you not have waited a little longer?" she murmured to the heavens, although she did not begrudge a reason to snuggle closer to Edmund's warmth. He pulled his cloak even tighter around her.

Would it be so wrong to marry him for her convenience? Did she care enough for both of them? He would be an easy husband, even if the church was his first love. She had no doubts on that score.

"What are you thinking, Isabella?" he asked.

"How can you tell I am thinking instead of sleeping?" she countered.

"A sixth sense, perhaps," he said with hints of laughter in his voice.

"Pray tell," she insisted, daring a glance up at his face.

He looked down at her with a devastating smile. She did not know if she would be strong enough to let him go were he to offer a second time.

"Very well, you were wriggling and making little noises, as though conversing with yourself."

"I was not!" she protested.

"You most definitely were, but I find it very endearing."

She felt warmth in her cheeks at his words, which the steady rainfall did nothing to cool. She tried to take it all in—his masculine scent, which was earthy and part horse—his broad shoulders and his strong arms. He was just the combination of kindness and gentleness, with fine form and affection that the hero of her dreams would have.

As the rain fell harder, it was impossible to speak and Edmund increased the pace of the horse so they might reach the house faster. Isabella was tempted to scream that she wanted to stay like this in his arms forever, but decided it would take entirely too much effort. Instead, she inhaled a deep breath and burrowed even closer, finding peace and rest in his arms.

# CHAPTER ELEVEN

A S EDMUND HELD Isabella in his arms, he knew he would not cease until she was his. He sensed her attraction to him, but also her hesitation. While he was beginning to think he understood what was causing her hesitation, her supposed ruination mattered not a jot to him.

By the time he drew rein at the house, Isabella was limp in his arms and his throat grew tight at the thought of what had almost happened to her. Her breaths were shallow and she trembled with weakness.

Rowley was waiting at the front steps and lifted her carefully from Edmund's arms while he dismounted.

"How is she?" Rowley asked, though it was clear she was not well.

"Weak, but in good spirits. She had not eaten in days, and became lost while trying to find her way back. With rest and nourishment, she should recover in a few days."

"Thank God," Rowley responded as he carried her into the house, where Emma was waiting anxiously. "I will have it ever on my conscience I did not consider looking beyond the ridge. I am afraid it did not occur to me she might have known of the hut. I was astonished Emma remembered its existence."

"To be fair, it is the most secluded place I could think of," the duchess remarked. "If only I had realized she was missing…"

"You were rather occupied with George," Edmund reminded her.

Emma smiled faintly. "I have had one of the guest chambers prepared for her."

Rowley was still carrying Isabella, and Edmund selfishly wanted to take her back, but that would be ridiculous. Instead, he followed the little party upstairs and saw her safely placed on a large four-post bed in a comfortable room overlooking the gardens. She looked like a small waif on the large bed, all dirty and disheveled, yet she nothing could hide her beauty. A fire had been lit and a maid was waiting to attend to her. As Rowley set her upon the silken covers, Isabella opened her eyes. It was a measure of encouragement to Edmund that her eyes immediately searched for him. Rowley stepped back to let Edmund draw closer.

Isabella reached for him and he took her hand in his. "Thank you for saving me." She smiled. "You are a true Knight."

"Alas, I forgot my shining armor today." The fact her words gave him such pleasure made Edmund feel like a silly schoolboy. "I will leave you in Mary's capable hands. If you have need of me, you need only to say the words."

As he stepped out of the room, he was reassured when he heard her ask for a bath and dry clothing.

He followed his brother back down to the study, where he collapsed into a chair with relief. His brother's hand squeezed his shoulder from behind.

"I think she has come to no great harm."

"Yes," he agreed, but they both knew what a near thing it had been.

Rowley walked over to his desk and picked up a letter. "I have had word from Ruskington."

"What has he to say?"

"He says people are beginning to ask after Isabella—demanding she be presented. He believes her reputation will be irreparably damaged and her hope of contracting a good marriage is ruined."

"I am not surprised. We said much the same when we first learned of the affair."

"He begs for our support with her once this ludicrous situation is over. He is unsatisfied in his efforts to find her a husband. The only—ah—*gentlemen* willing to attach their name to hers as a matter of some urgency are unworthy of her, he says."

"You must help me convince her, Rowley. I think she is not averse to my suit, but she fears she will darken my name and prospects in the Church."

"Ridiculous!" his brother exclaimed. "Your position is assured. I do agree, nevertheless, if you are certain it is what you want, then we must convince her of the sincerity of your feelings. You have always proclaimed the Church to be your choice, and I would not see you shackled for life to someone you have felt compelled, by your good nature, to rescue."

"I would not!" Edmund insisted, sitting upright in protest.

Rowley gave him that all-knowing look which disagreed without words needing to be spoken.

"Perhaps I would," Edmund conceded, "but not for such a situation as this."

Rowley narrowed his eyes as if amused. "I do consider Lady Isabella to be a lovely girl and a suitable match, and I will do my best to promote it, if it is what you wish."

"Very much so, Brother."

"I thought so, but I wanted to hear the words from your lips. I have taken the liberty of sending to the Archbishop for a special license. I would like to return to London to support Ruskington with the marriage already *un fait acompli*."

"I hate to seek to persuade her when she has been through so much," Edmund wavered.

"Now is not the time for prevarication. It will be up to you to ensure her happiness after the fact."

The idea was temptation beyond comprehension. Soon this heinous situation would be over and he wanted her to desire him beyond gratitude.

"Very well. We—I—convince Isabella to marry me. What then?"

Rowley held up the letter again. "It forces Frompton's hand. Isabella arrives in London as Lady Edmund Knight, and her part in this is done."

"What of her father's consent?"

"I have had a letter from Ruskington explaining the situation to the Archbishop. Besides, you marry the morning of Lady Isabella's birth date, and who could argue your suitability as a husband? Frompton has little credit left following his involvement in this shocking affair."

"The thought of returning to London is not so appealing just now," Edmund admitted.

"You will take the living here, at last?"

"I confess I am considering it. London has been hostile of late."

"Dare I ask?"

"Suffice it to say it involves broken windows and the floor of the vicarage being covered in sewage."

Rowley raised his brows in interest. "One of your angered procurers?"

"The one who stole the four doves now ensconced in your cottage, and the one who was using the boy."

"However did you get them away?"

Edmund smiled mischievously. "They were ushered, one at a time as parishioners, from my Sunday service into a nearby carriage. The curate took them away while I performed my duties in front of any watchful eye."

"Well done. I do hope you will consider the living here. If not, I would be pleased to have you manage Stonebury. It is not too distant and a lovely estate on which to bring up children. You would not need to shed your vestments, but also would not rely upon it for your daily bread."

"I do not know how to answer you, Brother."

"Consider it. Although, with Lady Isabella's portion, you may wish to find a property of your own."

"It is all planned out, is it not? Now to convince the bride," Edmund remarked sardonically.

"Stop thinking like a clergyman and instead behave like a normal man. Women want to be wooed. You read sermons for a living and have the most eloquent speech of any of us."

"I am a normal man!" Edmund protested. "While I confess I bungled the first proposal, I am waiting for the right moment to speak again."

"Were you not just alone with her for several hours?"

"She was near starvation and hardly in a fit mind to be proposed to!" Although, he admitted to himself, there had been the one moment when he had almost done that very thing.

"Promise me you will do so before my man returns with the special license."

"Do you not think she is safe now? The runner left; surely the danger to her is past?"

"To be frank, I do not think we have seen the last of him." He held up the letter again. "Ruskington also wrote that the runner, upon returning to London, informed Frompton he was certain she was being hidden in one of my households."

"I do not want her to know that," Edmund said. "Mr. Smallbone is more clever than I gave him credit for."

"I agree. I want her to marry you because she wishes to, not because she has no other option."

"Perhaps we should place guards around the house?" Edmund suggested.

"I have already asked all the grooms and footmen to be on alert.

Posting sentries would unduly raise suspicion about her. I can trust my long-serving servants implicitly, but it only takes a single tongue loosened by drink…"

"I cannot imagine speculation is not already rampant in the servants' quarters."

"There is little I can do about that now. Emma insists on treating Lady Isabella as a guest, and after her disappearance, coupled with the runner nosing about the house, complete secrecy is a lost cause."

"Mm," Edmund acknowledged, somewhat vaguely. "Though it does not mean we should not be cautious."

"She is safe enough in her chamber for the night. I suggest you spend the rest of the evening devising a strategy for tomorrow," Rowley advised. "Then we may proceed with our plans to assist Ruskington in London."

"Why do I feel as if I need a battle plan?"

"Because it will affect the rest of your life."

"A guide would be most welcome. This is one area in which the Bible is not prolific," Edmund pointed out, with a rueful twist of his lips. "I know she will be an excellent mate."

"Ah, but you have to convince her that *you* are," Rowley added wryly.

ISABELLA AWOKE THE next morning and found herself without employment. The duke and duchess insisted she be treated as a guest and so she was now resting on a chaise longue in the conservatory, trying to read a book. The conservatory had always been her favorite place in the grand house when she would on occasion bring Lord George there, with its glass walls allowing natural light. The room was filled with greenery and exotic flowers and was scented with hints of citrus from the orange trees.

Reading was what she had hoped for when she been in the hut all alone, but now she could not concentrate on the words. Her strength was already improving, but there was too much on her mind with her future so uncertain.

When Edmund found her, some time later, she was staring, unseeing, lost in thought.

"Penny for them?" he asked, startling her.

She smiled up at him. "I am mostly grateful to be safe here at the house again, but I confess I am worrying about my future."

"Very understandable. May I join you?"

"Yes, of course." She sat up and slipped across the padded seat to make room for him. She felt very pleased that he had sought her out, but also a little self-conscious.

"How are you feeling?" he asked.

"Much better, thank you. I have far more sympathy now with the waifs I see on the streets in London. I understand why you fight so hard for them."

"Indeed, nothing else matters a great deal when you are cold and hungry."

"I admire your work very much." *And you*, she wanted to say but was not so bold.

"That is what gave me the excuse to come and visit you here, Lady Isabella."

She frowned, furrowed her brow. "What do you mean?"

"I have brought four girls here who were in a similar situation to you. And a young boy," he added.

"Are they unharmed?"

"They seem to be, but they have been found once. I had taken them to the house in Kent my brother and his wife established for them."

She gasped. "How awful! How frightened they must be! May I visit with them?"

"I think that would be acceptable," he said. "I need to see how they go on, anyway. You are certain you feel strong enough?"

"It is nothing compared to what they have suffered," she replied. She needed to remember that, she told herself. At least she had been rescued before her body had been abused.

"Such fortitude, Lady Isabella," he remarked, helping her to her feet. They were standing very close together and he still held her hand. He raised his other hand and tucked a hair back behind her ears. For a moment, she thought he was going to kiss her, and was uncertain how she felt about that. While she wanted him to do so very much, the time and place were hardly propitious.

"Would it be acceptable if I..." He leaned forward and his lips briefly touched hers.

"Cor, you ain't gonna kiss her, are ye?" a little voice asked from behind an orange tree.

Isabella giggled.

"Johnny," Edmund said in the tone of voice universally used by exasperated parents. "What are you doing in here?"

Johnny had the grace to look sheepish, and murmured, "'Is Grace said to make meself at 'ome."

Isabella's heart was completely in this little boy's hands. She knelt down before him.

"Did you want to try an orange?"

The little boy nodded guiltily and pulled his hand from behind his back, revealing the remnants of the fruit.

"I cannot blame you, for oranges are delicious, but you will never go hungry, you know, living here. You do not need to sneak about like a thief, do you understand? You must be trustworthy and honorable in order to remain here," Edmund said sternly.

"Yes, sir," he said, looking frightened.

"No one is angry, Johnny," Isabella said, pulling him into her arms. He was as stiff as a board, but she tried to cuddle him anyway.

"Are you supposed to be doing anything in the stables this morning, Johnny?"

He nodded. "I am 'posed to brush the horses down when they're done exercisin' them."

"Then you had better get back to your task."

Johnny nodded and hurried away.

Isabella smiled after him, but then turned to Edmund and frowned. "Was he being abused?"

Edmund shook his head. "I do not think so. His mother died just before I met you the first time. He was the messenger Heath sent to let me know about your... predicament."

Isabella's hands went to her chest. "Oh, the dear! I am so grateful you are helping him. Maybe I will be able to do something for him when I am free."

"I would do anything to help you, Lady Isabella, if you would allow me to."

She bit her lower lip. She wanted that very much, but she was not quite ready to answer.

"I know, thank you."

"Shall we go and call on the girls?" he suggested. He gave her his arm and she took it as he led her out to the stables. A groom harnessed a roan gelding to a gig and they climbed in.

"It is not a long ride, but I do not wish to tax your strength so soon," he remarked.

She smiled gratefully. "I believe I have seen the cottage you speak of. It is referred to as Primrose Cottage, is it not?"

"It is," he said. "Aptly named for the flowers that grow in a thick blanket around the meadow here each spring. There is a living here with the estate and that would be my home if I chose to take it."

He tooled the carriage with ease down an earth path which went beside the lake. It was in the opposite direction from the ridge, and pretty in a different way, being surrounded by dense woods of beeches, walnuts, and alders. The air was thick with the smell of freshly cut grass and wildflowers dotting the undergrowth with brightly coloured blooms, much like those near her hiding place.

They drove along in silence for a while—Isabella feeling too nervous to speak and not wanting to ruin the moment of being with him. She confessed to herself that she wished he had come solely for her, but she was also grateful for the type of man he was, to risk so much to help unfortunates.

"You have grown quiet again," he said, looking at her skeptically.

"I suppose it is because, having had no one to talk to besides myself for several days, I do not know what to say."

He chuckled. "Whereas I am never at a loss for words. I try to be mindful of it with my sermons."

"I am certain your parishioners appreciate that," she quipped.

"It is beautiful country here, is it not? Sometimes I am tempted to leave London behind and take up a simpler life."

"Then why don't you?" she asked, turning to look at his lean profile with the square jaw and aquiline nose which had become so dear to her.

He waved one hand in gesture. "A sense of purpose, I suppose."

"Do you think you will be less satisfied? Is there not good to be done anywhere if we look for it?"

He looked down at her, his expression making her insides melt. "You are right. Perhaps I fear loneliness."

His words held a deeper meaning, she was certain.

"Isabella," he said, beginning to slow the horse. "My desires have not changed. My heart is constant once it sets its course. What must I do to convince you to be my wife?"

Her heart had also set its course and that organ tightened in her chest, as if in protest with her warring mind.

As if he sensed her hesitation, he transferred the ribbons to his right hand and reached over with his left and took hers.

"I should have waited to speak. My mouth jumps ahead of proper thought when it comes to you."

Tears threatened, but she spoke anyway. "It was perfect."

"I wanted you to know that I am not asking you out of some exaggerated sense of honor and duty. I truly want to be your husband."

She could not speak. She had been holding her breath, listening to him as he erased all her objections with his speech. He was watching her warily, so she reached up and pulled his face, his lips, to hers in answer. She had never, willingly, done anything so bold in her life. It felt as though fire was running through her body at his touch. His response was eager and she felt encouraged that he might indeed desire her. She became emboldened as the kiss grew deeper and yet she still felt completely safe with him through the tenderness he showed her.

Edmund pulled back enough for their foreheads to meet and then smiled at her. "Please tell me that is a yes, for I will not easily accept a refusal after that taste of Heaven." His eyes crinkled at the corners with a devilish smile.

"I will say, sir, at first I thought your offer was mercenary."

"And now?"

"I would like to be your wife very much, but are you certain you know the difficulties we face?"

"None of it matters if we are together. Most of the problem will go away when we marry."

"I hope you are right."

# CHAPTER TWELVE

EDMUND GAVE THE roan the office to walk on again and in a very few minutes turned up the drive to Primrose Cottage, drawing to a halt before the substantial dwelling. "Cottage" was rather a misnomer for what was a lovely home.

He felt as though he was floating on air, a notion he had always thought silly before. Not only did Isabella reciprocate his feelings, she also wanted to be his wife! He would have rather driven on, to spend more time alone with her and steal more earth-shattering kisses, but they were here and he still needed to see how the four girls were getting along.

"It is a lovely house!" Isabella exclaimed. "I would not mind living here at all," she said, giving him a bashful look.

"We can certainly reconsider my parish in London. I do not think it an ideal place to bring up a family."

"Oh, Edmund, do you—do you think it is possible? That we can soon put all of this trouble behind us and be happy together?"

"I intend to do just that. What hold can your father have over you once you are wed?"

"He gave up his rights to my loyalty when he tried to sell me."

"I have quite enough family for us both, and they already adore you. And you have your brothers."

"I wonder how Alex is managing affairs at the moment. Father cannot be easy in his mind as the date of my majority approaches."

"No," Edmund agreed. "Rowley had hoped to return to London to support him, with you and I already married."

Isabella stiffened on the seat beside him. "So soon?"

"We will talk about it more. You will not be forced into anything, I promise."

He jumped down, hitched the horse to a nearby post and then turned to help Isabella to alight. As she rose from the seat, he stilled for a brief moment, considering, and then placed his hands on her waist to lift her down. Her blush, in addition to her unlooked-for kiss, dispelled all thoughts in his mind of any unsuitability and any lingering doubts of indifference. It would be a very compatible match. He gave her his arm, and led her to the front steps of the cottage. There was no answer, so Edmund opened the door.

"Shall I go in first to make sure all is well?" Isabella asked.

"That would probably be best," Edmund said, not remarking out loud what he thought might be going forward in a place occupied by four females who had been living in a bawdy house.

He waited on the portico, looking out over the surrounding vista. Truly, there were few places more beautiful than the southwest coast of England. A feeling of peace came over him; a sensation that, come what may, it was right for Isabella and he to marry.

Isabella returned, a smile shaping her full mouth. "All is safe, my lord."

"My lord?" he asked, casting her a curious look.

She looked sheepish. "I am uncertain what to call you, and I confess to being a bit shy about our dealings with each other."

He took her hand. "I want you to promise me that you will feel free to tell me anything. You need never be afraid of me. We will make sense of things together."

"Yes, Edmund." Those stormy blue eyes looked up at him and feelings of desire, and something even deeper, stirred within him. He kissed her hand before he forgot who he was. "Shall we?"

"They are in the kitchens," she explained, leading him along the hall to the roomy domestic quarters. When they walked in, the four girls stopped in the middle of their chores.

"Good morning, Kitty, Martha, Bertha and Susie," he said cheerfully. "How are you settling in?"

The four girls curtsied and chorused a return greeting.

"This is Miss Thatcher," he said, "if you did not make her acquaintance a moment ago."

"I did not mention our connection. I have also been rescued by the vicar," Isabella surprised him by saying to the girls, but he could see the four girls immediately relaxed at her words.

"Please, have a seat," Kitty said, as if practicing her manners. Edmund knew it was important to let them show him and he held out a stool at the wooden table for Isabella.

"Would you care for a biscuit, sir, miss?" Martha asked, looking proud as she held out a small tray of her creations.

"Someone must have told you of my weakness," Edmund said, delighted, as he took a piece of shortbread. Isabella took one as well and Susie offered them tea. She was the shyest of the four and he could not recall having heard her speak more than five words.

"Delightful," he remarked as he finished his first biscuit. "I see you have already learned a great deal."

Martha beamed. "I always wanted to be a cook," she said. "Mrs. Baird says I can start helping her here."

"I be getting to go home and take Susie with me," Kitty said, looking very young. "His Grace sent someone to talk to me pa, and when pa heard about my arm, he was that angry he agreed to take me back. He said Susie could come because I don't as like to leave her on her own."

"That is extraordinarily good of him. I am very pleased for you both." Edmund suspected Rowley had offered handsome compensation to the man to make it an easy decision, but he would never say so.

Isabella was talking to Bertha. "And what will you do?"

Bertha was the prettiest of the four and the one he was most concerned about. Many of the households in which she might be placed would think her fair game.

"I don't know as yet," she replied a little sadly. "I would also like to return home, but I don't know if I'd ever be accepted."

Edmund did not know Bertha's story. "I will look into it if His Grace has not already done so."

"I am from Cheshire, sir, and I believe His Grace sent someone to speak with my family."

"Cheshire is not very close to here, it probably takes some little while. Do not fret just yet."

"Don't you worry, Bertha. Tommy will take you back." Martha tried to reassure the girl.

Bertha's eyes filled with tears; shaking her head, she went out of the kitchen door into the yard behind the house. Martha followed her.

"She was stolen from an inn where she worked as a maid," Kitty explained. "She had a sweetheart and they were engaged to be married."

"I pray her beau will be understanding, then. When are you to leave?"

"His Grace wants a doctor to look at me arm first; perhaps today, if he can spare the time."

"A wise decision," Edmund said, feeling eternally grateful to his brother who had been very busy whilst Edmund was caring for Isabella. "We will return to say goodbye, then. I am happy for your good fortune, Kitty and Susie." He and Isabella stood up to leave and Kitty threw her arms around Edmund. He laughed. "All will be well, my dear," he said as he returned her grateful hug. She was near to sobbing. "There, there."

"I never thought I'd get to go home again. God bless you, sir."

He looked over her head and met Isabella's eyes full of empathy. She understood.

Once they regained the gig and were driving back to the house, they said little, but Isabella sat closer than was needful—almost snuggling against him. His heart was full.

"I do not want you to give up your work, Edmund," she said.

He turned to look down at her face. "Do you wish to live in London?"

"I am not certain," she confessed, "but I know it would be wrong for us not to help girls like them—like me."

Perhaps God knew what he was doing by putting them together, after all. "We do not have to decide now," he answered slowly. "My first concern is to see you safe, and married." He could not help but lean over and kiss the top of her head.

She was watching him with those big blue eyes, so trusting in their hope... in—could it be—love? He wanted this moment never to end, but life must carry on, and there was much to be arranged.

"Ruskington has asked us to return to London to help him. I fear it will not be an easy matter for him or your father in dealing with Wethersby."

"Do you mean before we are wed? My birthday is still a few days away. Can my father contest our marriage if we wed before that date?"

"I believe the plan is to travel to London and wed as soon as you reach your majority. Our brothers are working on obtaining a special license."

"So you intend for us to wed on my birthday and present ourselves as Mr. and Mrs. Knight?"

"Yes. It will force your father's hand. He will have no right either to give you away or annul the marriage."

She nodded. "It makes perfect sense."

"Rowley is excellent at arranging such schemes to one's satisfaction." He took her hand and squeezed it. "I am sorry it has come to this and that the happiest day of my life will be overshadowed, for you, by this tragedy."

"As am I," she said sadly, "but please believe I do not regret marrying you."

"My dear Isabella, I will make it my life's purpose to see that you never do."

⁂

ISABELLA'S MIND WAS in a constant state of flux. One moment she was giddy about her upcoming nuptials, the next she was forlorn about her father's impending ruin. He had made his own bed and had to lie in it, as the saying went, but she knew it would forever be a dark cloud over her family's name. Would Wethersby kill him? It seemed very likely. She could not see the situation ending in any other way. What would happen to her mother—and to Alex—should the worst occur? At least the affair would be resolved soon.

They were to leave for London the next day. The duke and duchess preferred to travel by boat as far as possible, and thought it a safer method by which to hide Isabella. They were to take the carriage to Exeter, and the yacht as far as Brighton so that they might sleep more pleasantly on the ship and avoid the need to stay at inns.

Isabella was a little frightened, yet fascinated at the prospect of sailing on a boat. Since sleep was elusive, she was happy when morning finally arrived and she could set about ending the fear of what her father would do with her. When they rose from the breakfast table, the carriages were being loaded at the front of the house to take them to Exeter. She held Lord George while the rest of the family gathered, simply happy to be with him.

She would miss George terribly when she was no longer a part of the duke's household, but consoled herself that she would soon be the child's aunt. She sat on a bench in the garden and held George upright upon her knee. He was trying to bounce in her lap a little, quite amused with himself, when she thought she heard a rustling nearby. Thinking that perhaps one or more members of the party had left the house by way of a different door, she walked around to peer at the front drive. A gentle breeze was blowing towards her and the noise appeared to be coming from a line of bushes separating the garden from the forecourt.

Immediately, she stilled and put her head down. George began to pull at her bonnet, which was the worst thing that could happen. Was someone in the bushes? It took all her strength of will not to turn and look. She huddled George against her and hurried back into the house, only noticing how heavily she was breathing once they were safely behind the door. Leaning against the wall, she tried to catch her breath. George succeeded in pulling one of the ribbons on her bonnet loose and began to suck it.

"No, no, George," she said. "What would have happened if someone had seen me?"

"Is something wrong, miss?" Quincy asked as he came into the entrance hall at that moment.

"It is probably nothing. I heard a noise in the bushes and it frightened me, that is all." He must think her completely addled after her previous mishap, she thought ruefully.

Quincy frowned, then turned to one of the footmen. "Thomas, go outside and ensure there is no one lurking in the grounds. It was most likely an animal of some kind, but we will make certain."

"Thank you, Quincy. It was very likely an animal, for who would be so bold as to spy on the house with the servants busying about, loading the carriages?" she said—as much to herself as to the butler.

She made herself walk around the ground floor, bouncing George on her hip and playing with him to keep her mind off her worries. She was becoming as nervous as a cat. The duke and Edmund had promised to keep her safe, and she trusted them.

It was not long until the family was ready to leave. She joined them again in the entrance hall, where the footman and butler were whispering to the duke. His Grace smiled and greeted her, but did not say anything about intruders. She must be imagining things.

"Good morning," Edmund said from behind her, and she turned to smile at him. Her worries seemed to lessen greatly in his presence. "Are you well today?"

"I believe I shall be, as soon as we are on our way. I am ready to have done with this whole sorry affair."

He looked at her in astonishment.

"I do not mean to refer to our wedding, of course. I merely wish to have this other wretchedness behind us."

He touched her arm. "Of course you are. It will not be long now."

She prayed he was correct. The family, their trunks and various servants were soon loaded into two carriages and a baggage wagon for the journey to Exeter. It would be a very full day's travel and then, hopefully, they would be able to sleep on the yacht. Isabella began to feel silly, but she could not shake the feeling that she was being watched.

Once settled into the crested traveling coach, it was easy to allow herself to be distracted by George or the duchess. Knowing the duke was suspected of harboring her in his household, Edmund and the duke rode alongside the coach, and Isabella could not help but wonder if they did so in order to keep watch.

If the duchess sensed Isabella's anxieties, she did not say so, and they spoke amiably about such topics as their childhoods while passing George back and forth between them except when he was napping. When they stopped to change horses, take refreshment or use the necessary, Isabella was never alone. Once or twice, she had the sensation that someone was watching her again, but she tried to keep her bonnet pulled low over her face and maintain a calm appearance, not look around nervously or with suspicion. It was difficult, knowing she was suspected to be living in the duke's household.

Never again would she venture out on her own, unless she felt harm would come to her new family. She could not risk those whom she now loved as much as her own; more than some of her own, if truth be known. It still pained her to conjecture on what she had done to cause her father's betrayal, but she could think of nothing. Surely, there was nothing anyone could do to deserve the fate he had tried to hand out to her?

"Is something wrong, Isabella?" the duchess asked. Concern was etched upon her face.

"Nothing new, ma'am. More and more I find myself questioning what motive my father could have had to punish me so."

The duchess reached across the carriage to take Isabella's hand. "Do not blame yourself. I suffered for my father's sins for a very long time, and paid a very dear price. I was too proud to ask for help, and I shudder to think what would have happened if my godmother had not rescued me."

"I feel the same way about Edmund and Your Graces. I only hope that my story will have a happy ending, as yours has. I am convinced that even though I am to marry Edmund, something dreadful will still happen to my family."

"I cannot pretend it will not be so. Your father has been playing a very deep game with Wethersby and for a very long time. Feuds such as theirs rarely end well. But know this, my dear, when all this unpleasantness is over, you will have a husband and family who love you very much."

"It still seems too good to be true." Isabella wanted to tell the duchess her fears about being followed, but as George chose that moment to awaken from his nap, she decided against it.

Edmund and the duke drew their horses alongside the carriage.

"We are almost at the quay," the duke said. Spotting his father, George at once stretched out his arms, reaching towards him.

"Papa," the duchess repeated as she waved George's little hand at the Duke.

George made a reciprocating noise of glee and tried to grasp the window to watch.

"I confess I will feel great relief once we are aboard the ship," Isabella murmured.

"I know you will," Emma replied. "I do not think anyone could harm you with the entourage Rowley has placed around us."

There were indeed a great number of outriders and postilions, but to judge by the other occasions she had traveled with the duke and duchess, it always seemed to be the case. This uneasy feeling would end once she was safely Lady Edmund Knight, she was sure. What a beautiful thought that was, and she tried to dispel concerns of what could still happen between now and then.

The carriage slowed to a halt and they waited inside until Edmund and the duke came to escort them to the boat. It was a two-masted ship with a cabin in the center, and Isabella was still a little dismayed about its ability to stay afloat with so many people on board.

"Are you nervous?" Edmund asked from beside her.

"A little; a mixture of that and excitement," she confessed as he guided her up a narrow gangway onto the deck. She wobbled as the boat moved and looked to him for help.

"You will soon get the feel of it," he assured her as he leaped across onto the boat with ease. "It will be an adventure," he added, smiling down into her face.

*Soon, very soon, he will be mine*, she comforted herself as his arm slipped around her waist and he began to explain the workings of the sails as the crew unfurled them and maneuvered the ropes and rigging.

At once, the wind caught a sail and it snapped into place as the boat moved forward.

"We are fortunate to have caught the tide," he explained. She had heard enough to know that was necessary for a ship to sail.

"At last, a bit of luck," she said, feeling joyous as she looked into his loving eyes—until she turned to look back at the receding coastline and saw an unknown man watching her.

# CHAPTER THIRTEEN

EDMUND SAW NED Smallbone standing on the quay and quickly moved Isabella from the railing towards the cabin, praying she had not also seen the man. She was already frightened to death, and what would that do to her? Many thoughts flitted through his mind, but getting her down to the cabin, out of sight, and alerting Rowley were his first priorities.

Isabella went willingly, and once they had climbed down the ladder below the deck, she looked him in the eye.

"I saw that man, Edmund. Who was he?"

"I was hoping I had been quick enough," he confessed. "That was Mr. Smallbone, the Bow Street Runner."

Having already attained the confined space, Rowley and Emma could not but overhear and turned towards them immediately.

"Was he alone?" Rowley asked.

"He appeared to be," Edmund replied. His brother's eyes met his and many thoughts seemed to pass between them without a word needing to be said.

"Stay below decks, at least until we are far off the shore," Rowley commanded.

All Isabella seemed to be able to manage was nodding her head in affirmation. She looked like a frightened rabbit about to be devoured by a fox. How he longed to take her in his arms and love her fears away, but that was a trite, arrogant thought. He would be of more use by keeping her away from the clever investigator and the devil of a father who sought after her. Instead, he pulled her into his arms for a quick embrace.

"Try to rest," he murmured. "He cannot harm you on the boat." He kissed the top of her head and went above decks with his brother to speak privately.

Rowley was watching the shore in the distance.

"Can you see anything?" Edmund asked.

"No. He is doubtless speeding away towards where he expects us to land. Brighton is an unlikely port, and I pray he will not discover I often dock there."

"I would anticipate that he will be there when we arrive."

"Indeed. It is best to prepare for the worst outcome," Rowley agreed. "He is a busy fellow."

"Should we change course?" Edmund asked.

Rowley narrowed his gaze, as he did when in thought. Edmund knew to wait.

"I will speak to the captain, but I do not think there is any way Smallbone can beat us to Brighton, even riding like the devil. He cannot simply steal her from us, as bold as brass."

"But he could send word to Frompton while he travels to intercept us. At the very least, Frompton would be waiting for us in London. For all we know, Smallbone has a small army with him, prepared to head to every port."

Rowley cursed. "This is a disaster, but I will not fail you and Isabella. I must be careful, however, given I am harboring one of my peers' daughters." He held up his hand. "You need not say he forfeited his right to her. I agree with you, but it is a very fragile situation since the law does not."

"Shall I take her somewhere else?" Edmund asked. "There is still a week until we may wed."

Rowley turned to place his back against the railing and crossed his arms over his chest.

"Where could you take her that would find her safer than being under my protection?"

"I do not know," Edmund admitted openly. "They seem to find us no matter where we are."

"Perhaps a disguise? Emma is gifted at such arts," Rowley suggested.

"That will be of benefit once we are in London. What of the journey there, however?"

"We travel differently," Rowley said, as though thinking out loud.

"All of us travel in disguise as poor farmers?" Edmund laughed as though the thought was preposterous. "It will never work."

"We must decide tonight. With fair winds, we will reach Brighton mid-morning."

"Then I believe we should seize the opportunity and engage to hire a farm cart. The ducal entourage will proceed as a distraction, while one of us drives the cart—with adequate protection—on a different path."

"I do not like the notion of separating. It weakens our defenses."

"We cannot take the chance of staying together. We might succeed, it is true, but they know she is with you."

"Very well. Inform Isabella of our plans. I will arrange for some of my men to follow you discreetly."

Edmund went back below decks to find Isabella. He did not like this one bit. Dividing meant less protection, but arriving in London as quickly as possible was for the best. They could hide his betrothed at Aunt Hambridge's house, with Eugenia.

When he found Isabella, she was alone on a bunk, curled up with her knees to her chest. She looked so small and vulnerable, in the flickering lantern light, that any strength of will he had thought he possessed was lost at sea.

"Propriety be hanged," he said to himself as he climbed onto the bunk with her and took her into his arms. She burrowed into his chest and he kissed the top of her head; her lithe form was shaking with fear.

"Hush now," he whispered. "I will do everything in my power to protect you. Rest now, for he cannot harm you while we remain on the boat."

"What will I do if they catch me?" she whispered.

"I will not let that happen, but know that I would never stop searching for you."

She blew out a shuddering breath.

"This will end soon, Isabella, and neither man—I hesitate to call them gentlemen—will be able to hurt you."

"I hope that my mother and brothers will still accept me."

"I think Ruskington has already proved that he will," Edmund reassured her.

"Yes, as long as nothing happens to force him to choose. Do let us talk of something else. I need a distraction from my maudlin thoughts."

Edmund had a dozen or more unwholesome ideas of how to distract her before he was able to conquer his wayward thoughts. The last thing Isabella needed was to be taken advantage of, even if they were betrothed. Instead, he cherished both the feel of her in his arms and her trust in him. He almost laughed to think that his brother seemed to consider him abnormal and incapable of primitive human need and touch.

"What would you like to talk about?" he asked, gently stroking her hair.

She was quiet for so long, he thought she had fallen asleep. "It is horrid that I cannot turn my mind to anything else. I have been trying to think of our wedding, or what our children might look like, but then my mind turns back to how sad it will be not to have my family present or that our children will not know their grandparents."

"Alas, those things might be true." He could hardly offer her false assurances. "However, we can make certain our children have a happy childhood full of love."

"Yes." She smiled up at him. "Dark curls with blue eyes?" she proposed.

"I think that is a safe assumption. I would adore a little girl who looks like you."

"I should wish for a little boy, who is as handsome as his father and blessed with his generosity of spirit," she answered at once. "Edmund?" She looked up at him, the question reflected in her eyes.

Before he thought better of it, he shifted her so their mouths could meet. Gentle and tender, he brushed his lips back and forth across hers, allowing her to explore and be reassured by his gentleness and love. He was loving by nature, but this was a far deeper degree of feeling than he had ever felt before, and he knew she was necessary to his future happiness. Her hands started to roam dangerously, hungrily, as though seeking reassurance, and he doubted she knew what she was doing. He pulled her hands back to hold them to his face and determined the kiss would go no further. Thankfully, the boat had taken to rocking against the swell, enough to make him feel tired.

"Sleep, my love."

"You will not leave me?" she asked drowsily.

"Never," he said, as he tucked her into the crook of his arm and drew her close against his side. Even though sleep was beckoning to him, his mind was not so easy to settle. What lengths would he go to, in order to keep her from the runner or Wethersby? It did not sit well with him, as a man of the cloth, to acknowledge the truth, but he knew he would kill for her.

Perhaps it was time to reconsider his future.

THE NEXT MORNING, they arrived in Brighton. Isabella and Edmund were dressed as any common farmer and wife would in inexpensive but sturdy cloth the color of mud. He wore a plain shirt with a neckerchief and she a worn apron with a practical mobcap to hide her curls. She would not have recognized Edmund in his current attire were she to have met him on the street, and even she was now dressed in the oldest, most plain gown they could find. That had not been an easy task in a duke's household, where his servants were garbed more finely than many gentry. Nevertheless, she was well hidden and Edmund was well disguised.

They hired an old cart from a dairyman on Ship Street, in the back of which Isabella could lie down and be covered with blankets. Two of the duke's outriders were to follow discreetly, and the whole set-out was to go ahead of the ducal caravan of carriages.

"No matter what happens, Isabella, promise me you will not come out from hiding," Edmund exhorted her. Isabella stared at him. How could he think she would not try to defend him? He could obviously sense her thoughts, for the corner of his mouth twisted. "Under no circumstances will you let anyone know you are there. Promise me, please."

"I will do my best," she said, trying not to deliberately lie, but not certain she could promise to be idle while someone harmed him.

"I do not anticipate any problems; 'tis simply we are all on edge with the possibilities," he said.

"I know," she replied, climbing into the cart under the cover of a stable. The travelers had waited at The Ship and Anchor posting inn while the arrangements for her disguise had been made.

"It appears we have beaten them," Edmund said to Rowley as they chatted discreetly in the yard behind the inn, where carriages were waiting to convey them to London. Isabella waited in the back of the hired cart, trying not to be fearful of any odd sound she heard. It was hard on her nerves to be unable to see what was going on around them.

The face of Mr. Smallbone, the Bow Street Runner, had haunted her dreams throughout the night and even though she had been safe in Edmund's arms, she had still awoken with fright on a couple of occasions, thinking that it was the runner, capturing her, instead.

Edmund had reassured her back to sleep, but the dream only magnified her anxieties for their trip to London. They would not be able to travel quickly in an old cart, but they were definitely more inconspicuous.

The old wagon, drawn by two brown nags, pulled forward and it gave her an entirely new appreciation of the luxuriously sprung carriages she was accustomed to as a duke's daughter, and even servant. The miles passed slowly as she was jostled back and forth on the hard, wooden planks beneath her. Every bump was magnified and every rut in the road caused pain in her bones. Knowing it would be another long day, she tried her best to concentrate on breathing easily instead of feeling as though the blankets were suffocating her. Despite these troubles, she must have drifted off to sleep, however, for she was startled awake when someone called, "Halt."

"What—" Edmund said, moments before she heard an unnerving, loud noise of an object meeting flesh, as if he had been hit. Where were the outriders?

Paralyzed with fear, she tried to think of how she could help while still keeping her promise to Edmund. Strange thumping noises, mixed with a rocking of the cart, caused her to abandon that pledge and she pulled back the blanket enough to look up. Edmund was no longer on the seat; he had been thrown over a horse and was being led away!

If only she had some sort of weapon, she might succeed in stopping them, she moaned silently in anguish. What could she do? Before she could make any choices, the man hit one of the cart-horses on the rump before then galloping away. The poor creatures, startled out of their habitual placidity, careered along the road in a stiff-legged, jiggeting fashion that threatened to overturn the vehicle. Isabella clutched the sides and prayed for a safe deliverance.

Peering between almost squeezed-tight eyelids, she saw a hill looming ahead. The horses began to charge down the slope, the wagon lurching dangerously behind their erratic progress. Isabella had few choices. She could jump from the conveyance and risk broken limbs, or she could try to climb on to the seat and attempt to control them. Without further delay, she threw back the layers of coarse, dusty blankets and sacks of potatoes that had served to disguise her presence, and began the treacherous task of creeping forward on all fours. The cart swayed and bounced alarmingly over the washboard ridges in the road.

"Pray that the horses keep to the road," she muttered to the heavens, as the trees on either side passed at a more rapid rate than she would have thought these nags capable of.

She tried calling, in commanding tones, for them to stop. She tried speaking softly and calmly, using a soothing, musical intonation as her old groom had done. Neither approach had the slightest effect on the panicked jades. There was nothing for it but to throw herself over into the seat! For several seconds, she stared at the narrow wooden bench and the ground passing swiftly beneath the horses' hooves. If she slipped, she could be killed!

"There is nothing to be served by thinking like *that*, Isabella!" she told herself firmly. The momentum was increasing; she could wait no longer. Swallowing deeply, she lifted one leg over the front and gingerly stretched her foot towards the ledge which served as a seat. Her knuckles were white where she gripped the edge of the wagon. Then, a poorly timed rut propelled her towards the bench. For one, terrifying moment, she was sure she must be thrown beneath the wheels, but somehow her clutching fingers saved her. Her chin met the hard edge of the frame in a blow which rattled her teeth, but at least she had not fallen out! Clinging precariously to said frame, she set about untangling her skirts and placing her feet on the footboard.

At last she righted herself and looked about for the reins. By a stroke of supreme good fortune, they had caught about the handle of the brake. Trying not to think how easily they might have been flapping loose over the horses' angular backs, she grabbed the ribbons.

How did one stop a bolting pair? She knew it was not merely a case of pulling on the reins. That could make the horses pull harder. Panting with a combination of fear and the necessity for speed, she fumbled to gather the reins correctly. At home in the country, she had been wont to ride rather than drive.

"Steady now, boys," she called, feeling the horses' mouths with a give-and-take motion on the narrow leather lines. "Steady." She drew out the last letter on the word, hoping it would penetrate the nags' instinctive fixedness on flight.

At first, it did not seem to have changed their ambitions to the slightest degree. Hedges continued to flash by, as did scattered coppices. Mercifully, a hamlet was deserted when the wagon sped through, only a handful of ducks on a pond being disturbed by its passing. Isabella pulled all four reins simultaneously.

"Woah!" she cried. Ahead loomed a bend in the road—a bend too tight to negotiate at this speed. "Woah!" she shouted, and forgetting her previous reservations, leaned back and hauled on the ribbons. Relief traveled through her with the force of a river in flood as the pair slowed a trifle. She pulled again. "Good boys. that's the ticket!"

The two brown nags were all but bottomed, she could see, for once they consented to listen, they came back to a walk within a few hundred yards. Lathered in sweat, with heaving flanks, they dropped their heads into their collars and plodded like oxen. Isabella wiped her brow, offered up a silent prayer and sat back to consider what she should do.

Now that the horses were once more under control, should she wait for the Knighton carriages to join her, or should she try to follow

Edmund? Supposing she herself were caught? She would be no help at all to Edmund, if that happened! To think they had been worried about her safety, and now they had taken him. What a counter-turn, to be sure.

What could they mean by doing that? Did they hope to find her through him? Little did they know she would have been perfectly willing to offer herself in exchange.

"Drat the slowness of this cart!" she grumbled, neatly forgetting her previous alarm. Even when racing out of control, the lumbering wagon was no match for a rider on a horse. Before she had to decide on her course of action, however, she heard someone giving chase. In some disquiet, she turned to look behind her. A cloud of dust slowly cleared and then a horse pulled up beside her. Knighton had come to her rescue! "Thank God!" she declared.

"What has happened?" he asked.

"Someone has taken Edmund!"

"Did you see who it was?" He was alarmingly calm.

"It happened so fast. I saw the rider only from behind, once I had realized what was happening. Edmund was ambushed and carried off, tied on a horse, but the whole incident was over with exceedingly quick. I am certain we were attacked from behind, but I would swear it was not Smallbone, for the man seemed larger."

"We came across the outriders. They had been tied up and their horses scattered."

"Why would they take Edmund? I thought they were hunting me."

"Edmund has some enemies. It could be completely by chance that they have discovered him at the same time."

"We must hurry—I fear he is harmed."

"What makes you say so?" he asked, looking eerily composed. "Not that I believe he would have gone willingly and left you unprotected."

"I thought I heard sounds of him being hit, followed by a groan." She closed her eyes against the pain of reliving those moments. "I wish I might have been prepared."

"You could not have known. We had no reason to believe anyone was after him. It brings a new perspective to the proceedings."

"It does?" Isabella questioned—because she was more confused and afraid than ever.

"It would appear we have two foes instead of one. Edmund had fled to the Grange in order to avoid one of them. The vicarage had been attacked and damaged. We must make haste. If he is truly harmed, we must find him. Did you overhear anything at all?"

"Very little, I am afraid. I am sorry I can be of no better help, but as I told you, it happened very quickly. I saw only one man riding away."

In due course, the carriages joined them, and the duke hurried away to speak to his drivers and then the little boy, Johnny. One of the coachmen handed the reins to a groom, and another jumped down and came towards her wagon.

"You must remain hidden, Miss Thatcher, especially as we are nearing London," the duke insisted. "One of my men will drive you. If my suspicions are correct, Johnny can help me find the man who attacked my brother. As you can see, this complicates matters greatly."

"Please do not concern yourself about me. All that matters is that Edmund is found safe."

The duke gave a curt nod and rode off with several of his men. Perched on the horse in front of him, the little boy held tight looking terrified.

Isabella sank back down into the bed of the cart, now willing to trade her soul for Edmund's well-being. Nothing else seemed to matter anymore, not when something may have happened to him.

# CHAPTER FOURTEEN

EDMUND AWOKE TO a brutal pounding in his head and overwhelming nausea. Whatever ailed him? He tried to think, but the pain was devilish. In fact, opening his eyes and moving his head felt well-nigh impossible. Some basic instinct told him he needed to try to determine what was going forward, so he fought the urge to return to the black sleep which was pulling viciously at him.

*Isabella.*

Her name woke him up in a hurry. He had been trying to sneak Isabella into London in a farm cart when he was attacked. Where was he now? More to the point, was he alone and where was Isabella? Had they found her and hurt her?

He was surrounded by darkness in a thick cloth and his hands were bound, as were his feet. He was completely helpless. *Please, God, keep Isabella safe.* He would give anything to make sure she was unharmed.

He swallowed hard in an effort to quell the nausea and then lay quietly, hoping he could somehow sense where he might be or determine if he was alone. The last thing he wanted to do was alert his attackers if they believed him to be dead.

Who had done this to him? Was it some sort of message or warning with respect to Isabella, or had Old Ben caught up with him? He would not have thought the scoundrel resourceful enough, though he had managed to find the four girls in Kent. *No good deed goes unpun-*

*ished.*

Nevertheless, he would do it again. He would not have met Isabella otherwise. He swallowed again and tried to rally his senses in order to provide some clues as to his whereabouts. It seemed he was on the ground, for a certain earthy dampness sought to pervade both his nostrils and his clothes beneath him. Sounds of nature were present, once he listened: the occasional, distinctive warble of a robin or the chirping of crickets. Had he been beaten and dumped in the woods to rot? Left for dead? His faculties were dull, yet sensed no other person close by.

He worked his hands against the rough ropes, but they were bound so tightly that he had very little feeling in them at all. His ankles were not tied as fast, although, without hands with which to work the knots loose, he was of no use to Isabella until someone found him. It would be easy to panic, though that was not his nature. Struggling would only tire him out and make him more vulnerable. What, then, should he do? He pondered the question while trying to keep his breathing to a calm enough pace in order not to suffocate.

If he was in the middle of a wood somewhere, it would be days, most likely, before he was found—if some form of wildlife did not find him first.

What could he do? He could hear no traffic or evidence of roads nearby, so yelling would be fruitless. However, supposing Isabella lay nearby?

"Isabella?" he called softly. There was no response, not even the rustle of a leaf. "Isabella?" he called again, a little louder, but there was still no answer, no corresponding movement nearby.

He had to think. He could lie on the damp ground and pray for rescue, but even though he believed in divine miracles, he never relied on them.

The last he could recall, they had been at least an hour south of London. Was he perhaps somewhere on the Thornton Heath?

He did not know if it was night or day, though some instinct made him think it was not nightfall. For all he knew, he could already have been lying here for days.

It was too easy to slip into a trough of moroseness when helpless— too easy to think of everything he had done wrong and what he wished he had done better. Isabella would be safe under Rowley's protection, but had she also been harmed? That was what pained him the most, the not knowing how his beloved fared.

Unable to lie there without trying to help himself, he writhed against the ropes that bound his hands. He managed to roll his body over which gave him some purchase against the bindings. After a great deal of rubbing and scraping, he managed to free one thumb. A small victory.

It did appear, however, that he was quite alone. After all the struggles he had undertaken to free one appendage, if anyone had been about, they would have at least laughed at his expense.

His head throbbed sorely after the movement and his eyes felt heavy. It was sometime later when he awoke to something nudging his side. He stilled with fear. Was it a wild animal come to see if an easy meal was before him, or merely a deer that was curious?

He was as near to panic as he had ever felt in his life before, but he found his voice enough to speak.

"Who is there?"

Again, there was no answer. He tried to feel, but he still had little movement. "Please help me if you can. There will be a reward for your kindness, I assure you."

His voice must have scared the animal away, if animal it was. He heard the steps scampering off and his emotions deflated further. Fully awake again, as attested by the painful drumming in his head, he worked more on his half-numb hands until he freed another finger. Soon, he would be able to free his hand, but the effort required was great because of the injuries he had suffered. It seemed probable he had been bludgeoned by some kind of hammer or cudgel. He was able to come up on all fours, but only just. Suddenly, he understood. Whatever sack he had been tied up in was not large and smelled of molded grains.

"At least they did not throw me in a river to drown," he muttered, in a dry attempt to lift his spirits.

If only he could free his face to breathe fresh air, he mused, he would never take it for granted again. As he considered those simple gifts from the Almighty, a clap of thunder startled him and shook the earth beneath him.

"That is all I need now, God. For whatever penance I am paying my dues, please do not let me die from the elements in the course of it."

Lightning flashed so brightly that a faint glimmer of it was discernible within the captivity of his sack, and he knew the heavens were about to open upon him where he lay, with no shelter bar that to be had from such trees which might be nearby.

His chances of rescue were now greatly diminished, for if anyone were to try to find his scent with dogs, the rain would wash it away.

Large drops began to land and then beat on him. Soon it was pouring. It rained so long and hard that in no time at all he was lying in a puddle of water. He worked again on his hands and freed another finger, but the bindings were still too tight around his wrist to release the whole hand. He rested them in the water for a while to cool the burning, but then was so overcome with weakness, he had to roll over and lie on his back for fear he would swoon and drown in the puddle.

The position was hardly better, since the sack adhered to his face. He rolled to his side and settled there, still trying not to despair. But it was the hardest trial he had faced yet. Eventually, the rain stopped and more darkness closed in, bringing with it a chill that Edmund feared would be the death of him.

>>>><<<<

ISABELLA COULD NOT bear to sit passively while Edmund was out, who knew where and very likely hurt, if her suppositions were correct. While she knew the duke and his men would do everything in their power to find him, she could not be idle. Yet what could she do?

The duke would not allow her out of his sight again after she had been missing before—even if that had been an unfortunate misunderstanding. Now she was being ridiculous, she told herself crossly, but she wanted so desperately to be able to do something to help.

Isabella began to pray; as if in response, a loud clap of thunder shook the cart. Was God speaking to her? Surely a thunderstorm was the worst thing that could happen at this moment.

Rain began to pour down, soaking her coverings and plastering them to her body and face. She sat up and decided that her disguise was in no more danger to her person than drowning would be.

As she pulled the wet blanket from her face, she tried to keep down, but at least be able to see. Watching the road and surrounding woods made her feel as though she was doing something, however small.

The rain poured down unmercifully. Soon she was thoroughly soaked through and the wagon began to fill with water. The cart was forced to slow down as the roads became muddy and rutted. Would they have to stop for the night somewhere?

It was difficult to hold her eyes open and see where they were going, let alone search for any sign of Edmund. Where could they have taken him? She still did not understand why he had been captured and not her. Was her father truly so ruthless as to harm Edmund? Frompton did not even know that Edmund had saved her from the brothel, so it made little sense.

Perhaps Edmund truly did have enemies, but she could not think they would grant him any mercy if they had gone to the trouble to seek him out this far from town and find him in disguise. If it were so, they were going to kill him.

That realization tore at her insides. *No, God, no.*

She noticed a horse approaching and the driver pulled up to speak with him. Her heart jumped on recognizing the duke. Had Edmund been found so soon?

"Miss Thatcher, I think it would now be safer for you to ride in one of the carriages," he informed her. "I can barely see five feet in front of me."

"Have you any news?" she asked, blinking away the rain.

"Based on the descriptions I could proffer, it seems the blackguards continued north for some way, but only a single rider was seen beyond Thornton Heath. My men are searching the Heath at this moment. It is the most likely place for the kidnapper to have left Edmund. At first, I wondered if they had kidnapped him to seek a ransom. It is still a possibility, but I am beginning to think they meant him harm."

"I am inclined to agree with you, sir." She was shivering and could hardly speak for her chattering teeth, although more from fear than the cold. "How may I help? I cannot simply sit here and wait!"

"I would like you to join the duchess in her carriage and she will take you to my aunt's house where no one will think to look for you. I cannot have you out here where I cannot keep you safe," he said. His tone was insistent. "You can help Edmund the most by protecting yourself."

"I had not considered we might need to be concerned for him."

"Nor I. I must go now, but I have sent for more men. I will do everything in my power to bring him back to you, Isabella." He looked her in the eye. His expression was grave and determined. She would not care to be on the wrong side of his wrath. He held out his hands to assist her and lifted her from the back of the cart. To her surprise, he then carried her to the carriage and placed her inside, thus saving her from walking in the mud.

"I will send word as soon as I know something," he said to Isabella before turning to the duchess. "Use the guns if necessary." Leaning forward, he kissed his wife and the baby before closing the door.

The duchess smiled half-heartedly at her as she stroked the sleeping George's hair. "I wish we had stayed together from the beginning, but it does no good to be wise after the event."

"No, we did what we thought was best. How could we have known someone was after Edmund as well? And, for all we know, we may have thrown the runners off the trail, if they were watching the ports," Isabella responded. "What will I do if something has happened to him?" she added, trying not to despair although her voice cracked on the words.

Emma moved closer, even though Isabella was drenched. "We cannot fret over what has yet to happen," she said gently. "For now we must keep you safe, and pray."

"Would you be able to sit back and watch were the duke in trouble?"

Emma bit her lower lip, then shook her head. "Of course not. But your own safety is in jeopardy."

Isabella swallowed hard and looked out of the window. "I cannot just sit here and do nothing!" she said firmly. "I wish I might at least wait nearby while they search," she begged.

The indecision was written all over the duchess's face. "Very well. I will accept the consequences, but you must not leave my sight."

"Thank you, Your Grace," Isabella said. Taking Emma's hands in hers, she bowed her head over them.

"Please do not make me regret this, Isabella. I could not bear to have your blood on my soul."

"I understand, that is how I feel about Edmund."

Emma rapped on the roof and ordered the caravan to pull into the nearest inn.

The postilion looked extremely nervous. "I had a direct order from the duke not to stop, no matter what, Your Grace."

The duchess did not blink. "I am directing you to stop at the nearest inn, and I will bear the consequences. Do I make myself clear?"

"Yes, Your Grace." The servant slid the latch shut.

"Will he be very angry with you?" Isabella asked, having second thoughts.

"Of course he will, but I can manage him," she said with a sly smile. "I can blame it on the mud, if nothing else."

At least another mile went by before they stopped. "You must remain disguised, Isabella," Emma warned.

"I am well aware of the need for caution. I do not intend to make use of the public rooms. I merely wish to be nearby if he is found."

"He could have been taken to London," the duchess warned. Underlying her words was the unspoken statement that he might never be found if that were the case.

"It would be an enterprise full of risk, to carry an unconscious passenger thrown over a horse. Besides, Knighton believes he is here."

"If his informant was accurate," Isabella argued before sliding back the latch to request refreshments and information as soon as it was available.

A young serving maid returned some few minutes later with tea and meat pies on a tray. "There is a private parlor if you would care to use it, Your Grace," the girl said, blushing.

"Perhaps when the baby wakens," the duchess said kindly.

Isabella welcomed the tea to help warm her, but felt guilty that Edmund was possibly still out in the elements. She ate a few bites of the pie, and then watched out of the window for any sign of news. The inn was a two-storeyed wooden building, with a sign swinging back and forth in the rain proclaiming it "The Crooked Crow."

"I can wait no longer," she said after a few minutes of staring at the sign, and at once began climbing down from the carriage.

"Where are you going?" the duchess asked. George was still fast asleep in her lap.

"Not far, but I must do something!" Isabella exclaimed.

"Then you must take one of the men with you for this is not a safe area," Emma insisted. Isabella was grateful that the duchess did not attempt to prevent her.

Isabella chose not to notice that her boots sank deeply into the mud. One of the servants followed her as she lifted her skirts and charged in a most unladylike fashion through the now ankle-deep sludge. She did not know where she was going, but it felt better than sitting helplessly in the carriage.

It was still raining, but not as heavily as it had been before and she knew someone had no doubt already searched here—wherever here might be. In the distance ahead of her, she could see the duke's men searching methodically through an area of woodland.

"Where are you, Edmund?" she asked, staring at the leaden sky. She was beginning to feel frantic inside. "Now would be an excellent time for a sign from above," she muttered.

They had to find him soon. If he were still alive... the unthinkable intruded, and yet something in her heart told her not to give up hope. Edmund had helped her in her darkest hour and she would do the same for him. She plodded determinedly on, trying to think like the dastard who had done this to her beloved.

"Where would I leave someone if I did not wish them to be found?"

In the woods, far off the beaten path, was the obvious answer—which could be anywhere. She began to head determinedly for the woods, beyond where the horses' hoof prints stopped, leaves and twigs crunching beneath her feet. Wet branches whipped her in the face. Then she heard the sounds of rushing water, and it was growing louder. As she walked, another set of fears began to crowd her anxieties as she hurried towards what must surely be a river.

"Please let it not be so," she muttered as she all but ran in the direction of the water, unaware if the servant was even still with her.

Her feet led her to the edge of an embankment, where there was nowhere farther to go but down to the rushing water. She fell on her knees, feeling hopeless. Why had she thought she would have some sixth sense that would lead her straight to him? She was ready to collapse with despair as she watched the torrent of water down below. Had he been thrown into the river and cast out to sea?

"Miss!" the servant called.

She looked up to see him pointing towards a large sack. Was it perhaps large enough to hold a body? It looked to have been caught on a ledge.

"I am going to seek help."

"I will stay here. I cannot leave him just in case." It was going to take a miracle to retrieve whatever it was from the ledge. She imagined the sack being tossed over the embankment and coming to rest there instead of falling into the water. That in itself was a miracle. A tiny flicker of hope sprang to life within her breast as she watched the object below—except it was inanimate, and night was falling.

# CHAPTER FIFTEEN

ISABELLA EXAMINED THE lifeless object down below and soon grew impatient. She began to look around, wondering how they would reach the sack. It was at least ten feet to the ledge which was already awash with the rain. The bank would swiftly become mired and slippery, offering no purchase for the rescuers. Now would be an excellent time to have men, ropes, and horses, she reflected wryly. She scanned the tangled woods behind her, and wondered if a horse could reach such a spot, but then reminded herself the attacker had somehow managed to bring Edmund—if indeed Edmund was in the sack— here to dispose of him.

Isabella swallowed a huge lump in her throat. She had to find out if he was inside that horrid gunny sack prison.

Where were the men? The rain increased again and she could suffer this waiting no longer. What if he was lying face down? He could be drowning!

*Perhaps he is not down there*, a little voice inside her whispered hopefully. *But supposing he is, every moment could matter*, she argued.

She turned onto her stomach and began to look for a way to climb down. There were a few roots sticking out which she thought she could hold onto. Slowly, she began to slide backwards, praying she would not slide into the river below—or worse, knock Edmund down there. She saw a tree root a few feet away and, her heart thumping, decided to make the attempt. Reaching as far as she dared, she gave a little push with her toes and launched herself towards the handhold. Grabbing the gnarled wood with the tips of her fingers, her heart pounding in her ears with fright, she gulped a breath and adjusted her grip. She still had a long way to go, but the closer she was to the object, the more convinced she was Edmund could be inside the rough brown sack. It gave her the courage to continue.

She tried not to look down at the speed of the water or the ragged edge of the embankment. Her hand began to slip, so she reached with her foot for the next root jutting out of the bank, but the bark was slimy and her boot slipped. She squealed as her body slid down the slimy, sodden earth until she could snatch hold of something else. It was difficult to catch her breath, and she was sure she could feel scrapes and bruises forming under the layer of mud that covered her. Not that her appearance mattered one whit! She glanced down at the ledge, to see the shape of the body within the sack. Nothing could have more effectively firmed her resolve.

Looking down had been a mistake; she panicked at the distance. It had not seemed so far from above, but now she recognized that if the men did not arrive, she herself would be trapped.

"Do not think of it," she said to herself as water poured off the brim of her bonnet. "They will find you."

Her arms were shaking with the exertion and she knew she had to reach the ledge. She could see nowhere for her hands or feet to seek purchase, so she closed her eyes and whispered a prayer as she slowly let go and began to slide downwards.

Although her feet hit something which felt solid, she scrambled and slithered sideways until she was certain she was on the ledge and would not fall. Desperately, she turned and surveyed the object. Head, arms, legs… the contents were definitely human. She paused with fear. What if these were the remains of some other poor soul?

"Do not be lily-livered now," she chastised herself. She touched the object softly. "Edmund?" There was no response. She moved her hands over the cold, sodden sack and found a rope tying it. She had no knife with which to cut it—she had no weapon, in fact—and felt every ounce of her recklessness, combined with almost overwhelming helplessness. Tears streamed down her face; she feared he was dead. Her drenched, filthy hands were growing numb with cold, so she chafed and blew on them, then attempted to undo the knots in the rope.

"Please, please come loose," she beseeched the inanimate rope that was her barrier to Edmund.

She tried to work the rope free with her fingers and then her mouth, but it was no use. In desperation, she looked about her for alternative ideas. The ledge was no more than a yard or two wide and bare of anything apart from the sack and saturated earth. Perhaps there was a tear or opening in the cloth somewhere, she thought hopefully. Gingerly, she rolled the body onto its back, but the fabric then plastered itself to the prisoner's face.

"That will not do," she muttered, now intent on seeing that same face. She tipped the heavy form back the other way, and found a slight rip behind the head. The fabric was rough hessian of the type used for provender and would not be easily torn. She stood up in an effort to use her weight, but she only managed a small rip.

A groaning noise came from the body, renewing her resolve. "I am here, Edmund. I am here!"

Although need lent strength to her fingers and she made several more attempts at tearing the cloth, they met with little success. Where, oh where, were the men?

Standing up again, Isabella placed her feet on either side of the huddled man and tried to determine if she could maneuver the hole over his face.

"If only I had a knife!" she wailed.

"Mm," the figure mumbled. Isabella's stomach lurched in response. She had found him!

"I cannot understand, dearest." She found it hard to keep calm. "Help is on the way, if they ever reach us here."

"Knife," he managed to convey.

"You have a knife?"

"Mm. Boot."

"How am I to reach it?" she asked. The hole in the sack was very far from his feet.

Edmund began to writhe, but moaned as he did so.

"Stop, you are hurting yourself. Let me try again." Gritting her teeth, Isabella ripped another section of the sack. While not achieving above an inch or two, the hole was now wide enough for her to be able to get her arm inside. She pressed the side of his face, which was cold and damp, but then felt a sticky substance.

Blood! Good God, it was a miracle he was still alive.

However, there was no possibility of her reaching a knife in his boot, so she continued this slow toil of ripping away at the cloth. Finally, she was able to uncover his face. He looked horrible. Trying not to look at his pale, waxy skin and the swollen, bloody half of his face, she leaned forward to kiss him.

"Fight for me," she ordered as she continued tearing at the cloth.

"Who would have thought these would be so tough?" she asked, not expecting a response. He was trying to watch her, but she could tell it took effort for him to not slip into unconsciousness. She was no doctor, but had no need of being learned in medicine to know he was near death.

"Isabella!" She heard her name called and looked up to the most welcome sight of the Duke of Knighton and several henchmen.

"He is alive, but hurt very badly. I have no knife with which to free him."

"Is there room for me there?" he asked.

"Not safely," she answered with regret.

"Do any of you men have a length of rope with you?" he called over his shoulder.

"No, sir."

"Nay, Your Grace."

Isabella heard other murmurs of apology and could imagine the shaking of heads. The duke smiled reassurance.

"Lacking the wherewithal to lower it, then, I will slide my knife down to you while we attempt to find something with which to hoist him up. Are you ready? Take care not to slip."

Isabella nodded and watched as the sheathed knife slid towards her. She caught it without mishap, then pulled it out of the leather cover and began frantically cutting away at Edmund's prison, trying not to slice either of them as she did so.

What she revealed was even worse than she had imagined. Once she had released his hands of the wicked bindings, she chafed the mottled, frozen flesh for a while and then began to slice away at the bindings around his boots.

"Hurry," she called, looking upward. She could see nothing, but knew the duke and his men were working on something. Sundry shouts and sounds of industry echoed in the forest above.

At last, his face appeared over the edge. "I am about to send down some knotted ropes. Keep the sacking underneath him and try to place the ropes under his wrapped body. We will use the horses to hoist him up."

Isabella was worried about dragging him along the side of the embankment, but it was their only choice, she knew. No one would be able to carry him up the side due to the mud.

Two large ropes were sent over the edge, with a loop and knot that resembled a noose. She picked up Edmund's legs and slipped the first loop down to below his knees. The other would be more difficult. His eyes were closed again and she knew this would pain him horribly.

"Your brother is here," she told him as she lifted his head, causing both a grimace and a groan.

"We must lift you by horse and it will hurt, I am afraid." That was an understatement.

She slid the second loop down beneath his back and then looked up and gave the signal.

The ropes grew taut under the strain and moved him slightly. She did her best to add support beneath him, in an effort to ease the brunt of the pull, but he was much too large for her to do any good.

As the horses pulled, he began to lift and be dragged up the side of the embankment. It was difficult to watch, knowing what he must be suffering, though the manoeuvre was impressively controlled.

His body disappeared up over the side and Isabella wept with relief. At least he would not die out here alone if his injuries proved fatal.

It was hard to stay composed, but she knew it would soon be her turn.

The duke leaned over the side and called her name, as rain dripped from his hat and greatcoat.

"We will do the same for you, Miss Thatcher."

The two ropes were lowered again, and she placed one under her knees and ran another behind her back. She gave the signal for them to pull, then braced herself as she slid against the side, feeling every tree root as she did so. Mud oozed into the sides of her dress, feeling vastly unpleasant against her skin, but there was little she cared about except Edmund. Once at the top, she was lifted out of the ropes. Edmund was already in his brother's arms, mounted on a horse. She herself was quickly lifted in front of one of the duke's men and she near collapsed with relief as they made their way back to the inn. *Thank God, thank God.*

WHEN THE SEARCHERS arrived at the inn, the duchess was waiting. She and a maid ushered Isabella inside the hostelry and upstairs to a bedchamber, when all she wanted was to take care of Edmund. A warm bath was waiting for her and some clean, dry clothing, and another of the maids was waiting to fuss over her. She did have mud everywhere—she could feel it in undesirable places—and was in dire need, it was true, but she was too worried to take pleasure in the task.

The maid helped her out of her boots and stripped off her gown. Even in her brother's most rambunctious days, Isabella could not recall either of them being covered from head to toe in mud like this.

She lowered herself into the warm bath as the maid began to take down her hair, clicking her tongue and muttering. Isabella scarcely heard her. She took the bar of soap and scrubbed away the remnants of that horrible experience as the tub became clouded with mud.

The maid poured some water over her head, massaged some soap and oil through her hair, then Isabella stood mindlessly to be rinsed, and afterwards, dried.

Once clothed again, she picked out her curls with a comb while sitting before the fire, desperately hoping someone would come with news. Instead, the maid left and later returned with a tea tray.

"Have you heard any news of the gentleman who was hurt?" Isabella asked, despite knowing it was vulgar to question the girl.

The maidservant, who was not part of the duchess' retinue, looked a little wary. "The doctor is with him now, miss."

Isabella sighed with relief. "Thank goodness he was able to come quickly."

"Aye, the duke sent for him afore they went searching. His Grace sent several notes off and now there be many people here to help."

"Sometimes it is good to be a duke," Isabella muttered, wondering who else he had sought.

"Aye, that it is," the girl replied, clearly bedazzled.

"When the doctor leaves, will you please ask when I might see the gentleman?"

The girl looked nervous, her eyes wide. "I suppose I could." She curtseyed and began to back from the room, carrying one of the jugs that had held water. "Oh, there is a gentleman asking to see you, miss. Should I send him up?"

Isabella immediately stilled. "Who is he and whom did he ask for?"

"I don't rightly know. He didn't give his name. He said, 'Please tell me when the lady is ready to receive,'" she mimicked.

"Tell no one anything about me, except the duke," Isabella said sternly. "No one must know who I am or why I am here, is that understood?"

The girl looked chastened, so Isabella tried to soften her words. "Some bad men are after the gentleman and myself. It is better for everyone if no one knows who we are, or why we are here."

"Yes, miss."

Now Isabella needed to know who wanted to speak with her. Had the runner found her so soon? It was possible, for she had hardly been aware of her own concerns while searching for Edmund. Would it be necessary to escape yet again? She was dog-tired and weary of having to hide. The duke would protect her, she reasoned, while debating what might be her best course of action. Forcing herself to her feet— she ached everywhere—she walked over to gaze out of the window. It was more than fifteen feet to the ground and she was so very tired of running.

Her room looked out over the woods and wild, grassy areas of the heath, and she could even see the river in the distance. How peaceful and innocent nature looked when you were not at its mercy!

There was a knock on the door, and Isabella prayed the runner had not forced his way upstairs before reflecting that he would hardly bother to knock if he thought he had found his prey.

"Stop being ridiculous!" she chastised herself. "The duke would hardly allow such a thing with his own family here in the inn!"

"Enter," she called softly. It was only the maid.

"The man says he is your brother. I took the liberty of asking His Grace's man and he said he is who he says he is."

Relief flooded through Isabella. "Send him in."

Isabella practically threw herself into her brother's arms as soon as he walked through the door. The only sight more welcome to her would have been Edmund standing there, hale once more.

"Alex!" she almost wailed as she tried to fight her emotions. "I will not even ask how you come to be here so quickly."

He held her tightly and stroked her damp hair, whispering soothing comforts in her ear. "All will be well now."

"Have you heard anything about Edmund?" she asked, desperate for news.

"Very little, I am afraid. His injuries are very grave, according to the doctor."

"I know," she whispered.

Alex set her at arms' length and looked down at her. "How could you risk yourself in such a way?" He shook his head and then pulled her back into his arms. "Isabella," he said in an affectionate tone.

"Was I to let him die?"

He led her to the well-worn armchairs by the fire and she sat in one while he took the one opposite. He ran his hands through his unruly hair. He still had not done away with his wild appearance.

"Knighton told me of your adventures in Devonshire."

"Did he?" she asked, biting her lower lip and not meeting his eyes.

"He would have protected you, Isabella. The runner could hardly abduct you from the duke's land."

"I was foolish, I will not deny it, but I was so very afraid, Alex."

He reached over and held her hand. "I am merely a worried elder brother. I do not mean to scold."

"What will happen now? Edmund will hardly be in a position to marry me in six days, and it will be impossible to keep my presence a secret from Father after this."

"We shall try," Alex insisted. "I will not give you to Wethersby."

Isabella was both warmed by and afraid of the menace in her brother's voice. Never before had she thought him capable of such resolve. He had changed a great deal during his time in Canada. She squeezed his hand.

"This sorry affair will soon be over."

He gave her a lopsided smile.

"Do you think I might see him?" she asked, desperate for a glimpse of her beloved.

He opened his mouth to protest but then closed it again. "I will see what I can do," he said, standing up. He bent over to kiss her on the head. "Forgive me for not being here when you needed me." His voice was strained.

Isabella looked up into his watering eyes and had to fight her own tears. "You could not have known he would turn into a monster."

"Could I not? Looking back, the signs were there. I let my own stubborn pride come before you, Mother and Michael, though he can fend for himself."

"Please do not berate yourself, you are here now. That is all that matters."

He watched her for a moment before walking from the room. He returned a few minutes later and led her to a chamber further down the passage. The duke and duchess were inside the room. They looked up at her entrance, and the concern in their eyes was touching.

"Isabella," the duchess said quietly as she walked to her and gave her a heartfelt hug. Isabella closed her eyes and cherished the contact. She had had so little since that fateful day when this tragedy had begun. When she opened her eyes and drew back, the duke was standing beside them. He took her hand.

"You have my eternal gratitude, Isabella, although I wish you had not risked yourself."

"How could I not when he has done so for me? This is, in part, my fault." The duke's face took on a thoughtful look, but she continued before he could object. "How is he?" she asked, walking over to the bed and looking down at Edmund, who lay, almost lifeless, on the narrow mattress. He had been cleaned and bandaged, but her heart ached to see him in such straits.

"He sustained a very heavy blow to the back of his head," the duke said, "but we Knights are a tough breed and he has much to live for." He took her arm and helped her to sit in the chair next to Edmund's bed. She looked up at him gratefully as she took Edmund's bandaged hand gently into hers.

When she heard the others quietly leave the room, she put her head down on the mattress next to their joined hands.

"Oh, Edmund. Please fight for me. I cannot bear to live without you."

"Never," he answered in a low, raspy voice.

She looked up with disbelief and was hard put *not* to throw herself upon him.

"Thank God!" she said, rising and bending over him to place a kiss on his lips. "I thought you had lost consciousness."

He smiled quickly. "I do not seem to be able to remain awake for long," he confessed.

"Then I shall try not to tire you. It was such a shock when you were attacked after all our careful plans!"

"Indeed. So much for being inconspicuous," he drawled, before falling back to sleep.

# CHAPTER SIXTEEN

EDMUND FELL IN and out of consciousness, but Isabella's plight was never far from his mind. He knew they needed to marry soon and that it would not be long before news of their adventures reached Frompton.

His mind wanted to solve the problem, but his body would not cooperate. He could hear conversations happening around him, but it was too much effort to open his eyes and speak. It felt as though he was swimming through mud and could not see or talk properly.

"How long will he need to be kept here?" Ruskington asked.

"Days... weeks...?"

Edmund could hear the uncertainty in his brother's voice.

"Should I take Isabella away somewhere? I cannot like the lack of protection of an inn."

Boots sounded across the wooden floor as if their owner were pacing up and down.

"I cannot like either of them being here. Even with my men surrounding the building, it is too vulnerable. You cannot leave your father for long or he will grow suspicious and anyone concerned will expect me to return to Knighton House."

"Supposing somebody lets it slip in a—ah—*trusted* ear, if you understand me, that your brother died in the attack?" Ruskington asked.

Rowley paused. "That could work. It will mean convincing the landlord and his servants as well. I would trust anyone in my household, but not the people here."

"I agree that people are too easily bought when they have no allegiance. Perhaps you should purchase the establishment."

Knighton clearly ignored this facetiousness, for there was barely a pause before he continued.

"Yet what is to be done with your sister? Your father strongly suspects that I am complicit in hiding her," Rowley argued.

"It would almost be amusing to hide her under my father's nose, but it would be too fraught with risk. Isabella mentioned Lady Hambridge and your sister as a possible priest-hole."

Someone snapped their fingers. "Edmund had suggested that. It might serve very well."

"Convincing her to leave whilst your brother lies here, suffering, will be difficult."

Rowley sighed heavily. "Perhaps I should remove him to Town. It is ten miles, but if taken slowly, the journey would, I hope, not cost him too much pain. I do not like being here with my duchess and child, and leaving him is unthinkable."

Edmund thought he would like to be back in his bed at night, in his brother's house. For some reason, returning to the vicarage was not appealing.

"What of his attacker? Do you think it was a direct assault on your brother? And will whoever was responsible attack again? We are still vulnerable here."

"I do. The cur was threatening him and severely beat some of the girls Edmund rescued. The young boy who warned Edmund about your sister was his errand boy. He has given me a list of places where we might find that dastard."

Normally, Edmund would preach against revenge, but Old Ben needed to be stopped. After this cold-blooded attack, Edmund knew the persecution would not stop until one of them was dead. He was not ready for it to be him. However, he could not like Johnny's involvement. The boy would be beaten and killed for helping them. There were no second chances for orphaned boys such as he. Johnny would be seen as a traitor for not being loyal to the one who gave him food and shelter, meager though it was. Little though he wanted to.

"What can I do to help?" Ruskington asked.

"Keep your sister safe for my brother."

"With my life," Ruskington swore. Edmund knew it need not be said. He was in no position even to help himself.

"I have called upon Heath, Petersham, Perth, and Sir Martin to help. They helped destroy Emerson and will be glad to assist."

"What do you intend to do?"

"Firstly, we have to find this man and see who is behind him. Blackguards like him do not act alone."

"You suspect Wethersby?"

"I am uncertain on that score. Heath was suspicious because of Wethersby's acquaintance with Emerson and his presence the night your sister was auctioned, but my inquiries have revealed nothing more."

"I am not well acquainted with his lordship, but trust your judgment. Wethersby has certainly been a thorn in the flesh of my family since before I was born. I will confess to some bloodlust, but would not wish to wrongly accuse anyone. I will be deuced grateful when all of this is over. Why did I ever long for adventure?" he asked in a sardonic tone.

"'We would often be sorry if our wishes were gratified...' to quote Aesop."

"I would feel more comfortable if your brother was awake," Ruskington murmured.

"He seems only to awaken when your sister is near."

"Wise gentleman. How do you propose to tell of his death?"

"I don't." There was a pause, and then Rowley explained. "A rumor should suffice for long enough for Isabella to reach her majority. No one will bother me until I send out death notices."

"I suppose it could do the trick, and I can think of no better alternative."

Edmund had to speak. "Isabella," he struggled to say.

Rowley came over to his bedside.

"Did you say something, Edmund?" he asked.

Edmund struggled to open his eyes, for the light was painful, but he did it anyway.

"Isabella must be kept safe," he croaked.

"*Both* of you must be kept safe," Rowley corrected.

Edmund frowned.

"We will take her to Aunt Hambridge's. I would like to take you home, if you think you might manage the journey."

"Yes," he said with difficulty. His mouth felt as dry as an African desert.

Rowley held a cup to his lips. Never again would Edmund take drink for granted.

"You will send for the bishop?" Edmund's voice was stilted.

"I think we should wait until you are recovered," Rowley said, casting a glance at Ruskington, but Edmund did not miss it.

"I am still of sound mind. Are you concerned I will not be whole?" He closed his eyes again in pain. What would happen if he were not? Had the doctor said something?

"Do not fret, Edmund. We will not let anything happen to Isabella."

"I want to go, now, before Smallbone can find her." He tried to sit up, although the pain was excruciating, but Rowley put a staying hand on his shoulder.

"Not yet, let me arrange things, at least to my satisfaction. I must ensure both of you are protected... unlike last time."

"I intend to take Isabella to Lady Hambridge, as you suggested.

You still have my blessing to wed her, of course," Ruskington said before turning back to Rowley. "And, of course, you have my full support in bringing his attacker to justice." He held out his hand to Rowley and shook it.

Ruskington left, presumably to take Isabella away, and Edmund felt a tightening in his throat. He felt himself to be a failure and, when she needed him most, he was utterly useless!

"Stop fretting, Edmund. Perhaps this is the best way."

Edmund could not help but glare at his brother.

"She is with her brother, who is possibly the only one who can protect her from their father. I have no authority to prevent him from taking her."

"I want to leave now," Edmund insisted, closing his eyes.

"I must make arrangements, but I will do so as quickly as I may. It will serve our purposes best if those at this inn believe you have died."

"Then I shall play dead if it means we may leave here faster."

Edmund opened one eye in time to see his brother looking down at him with one of his rare smiles.

There was a slight knock on the door and Rowley hurried over to answer it, guarding the view into the room. He at once stood aside to reveal Isabella, and Edmund felt better just at the sight of her. He smiled and tried to look as healthy as he could for her sake.

"You have heard the plan?" she asked quietly.

"Yes, you are to go with Ruskington, and I am to feign death." She nodded as a tear rolled a path down her cheek. He weakly lifted his arm, intending to wipe it away, but shook with the effort.

"I do not wish to be away from you." Her chin quivered.

"Nor I from you, but our brothers think it is safest this way, and since your father believes you to be under Knighton's protection you will not be safe there. We have only a handful of days left." Feebly, he squeezed her hand.

"If that is your wish." She leaned forward and kissed him on the lips. "I love you, Edmund," she whispered and then turned and left before he could form the reciprocal words. The short conversation had exhausted him, and he fell back into oblivion. Pretending to be dead would not be difficult at the moment.

LEAVING EDMUND BEHIND was the hardest thing Isabella had ever done, especially so soon. He seemed a little improved, but the doctor was still cautious about saying anything encouraging. Her presence put all of them in danger, however, and Alex was her brother who had her welfare at heart. They waited until the last faint glow of the sun was retreating beyond the horizon, a strange counterpoint to the storms they had endured earlier. They traveled in the Frompton carriage with eight outriders to protect them, and Isabella could not help but be tense after her day's adventures—if one could call them that. How Alex was to call on Lady Hambridge and sneak her inside without anyone noticing, Isabella had no notion, but she was too weary to worry about such details.

This time, she had been disguised as her brother's valet, and was enjoying the freedom of breeches for the first time, though they felt strange and almost scandalous. She did not know if anyone was waiting there to abscond with her, but she walked into Alex's carriage without so much as a by your leave. To anyone observing, Lord Ruskington had merely stopped for refreshment and was now on his way back to London.

Alex gathered Isabella into his arms and held her while the carriage rolled back along the northern road. They scarcely spoke, but he seemed to need her comfort as much as she needed his. They arrived in London without incident, and pulling into the alley behind Lady Hambridge's house, stopped outside the mews. The stark smell of horses and straw, mixed with the thick odor of coal in the air, announced that she was no longer in the country.

Alex escorted her past the mews and along the path into the house, which was dark and quiet. They entered through the servants' entrance to attract less notice.

When they finally entered the kitchen, Isabella sighed with relief. "That was easier than I expected."

An older woman in a black bombazine gown and white collar, with a floppy mobcap covering her iron-grey ringlets, entered the kitchens. A look of horror at once crossed her face.

"I am Lord Ruskington, and this is my sister, Lady Isabella Hartmere. The Duke of Knighton was to have sent word ahead of our arrival, but if I could be shown to Lady Hambridge, I will explain everything myself." Alex hurried to take control of the situation.

"Yes, my lord," the woman said, bobbing a curtsy yet casting a look of disapproval at Isabella in men's clothing. "If you will follow me."

They were led up a flight of wooden servants' stairs to the family part of the house, and shown into a well-appointed drawing room. The housekeeper quickly lit a branch of candles, revealing pale green walls with white rococo plasterwork on the ceiling. It was late, and the lady of the house had apparently already retired.

"Please send my apologies to Lady Hambridge for disturbing her. If it were not for great urgency, Mrs...."

"Croft."

"If not for great urgency, Mrs. Croft, I should not consider—"

"Just a moment," Isabella interrupted. "Has Lady Eugenia yet retired? Perhaps we might spare Lady Hambridge's rest and speak with her instead."

The housekeeper seemed to approve of this notion. "I will enquire, my lady."

"Are you acquainted with Lady Eugenia?" Isabella asked Alex after the housekeeper had left.

"She only knows me as Miss Thatcher from my time at the Grange," Isabella replied, "but we are somewhat acquainted because of our closeness in age. It can be lonely in the country if one has no friends close by."

"The duke and duchess allowed this?" Alex wrinkled his brow.

"Once you have met Lady Eugenia, you will understand," Isabella answered with a wry smile.

Soon, Lady Eugenia burst into the room, a broad smile on her face. "Miss Thatcher!" she exclaimed and running over to Isabella, took her hands. "Is something amiss?"

"A great deal, in fact; we were hoping that His Grace's messenger would have been before us."

"If he spoke with my aunt, she did not mention it. And how do you come to be wearing breeches? How fast!" Lady Eugenia, of course, did not hesitate to ask. "I would dearly love to try them myself!" She seemed to notice Alex then and looked rather thunder-struck.

"Lady Eugenia, may I introduce my brother, Lord Ruskington?"

Lady Eugenia dipped into a curtsy as Alex bowed, eyes twinkling.

"Lord?" Eugenia did not mask her disbelief.

"As I said, there is a great deal to explain. I am actually Lady Isabella Hartmere, daughter of the Duke of Frompton."

Eugenia gasped as both hands flew to her cheeks. "You have been hiding under my brother's roof all along!"

"I see you know some of the story," Alex remarked dryly.

"It is all over Town," Eugenia informed him as she slipped into a chair.

The housekeeper entered with a tray containing tea and a plate of sandwiches. Alex went to relieve the woman of her burden and praised her consideration at this late hour. Mrs. Croft flushed, no doubt unused to praise from handsome young gentlemen, but Isabella knew it was just the right thing to have done. It could not but help to ease her way while a guest in the house.

"We can rely, I am sure, on your discretion to keep our presence to yourself?" he said, with a conspiratorial wink.

"Of course, my lord." She curtsied and left the room.

Lady Eugenia poured tea for both herself and Isabella. "I expect you would prefer something stronger," she said to Alex. "Aunt keeps brandy for my brothers." She went over to a cupboard, selected a glass and poured a good measure before handing it to Alex.

"I am much obliged, my lady," he said while warming it in his hands.

Eugenia looked almost bashful. Taking note, Isabella decided to consider the cause later. Alex was a handsome devil, but he was much older and, in all likelihood, still smarting from the loss of his family in Canada.

Eugenia invited Alex to sit down, and eagerly began asking questions.

"Tell me everything," she said, sipping her tea. "I did not even know Rowley and Emma were returning to London."

"His Grace had formed the intention of doing so in order to assist me with my father's situation, which, as you know, has become quite the scandal," Alex answered.

Eugenia nodded, not hiding her curiosity. "It is all anyone is talking about. Tonight, Wethersby publicly demanded to see Lady Isabella..." Eugenia looked over to her in wonder. "...and he has challenged your father to a duel on the twenty-first of this month if he does not meet his obligations."

Alex's face went as still as a marble statue, except for the betraying muscle twitching in his jaw.

"It has begun," Isabella said quietly.

"How come you to be here instead of your father's house?" Eugenia asked eagerly. "Oh, are we to hide you?"

"If you would be so kind. It would be only for a few more days,"

Isabella answered.

"You do not wish to go to Wethersby," she remarked as if it all made sense.

"There is one more matter," Alex said to Eugenia. "Your brother Edmund has suffered a blow to the head. Knighton is bringing him back to Town by slow stages."

Eugenia paled at the news, and Isabella instantly moved to her side. "Not Edmund!" Eugenia said, as though she had received her own blow to the head. "Will he survive?"

"I pray so," Isabella answered honestly. "He falls in and out of consciousness. The doctor will not promise anything... not only was the blow quite severe, he was bound and left for dead."

Eugenia closed her eyes as if absorbing the news. "Why would anyone wish to hurt him? He is the kindest soul ever to live." She shook her head. "At least they will be back here soon so I may see him!"

"There is yet one more thing," Alex said.

Eugenia and Isabella looked at him.

"Edmund will be believed to be dead or at death's door, in order to protect him from the blackguards who attacked him. It will be necessary to maintain the façade for the next few days, which will have the advantage of preventing curious callers."

Isabella had trouble maintaining her composure at this. Sniffing loudly, she then blew her nose. It was not to be hoped that Eugenia would not notice.

"Isabella and Edmund were to wed on the morning of the twenty-first, as soon as she came of age," Alex explained, "so she could not be given to Wethersby."

"That is something Edmund would do." Turning her attention to Isabella, Eugenia must have seen the longing in her face. "I will be your eyes and ears. I promise to take care of him, and then we will be sisters."

"I wish for nothing more." Isabella tried to force a smile.

"It is late, so I should be going if I am not to raise more suspicions." Coming to his feet, Alex bowed to Eugenia.

Isabella rose to kiss her brother on the cheek and see him out.

# CHAPTER SEVENTEEN

EDMUND AWOKE IN time to be carried inside to his old chamber at Knighton House. They had traveled slowly through the night and reached London by morning. Although Edmund was feeling a little stronger, sudden movements caused nausea and sometimes retching, in addition to dizziness. The doctor had pronounced him a miracle, adding the caveat that any other person would have been dead within hours of such a brutal blow.

Edmund had too much to live for to die. His first thoughts were of Isabella.

"Rowley?" he called out in the hustle and bustle of being transported.

"Did you suffer very much?" his older brother asked as Edmund was placed on the bed.

"I did not. I am grateful to be here. Have you received any word from our friend?"

"Ruskington arrived safely and ensured our sister was in good health." He answered vaguely with the servants being present. Many of them would have heard about the rift between Frompton and Wethersby, and though they were trustworthy, it would be foolish to tempt them.

Edmund smiled with relief and leaned gingerly back onto the pillow. "Thank you for everything, Brother."

Rowley inclined his head. "Get some rest, and I promise to keep you informed."

"I will—but only on that condition and if you will ask Cook to send up some raspberry tarts."

Rowley chuckled. "You must be feeling better, then."

Edmund watched his brother close the door, and then closed his eyes. He had some weakness in his left arm and leg and did not wish to worry his brother. He fell asleep while wondering when he would see Isabella again. Now was when she needed reassurance and comfort, and he was helpless.

When he awoke, there was a footman seated in a chair in his room. The man at once came to attention when he noticed Edmund was no longer sleeping.

"Would you be so kind as to fetch me some tea and biscuits?"

"Of course, my lord."

It was disconcerting to think that someone had been watching him sleep, Edmund mused, but he knew his brother meant well. In fact, Edmund was not sure he could manage to reach the bell-pull on his own.

A few minutes later, the door opened and the footman brought in a tea tray, followed by Edmund's sister, Eugenia wearing a white gown with multi-colored flowers.

"I have been waiting an hour for you to wake up!" she exclaimed as she walked across the room and sat on the side of his bed to fuss over him. She poured him some tea and set two raspberry tarts where he could reach them before looking over to the footman. "You may go for a while. I will stay with him."

"Yes, my lady." He gave a short bow and withdrew.

"How could you, Edmund?" Eugenia asked as soon as the door shut.

"I hardly asked someone to attack me," he said, in a rare use of sarcasm.

"I know, it is just more the kind of thing Heath would do. I would never have expected such foolhardiness of you. Will you make a full recovery? I confess I feared you would look far worse, based on what Isabella told me."

"How is she?" Edmund asked, a bit too eagerly.

Eugenia smiled knowingly. "She is well, but worried for you, of course." She took a napkin and dabbed at his chin as though he were an infant. He raised a brow in annoyance at her.

"More jam tarts?" she asked. "You have every cook in every household wrapped around your little finger."

"No, not at all," he corrected. "I simply appreciate them appropriately."

She gave a little, nonchalant shrug.

"Eugenia, that color is most becoming, but is more suited to one of my doves than to a girl recently out." His sister did not seem to intentionally defy convention, but she rarely followed the rules.

"I am delighted to see you have not lost your sense of tact," she retorted.

"Tell me what is happening, please. I know Rowley will try to protect me—and to that end will tell me nothing."

She pursed her lips as if to object, then changed her mind. "Oh, very well, but he will have my head if he hears I have directly disobeyed his order not to distress you."

"Has it ever stopped you before?"

"Not particularly," she agreed. "We were at Lord Worth's garden party, a couple of evenings ago, when Wethersby demanded Frompton bring Lady Isabella out. There has been a great deal of talk."

"And what are people saying?" Edmund questioned, trying not to sound anxious.

Eugenia chewed her lip for a moment. "Things you would normally scold me not to repeat."

Edmund swallowed a few choice words of censure. "Do not try

my patience, Sister."

Eugenia lowered her eyes as if suitably chastened, but a dimple peeped its own naughty truth. Edmund forbore to comment.

"There are rumors circulating that perhaps Isabella is not Frompton's daughter."

Edmund swallowed a sip of tea while trying to assimilate the possibility. The question had not occurred to him, but could explain a great deal of what had happened.

"Do people believe it? Or are they simply relishing some juicy gossip?"

"It is hard to say. Frompton's insistence on keeping Lady Isabella hidden is adding fuel to the fire," she answered. "Now I understand why," she added after a tiny pause, tilting her head in a thoughtful way. "To think she was at the Grange the whole time! And I had thought Miss Thatcher to be one of your doves." She laughed. "How clever you are! Frompton will be very angry when he discovers the truth, however."

"Eugenia," Edmund warned, placing his good hand on her arm. "Please do not say such a thing to Isabella."

She wrinkled her forehead. "Say what?"

"That you thought she was one of my doves."

"Well, Rowley said so, did he not, when you first brought her there? But still, she was the sweetest girl and did not behave in a vulgar fashion at all."

"Eugenia!"

She ceased her rambling and looked at him as if she had, in that very moment, understood what it meant.

"Oh no! The poor girl! Was it in such a case that you found her?"

"Yes, and we will speak no more of it."

Eugenia looked flabbergasted. Perhaps he should convey the details, yet he could not but feel the less she knew, the better.

"Is that all you have heard?"

"There is to be a duel. I am not privy to the details, of course, but rumor has it that it will occur on the twenty-first."

Edmund could only nod. When he tried, he saw two of his sister, and the Lord knew, the world could not handle two such beings.

"I should go." Eugenia stood up and smoothed her skirts.

She bent over to kiss him on the forehead and that was when he noticed Rowley and Heath standing in the doorway.

"Look who I found," Rowley said as Heath walked towards him on the bed.

"You are the last one of us I ever expected to see prostrate with injury," Heath teased.

"Forgive me for stealing your thunder," Edmund replied. "How is Cecilia?"

"Quite nauseous, I am afraid. I left her behind at Woodcrest where she might grow our child in comfort."

"Congratulations. Fatherhood will look good on you, but I can sympathize far too well with her queasiness."

"May I see your injury?" Eugenia asked.

Edmund rolled over onto his side, muttering, "Bloodthirsty wench," as he did so.

His three siblings made mixed noises of disgust and appreciation as the bandage was removed to reveal a large, sutured gash.

"I have come to discuss your nemesis if you feel up to it," Heath said as he pulled a chair next to the bed.

Eugenia turned to leave and Edmund called out to her. "Please give Isabella my love."

Eugenia smiled. "Of course. I would not be surprised to find her climbing in through your bedroom window, though. It was difficult to keep her away when she heard I was coming to visit."

"Isabella?" Heath questioned. "Clearly I am not privy to the entire drama."

"Only half," Rowley said. He patted his brother on the shoulder. "I will tell you later," he said as he escorted Eugenia out.

Once the door closed behind them, Heath spoke. "What can you tell me about Old Ben?"

"You do not want his ire to descend upon you."

"Well, he has mine fixed on him," Heath snarled. "He trespassed on my property and threatened people under my protection."

"I suppose he did," Edmund conceded with a sigh.

"What is it?" Heath asked, narrowing his eyes.

"I am growing tired of fighting a never-ending battle."

"There will always be brothels and perverse appetites, but let them be served by the willing, not by scared innocents stolen from the streets or tricked into it through indentured slavery."

"You are correct, of course. Forgive me, I am merely maudlin from my attack."

"Deservedly so. It must anguish you to be rewarded thus undeservedly for your good deeds."

"I was bound to reap my just desserts sooner or later," Edmund quipped.

"The man beat you and left you for dead. I am determined to find him."

"Heath, no…"

"Do not quote the scriptures to me, Edmund. I know their teachings well." His brother stood and walked to the window. "I believe he is part of the ring created by Emerson. Perhaps we brought only a part of it down, but I must finish what I started."

Edmund closed his eyes. "I wish I could do it myself."

"You will be with us in spirit. Petersham, Perth, and Hardy are champing at the bit to serve up some justice."

"Thank them for me. I am glad you will not be alone. Do you have a plan?"

"I have put a price on this Old Ben's head. I expect him to be practically delivered to my doorstep."

"And then?" Edmund asked warily.

"I expect him to squeak like a mouse that's been pounced on by a cat."

"Be careful, Brother."

"I will report as soon as we are finished."

ISABELLA PACED FRANTICALLY across the ivory and gold carpet. She was failing miserably at being held in captivity. She was not precisely a prisoner, but it felt as though the Chinese papered walls were closing in on her. Perhaps a little fresh air could be arranged… she looked out of the window longingly at the rose garden below.

There was a light knock on the door before Eugenia burst in and then shut the door behind her. She leaned against it, breathing heavily.

"What has happened?" Isabella angled her head as she asked.

"You will never believe it," Eugenia answered, walking into the room and sitting down in a green and cream striped chair.

"I think I would believe anything at this point," she said dryly.

"Now the rumors are swirling that Lord Wethersby has abducted you!"

"Where did you hear that?" Isabella asked, sinking into the chair opposite Eugenia and dropping her head in one hand. "I am completely ruined."

Eugenia was one of the few people Isabella had met who could screw up her face and still look adorable.

"I do not know about that," she answered. "If you emerge married to my brother, your father and Wethersby will look like the fools they are. We can spread it abroad as soon as the day of your birth dawns."

"What if my father confesses the whole—that he lost me? I doubt he will admit to trying to sell me."

"For some reason, I do not think he will admit he lost you, but nevertheless, this is certainly the greatest scandal to hit the beau monde in recent history.

"Lovely," Isabella retorted.

"The good news is, you will not lose Edmund, no matter what. He is head over ears in love with you."

"And you surmised all of this while visiting him on his sickbed?"

"Oh, yes. He did not look so sick, by the by."

Isabella's heart warmed at that revelation.

"My brother Heath arrived as I was leaving. They were already plotting a trap to catch the attacker."

"What? Edmund needs to rest!" Isabella suddenly realized she was gripping the arms of the chair with worry.

"It is of no use to protest," Eugenia said, as though she were worldly wise. "There is no gainsaying my brothers in anything once their minds are set on something. Besides, I do not think Edmund intends to participate physically. He is supposed to be thought dead, after all. I overheard Heath saying that several of his friends are to help. They all conspired to destroy Lord Emerson before." Eugenia continued to speak as though this were an everyday occurrence.

What kind of family would Isabella be marrying into?

"These men are dangerous! They have no conscience!" she protested.

"I think that is true," Eugenia agreed. She reached over to pull on the rope to summon a servant, who she met at the door a few minutes later. "I am famished. Would you send up tea and biscuits?"

Isabella watched Lady Eugenia move about with uncaged energy.

"So what else are the gossips saying? I have been abducted by Wethersby; is there anything else I should know?"

Eugenia blushed a little and attempted to smother a guilty look. She might try to pretend worldly sophistication, but she was still younger than Isabella.

"What is it?" Isabella insisted, feeling entirely comfortable with the girl now that her station had been revealed.

"I should not say. Edmund and Rowley will both have my head if they find out."

"I will not tell them. If it pertains to me, I have the right to know."

"I suppose that is true." Eugenia was pondering this when the maid returned with a tea tray and a plate of shortbread.

She poured the tea while the maid left the room and Isabella was very soon fit to burst with curiosity. She stared at Eugenia, waiting.

"Very well, they are saying you are a cuckoo."

"A what?" Isabella's jaw was gaping, but she did not care.

"You know, a cuckoo in the nest." Eugenia waved a biscuit-laden hand. "Frompton is not your real father."

Isabella paused, about to bite a biscuit, trying to absorb what she had been told. How could that be true?

Eugenia raised one brow. "Do you mean to tell me you know nothing of the ways of the *ton*?"

"Apparently not," Isabella said, deciding to console herself with a delicious bite of buttery goodness. Although she felt sick at the thought of having a different father, it would explain a great deal about Frompton's behavior towards her. "If that were the case, why would Frompton draw attention to it? He claimed me, after all."

"He could hardly do otherwise," Eugenia pointed out. "And if rumors are correct..." She looked heavenward. "... Frompton did not know until that card game when he lost to Wethersby."

Isabella wanted to be alone to consider what Eugenia had told her. Even if some of the tale was rumor, there was usually some grain of truth to be found. She was confused, but some things were beginning to make sense. "Thank you for telling me."

Eugenia looked as though she regretted it. "You must be distressed. Will you be—are you quite well?"

"I do not know. I need time to reflect." She also wanted—no, needed—Edmund very badly.

"What are you thinking?" Eugenia asked, as though she recognized a fellow conspirator in crime.

"You say Edmund is much improved?"

She gave a slight shrug. "He was awake and speaking with us, and he asked for raspberry tarts."

"I need you to help me visit him."

A mischievous gleam entered Eugenia's eye. "We could sneak you into the house."

"Supposing we are caught?"

"It is only two streets away. You can follow me, as my maid. No one will suspect a thing."

"Even the duke?"

"I can manage him," she said with a dismissive flick of her hand, much the same as the duchess had done the day before. Isabella very much doubted the severe duke was as manageable as they thought.

It was so very tempting. Isabella was quite desperate to see Edmund, yet the lingering threat of one Mr. Smallbone gave her pause.

"What of the runner?"

"You worry too much," Eugenia said dismissively.

"He chased me to Devonshire," Isabella reminded her. "He could clap me in irons and carry me to my father." Isabella frowned. "Whoever that is."

"Oh, I wish I had not told you that piece of tittle-tattle." Eugenia pouted. "I tell you what, we will take pistols and daggers and we will fight off anyone who dares to touch us."

"Do you know how to use either of them?" Isabella asked. opening her eyes wide.

"Of course I do!"

"Very well, then. I shall dress as a maid."

"After dinner, if you please. I have just returned from there and it might appear suspicious if I were to go now."

"Mayhap it would be better to go tomorrow morning."

"But then it will be daylight."

Isabella threw up her hands in defeat. "I await your convenience," she retorted.

Eugenia laughed. "I *do* like you!" She stood up and went to the door. "I will send up a maid's costume and we will leave as soon as my aunt retires for the evening."

Hours later, Isabella was prey to a bundle of anxieties, even though Eugenia's maid had instructed her most exactly on how to behave so as not to draw attention to herself. She was to walk a few paces behind Eugenia and be demure. Isabella had been an upper servant for nearly two years, so she thought she could succeed well enough. The hard part would be to keep her head down and not look around for villains about to jump out at her.

Once her ladyship had retired, they made their preparations. It was nearing half past nine and dusk was on the horizon; Eugenia's maid knew where they were going in case anyone should ask.

They crept down the servants' stairs and out through the entrance at the back of the house where Isabella had arrived only one night before. Lady Hambridge's bedchamber was near the front entrance and it would be too risky even though someone might question why Lady Eugenia was leaving through the rear door. Isabella stared at the back of Eugenia's gown, and only just kept from laughing out loud. Even though wearing a mourning lavender, the duke's sister somehow managed to look gaudy with her flounces and ribbons. She certainly had her own style. Perhaps she would have been well suited to the previous century, when the Duchess of Devonshire had made outrageous *à la mode*. At least Eugenia had not taken to wearing wigs bearing live wildlife or vegetation! She strolled more boldly than most young ladies, but as a duke's daughter, her credit was such she was granted far more license than a young lady of less exalted birth. Isabella would have been accorded the same luxury, except, were it ever made known, her shame would be beyond what was acceptable, even in one of her rank.

They crossed a street, skirting the edge of a park. Isabella had little knowledge of London apart from Hyde Park, where she had been on a few occasions during her last visit. She relaxed a trifle, for who would dare accost them in a public park? However, they crossed another busy street, returning to where the residences were, and where the sun fell behind the buildings, creating dark shadows. It all happened so quickly, that Isabella could scarce recount, later, what happened. An arm came from behind her and covered her mouth. Screaming was impossible. At the same instant, her arm was twisted behind her back and a voice growled in her ear.

"Be quiet or I hurt your lady."

She nodded her understanding through the excruciating pain.

"I knew ye would make a mistake," Mr. Smallbone said smugly as he stopped to tie a rancid gag over her mouth and bind her hands so tightly her muscles screamed from the stretching torture. "Ye 'ave to think like a criminal, I always say."

Isabella wanted to scream, but it was too late, and she would never forgive herself if Eugenia was harmed. Yet somehow Eugenia heard or sensed that Isabella was no longer following her.

Edmund's sister turned and ran straight at them, her pistol cocked and aimed in one hand and her dagger raised in the other.

Isabella had the wit to duck, while Mr. Smallbone did not know what was coming at him.

A loud boom rent the air, followed by a grunt and the thud of Mr. Smallbone's body on the ground. Finding herself released, Isabella turned. Blood was oozing from the man's chest in a bright red stain and she promptly fainted.

# CHAPTER EIGHTEEN

T HE MEN SET out just before dusk, eager to hunt.

"Are you certain we should take him?" Heath asked Rowley who was reluctantly staying behind should Edmund need him.

"Johnny knows Old Ben's movements better than anyone."

"Yessir," the boy nodded his head vigorously.

"And I trust he will keep you out of more trouble than vice versa."

Heath scowled at Rowley, but did not argue. The men were all dressed as inconspicuously as may be in dark colors with dark knit caps pulled over their heads in attempt to mitigate attention being drawn to them.

Sir Martin and Petersham were to go inside Madame Celeste's potential custom, and Perth and Heath were to go with Johnny to seek him out around the back where he resided. Not that Heath had any great expectation of finding him there. He was on the run if he knew what was good for him, and criminals like that had to be savvy to stay alive.

Perth's carriage dropped the three of them off a couple of streets away and then took Petersham and Sir Martin on to the front of the brothel.

Heath used to spend a great deal of time in this world, and now it fairly repulsed him. How had he not noticed how low he'd sunk?

He and Perth followed Johnny, who seemed to know this area like the back of his hand. They slunk through narrow alley ways that he would not have known existed. The stench of the slums was enough to make him hide his nose in his neck cloth.

They had reached the back of the brothel, but Johnny continued on to another set of doors that looked like they led to a rundown shack.

"Is this where he lives?" Heath asked quietly as they watched from across the alley. A guard was walking back and forth patrolling the backside of Madame Celeste's establishment. It looked considerably nicer from the front, Heath recalled.

"Do you think he is inside?"

"Not this time of night. He's usually inside patrolling," Johnny answered, his eyes darting back and forth, surveying everything around.

Perth and Heath looked at each other.

"I think I should go," Johnny said.

"What if he finds you there? I could pretend to be drunk and wandered into the wrong door," Heath explained.

"But the dog will bark something fierce at a stranger if I ain't there," Johnny said as if he just remembered.

"Very well, but we will be nearby. Shout if you need us."

Johnny ran across the alley with lightning speed when the guard had his back turned. Heath and Perth took turns strolling back and forth like drunkards in the alleyway. Something did not sit right with Heath about giving so much responsibility to the little boy. He should have done more for him that first night he had encountered him, but there were so many in his situation and they all could not be helped.

Johnny had been gone for several minutes, and Heath began to worry. What was taking him so long? He stopped and leaned his head next to the door Johnny had entered, debating whether or not to barge in.

"Psst. Sir!"

"What is it, Johnny?" Heath asked, hoping the guard would pay him no mind.

"I think you need to come inside."

Heath looked around and the guard had turned the corner for a moment. He signalled to Perth and slipped inside the door. Immediately he smelled the stench of a rotting corpse. It was very dark inside, and his eyes could not adjust. "Is there a candle anywhere, Johnny?" he asked as he heard the whines of an animal.

He heard some rumbling around as he tried not to retch from the odor. Johnny lit a taper and Heath immediately saw the large body hanging from the rafter that crossed the small room.

"Gor!" Johnny said as he saw the body with its eyes and tongue bulging.

"Go and find Lord Perth, Johnny."

Johnny gave a nod and was gone. The dog whimpered as he left, but stayed near the body. Amazing how dogs could be loyal even to scoundrels.

Heath busied himself looking around the small hovel for any kind of information about who Ben had worked for. He had little doubt that someone like Old Ben would have the funds or the wherewithal to run such an operation.

Whoever it was had rid the place of any evidence. It was disordered, but there was nothing to point any fingers that Heath could see. It was hard not to look at the body in the middle of the room, but Heath did not want to touch it. Once they had searched and made certain there was nothing to implicate the leader, he would send for the constable.

A noise behind him caused him to jump.

"Thank goodness," he said as Johnny entered with Perth.

"That is going to be a sight hard to erase," Perth said making a face of distaste.

"Indeed. If you would be so good as to take Johnny and send for the constable, I will finish up here."

"Do you have any belongings you would like to take first, Johnny?" Perth asked.

The little boy shook his head. "I don't have nuffink," he answered. "But who will take care of Mutt?"

"The dog?"

Johnny nodded, looking worried.

Heath knew they had to take it. He looked to Perth who simply shrugged his shoulders.

"He will have to come with us, I suppose."

Johnny smiled brightly as though there were not a grotesque dead body hanging from the ceiling, and gathered up the scrawny dog of unknown origins.

"If you take him home, I will go inside and inform the others. I think Madame Celeste and I need to have a heartfelt conversation. I have no doubt she could tell me everything."

"It will be hard to convince her to talk if she knows about Old Ben here. She will have her throat slit for her troubles."

"Come on little fellow," Perth said to Johnny. "It looks like your friend needs a bath and some scraps."

Johnny nodded. "I will share my scraps with you, Mutt. That's the only way Old Ben would let me keep him," the boy said proudly, and Heath knew he would be taking the boy back to Cecilia when this was over.

He did one last survey of every nook and cranny in the one-room shack – not that he expected to find much. It was hardly likely that the man had been literate and kept a journal of all of his crimes.

Heath had thought after dispensing of Emerson he would be done with bringing such low-lifes to order, however Edmund deserved retribution, even if someone had taken away the satisfaction of Old Ben.

Heath waited for the guard to turn the corner before he escaped and crossed the alley to hide under a meager overhang. However, he wanted to ensure the constable arrived before he went to find Madame Celeste.

Heath was about to give up and go find one himself when someone finally arrived. He stopped and talked to the guard who pointed him towards Old Ben's door. He escaped back across the alley around the corner while they were looking inside to discover the horrible sight.

He wanted to be the one to talk to Madame Celeste about Old Ben. He suspected she already knew, but would be able to tell by her reaction, however small.

Again, he wondered how he had ever found himself frequenting places such as this. Boredom, idleness – there were great truths that nothing good came from either. Now he had a purpose in life, he couldn't imagine ever finding pleasure in such debauchery.

He found Sir Martin and Petersham quickly and went straight to them. They were finishing a card game instead of sampling the wares offered. Petersham was newly married as well, but Heath had not seen him since his own wedding.

He sat at the table next to them and spoke quietly but over the din. "I must speak with Madame Celeste at once. I would like you to accompany me."

The three men rose together and found the owner, who almost appeared as if she was expecting them. She still had an attractive body, though she used paint to disguise her age. Up close, though, Heath could see the signs of a hard life.

She inclined her head at their approach. "Follow me." She led them down a corridor of many doors, and stopped at the one on the end. It was her own boudoir. It was more tasteful than one would expect of such a place, the colors were rich greens and purples and the room was heavily scented in a floral bouquet.

She sat on a round couch, crossing one leg over the other and leaning one arm back. "To what do I owe the pleasure of you three charming gentleman?"

"You cannot be ignorant of the attack on my brother," Heath began.

Celeste inclined her head. "I might have heard. My condolences." She betrayed no emotion, however.

"You might have also heard that it was Old Ben who lay in wait and attacked him on Thornton Heath."

"Ben had mentioned there was a personal matter between them." Her face remained impassive, but she began to sway one foot back and forth in an anxious motion.

"Then you might be surprised to know that I put a price on his head. Unfortunately, someone else got to him first."

A small flicker of her eyes betrayed her. She knew. "A pity. He was one of my best men. What do you want from me, Lord Heath? What can I do to keep your family away from my business?"

"Tell me who is behind it all."

She sighed as though he were a child who knew little of the ways of the world. "You might win small battles, but you will never win the war."

"What is your price, Madame?"

"I cannot be bought," she scoffed.

"Then name your benefactor and save yourself."

She paused for a moment as if debating. "There is no one else, my lord. Just me."

"You lie, and I will see you pay."

The three men turned and walked out.

"GET IN THE house, now, Eugenia!" Rowley said as he ran out into the square where they had been attacked.

"But she is tied up, I must help her!"

"I will see to her, but no one must see you. Get inside, now," he commanded.

Isabella was coming to as the duke scooped her up and began hurrying her inside a house. "Keep your head towards me," he ordered, before barking orders to his staff who had gathered at the loud noise. "Call the constable, and a physician to see to Mr. Small-bone. Carry him into the study. If anyone asks, he was attacking my sister and her maid. I witnessed all of it."

"Yes, Your Grace."

The duke carried her on into the house to a back parlor favored by the duchess. She was waiting there with Eugenia, who was shaking with shock. The duchess was placing a glass of brandy in her hand and commanding her to drink.

The duke set Isabella down in a chair and proceeded to cut off her bindings with a sharp knife. "Are you harmed?"

Isabella found that she was also shaking, but shook her head.

"I must deal with this situation, but both of you have a great deal of explaining to do later. Thankfully, I happened to see Smallbone attack you, Isabella."

A look passed between the duke and duchess and then he left the room. Eugenia began rocking back and forth in the chair, eyes wide.

"Drink," the duchess commanded. "You are in shock."

"What else could I have done? Is he dead?"

"I do not know, dearest. I know you were only protecting Isabella. He had no right to attack her like that."

Isabella felt wretched. It seemed like such a weak word for the misery she had caused everyone around her when they had done nothing but be kind. Edmund might now be an invalid and Mr. Smallbone might be dead because of her. It was too much to bear!

Somehow she had begun to hyperventilate in deep, gut-wrenching sobs. The duchess was suddenly kneeling before her trying to force brandy into her hands. "There now. You have both been through something no one should ever have to go through."

"Will I hang?" Eugenia asked. "I did not even think twice about whether I should shoot him. When I saw his hands on her..." She shook her head and could not speak.

"Your brother will not allow you to hang. We must not react prematurely. Mr. Smallbone might yet live."

"All of this because I insisted on seeing Edmund," Isabella confessed while she inhaled in a few ragged breaths.

"Well, you should certainly see Edmund since you have been through so much. It would cheer him. It will be sometime, yet, before we hear what is happening."

"Do you think it is safe to leave this room?" Isabella looked up from her glass to ask.

"Servants' stairs, my dear, and Mr. Smallbone is in no condition to hunt for you now."

"But will someone not wish to question us?" Eugenia asked, seeming to recover her wits somewhat.

"Your brother will do his best to prevent that. He witnessed the event, and a duke's word is generally not questioned. Come, let us go see Edmund." The duchess opened a panel that blended in with the woodwork and they all climbed the back stairway to the family chambers.

The duchess knocked on one of the doors and a footman answered. "Is Lord Edmund able to receive visitors? I think he will wish to see these in particular very much."

"I will inquire, Your Grace," he said, closing the door behind him. It was a few moments before he opened it again and held it wide for them to enter.

Isabella could barely restrain herself from launching at Edmund. His color was improved, and he was sitting upright.

"Oh Edmund!" She embarrassed herself by falling into his open arms.

"What has happened?" he asked his sister and Emma.

"It is all my fault," Isabella said, dabbing at her eyes with a hand-kerchief. "I only thought I was having a bad day having to be kept hidden, and was desperate to see you were well. I followed Eugenia disguised as a maid, and Mr. Smallbone attacked me."

He forced her back a little to look at her. She could feel a bruise forming on her cheek, and her hands had been bound much like his had with a coarse rope. Gently he touched her wrists and pulled her to his lips for a kiss before growling, "I will kill him."

"You will not have to," Eugenia answered.

"Please explain yourself," Edmund demanded when it looked like she would say no more.

"I shot him when I saw him attacking her. Rowley had him brought into the house and the physician is attending him now."

Edmund seemed to look at his sister with admiration. He tried to reach out with his other hand for Eugenia, but something was wrong and he could not make it. Isabella did not say anything, but she noticed and likely the others did too.

Eugenia propped her self on the side of the bed and leaned over to give her brother a kiss on the cheek. "This has been a tough time. I thought it was all over with Heath."

"We all did, and unfortunately there is still more to come to be finished."

There was a soft knock on the door and the duke was there with Lord Heath. Thank goodness it was a large chamber.

"Back so soon?" Edmund asked of Heath.

"May I speak freely?" he asked, looking at Isabella.

"Forgive me," Edmund said. "Lord Heath, may I present Lady Isabella, my betrothed."

"Ah, so much more makes sense to me now." He had been there the night of the auction. She could see the recognition on his face.

"What has happened?" Edmund brought his attention back to the present, thankfully.

"We found Old Ben, but someone got to him first."

"He is dead?" Eugenia asked.

"Very much so. We went in and spoke with Madame Celeste, and she insists she is working alone. I have no proof otherwise, but she was aware that Ben was dead."

"How and where?" Edmund asked.

"Hanged in his home. Johnny discovered him, but seemed surprisingly unaffected. Perth took him home."

"One could argue suicide, then," Edmund said, still considering the death.

"There is no proof otherwise, but there were no signs that he had done it to himself..."

Isabella shivered. This was a world that she had never known about before and it was pure evil. Pure, cold blooded evil. Edmund must have sensed her discomfort, for he pulled her closer.

"There is little we can do tonight," the duke spoke after hearing the information. "Madame Celeste is too clever to do anything for a while, and unfortunately she has come to my attention more than once. She will either reveal who is behind this to me, or she will no longer have any business in England. I must go and see how Dr. Evans is progressing with Smallbone."

"He still lives?" Eugenia asked nervously.

"The ball appeared to lodge between his ribs. If they shatter when the ball is removed, he will very likely die."

"I did not intend for him to die, but he was going to take Isabella away," she explained.

The duke's eyes softened and he gave his sister a nod. "Who is to say we would not all have done the same? There is no sense second guessing, for he most certainly acted beyond his authority. It will be handled, but for now we must wait and see. And there is still Frompton to be dealt with."

"How you must rue the day you laid eyes on me!" Isabella moaned.

"There will be none of that. You did nothing to warrant the situation you found yourself in, and now you are family," Edmund insisted.

She bit her lower lip as her chin quivered. She managed to whisper a "thank you."

The duke left the room and they all looked around at each other.

"What do we do now?" Eugenia asked.

"Sleep," the duchess answered.

"Who could sleep?" Eugenia retorted.

"Finish your brandy, and you will be out like a babe," Heath advised with a twinkle in his eye.

"But where?" Isabella asked. "Should we not return to Lady Hambridge's house?"

"I refuse to release you," Edmund said.

"I would like to consult Rowley on that, but I suspect the answer will depend on the outcome downstairs. For now, we shall all find our beds and if necessary, we will wake you in time to be returned before dawn," the duchess said, barely covering a yawn.

The siblings began to file out, but Edmund held on to her. "Stay."

"I do not want to be under the roof with that man."

"He cannot harm you now, and he was only doing what your father hired him to do, little though I approve of his methods."

"I can never be as good as you. If you keep talking, you will make this man out to be a saint."

"Never that. But I do not want to talk anymore."

"You are well enough?"

"For a kiss," he teased.

Isabella had never initiated anything in her life, but she placed her hand on his chest and felt his heart racing beneath it. His breath quickened, mirroring and mingling with her own. She touched her fingers to his lower lip and then followed them with her mouth in a sweet meeting of the lips. They traded soft brushes and warmth, until he pulled back.

"Did I do something wrong?" she asked, mortified.

"Not at all. It was so well done, I became disoriented."

Isabella was certain he was only being kind, but snuggled next to him and slept peacefully knowing no matter what the morrow brought, she would always have this.

# CHAPTER NINETEEN

MR. SMALLBONE SURVIVED the ball removal. The Chief Magistrate had retired Smallbone from the profession, and he was allowed a pension and house in the country, never to speak of the incident again. Rowley had persuaded the magistrate towards leniency, using the fact that he had been shot as excuse. It also kept Eugenia's name out of the matter.

Edmund was healing—far more slowly than he liked, but having Isabella nearby was speeding up the process. He had confessed his weaknesses, and the doctor had said that with time and exercise, he should make mostly a full recovery. Whoever would have imagined "mostly" could be such a terrifying word?

The duel was to take place tomorrow, which was no secret, and the household Knighton had kept to itself for the entire week. Rumors were spreading wildly, and there was much speculation about Edmund's death, but no crêpe had been hung on the windows or door knocker, and no straw was spread on the street to muffle sound, as would be normal for a house in mourning. Despite these lapses, no one went out into Society to quell the gossip.

There was a knock on the door.

"Enter," Edmund called.

"You have a visitor, my lord," the footman said. "What should I say?"

It could only be one of a few people who would be admitted into the house.

"I would like to dress and go downstairs," Edmund answered. "If you could please ask the gentleman to wait, and send someone in to assist me." Edmund had no valet. Few vicars had them, and he had always found it unnecessary, until now.

Dressing was difficult, but he managed with the help of his brother's valet, and felt more human than he had since the attack. He walked slowly down the stairs, with the assistance of a cane and the footman. He was exhausted, but he had done it! The thought flooded through his mind that perhaps he could still marry Isabella before the duel...

He entered the drawing room to see Ruskington waiting there for him. He turned and smiled.

"Excellent! I scarcely knew what to expect."

Edmund sank into a chair. "Forgive me. It is my first attempt at taking more than a few steps, but the doctor believes I will mostly recover."

He could see the relief cross Ruskington's face as it relaxed. He sat in an armchair opposite Edmund.

"Have there been any changes with your father?" Edmund asked, feeling himself slip into his vicararial demeanor in almost the same way he slipped on his vestments. He could sense that the man needed to unburden himself.

"Unfortunately, no. The seconds might as well have been speaking to the wind when trying to effect a reconciliation. The duel is set for tomorrow morning. Were I to sell tickets, I should, in all probability, be able to repay the debt," he added sardonically.

Dueling was now illegal, yet no one would stop a duke and an earl from settling a debt of honor.

Ruskington looked concerned, and Edmund gently encouraged him to open up. "What is it?"

"With regard to Isabella… there are more rumors." Ruskington clenched his jaw. "Have you heard?"

"Very little has reached my ears in my chambers. I have been fussed over and coddled, so no one would tell me much."

"They have been saying Isabella is not Frompton's daughter. My mother will not answer me. I wanted you to know; that is, if you are still considering the marriage?"

"Have you heard who her father might be?" Edmund asked, "Not that it affects my feelings for her in the slightest." He did not reveal he already knew, thanks to his garrulous sister, or that the more he had turned the idea over it in his mind, the more it explained everything which had happened.

"The obvious answer would be Wethersby, but I have not heard it confirmed." Ruskington stood and paced across the room. "He and my mother were in love, before her parents forced her into a more advantageous match with a duke. She bore him myself and my brother, and—I believe—sought love where she could find it later. My father is not an affectionate or easy man. Not that I am trying to justify my mother's actions, you understand, but it would explain a great deal."

Edmund nodded slightly, though the motion still pained him.

"It would also explain why Isabella was left in the country most of the time," Alex continued. "*Out of sight, out of mind*, and less chance for my father to realize he had been cuckolded."

"But somehow he found out," Edmund said softly.

"The dreaded card game." Alex agreed. "Now I understand why my father says Wethersby had cheated him. He did not mean at cards."

"So he thought to punish Isabella?"

"I cannot say for certain what he thought to gain by using Isabella so, other than hurting Wethersby and mother."

"Wethersby must have known it was her that night," Edmund

whispered. "'Tis why he wagered a fortune to win."

"I beg your pardon?" Ruskington was confused.

"The night of the auction. I had thought Wethersby merely a lecher, but I think he knew her identity and paid whatever it would take to win her. He had to have known she was Isabella—and his daughter."

"So Father was hoisted with his own petard, you think? I could kill him myself," Ruskington said, clearly seething.

"Nothing would stop me from marrying her. In fact, when I first saw you here, I thought you had come to tell me the marriage was no longer welcome."

"Never," Ruskington said, "though I believe we need to tell her everything and let her choose. She deserves every happiness."

Edmund fretted like a nervous boy as they waited for Isabella to join them.

She resembled a ray of sunshine when she entered the drawing room, finally dressed as a duke's daughter should be in pale blue sprigged muslin. His heart jumped within his chest and his insides felt as though butterflies were flooding every part of him. It was terrifying to be in love.

"Edmund!" she exclaimed as she came into the room, bringing with her the scent of lavender and vanilla. "Did you walk down the stairs?" she asked.

"I did. It was not a pretty sight, but I believe I will soon be able to manage without embarrassing myself."

She beamed at him, only then noticing her brother. "Alex!" She walked over to him and accepted his kiss on her cheek. "Has something else happened?"

"Not exactly, but there are some matters I think you should know."

"Have you found out who my father was?"

Ruskington paled. "You know?"

"I have heard the rumors," she confessed. She went to sit in the window seat and looked down at an embroidered flower on her skirt. "But I do not know who he may be."

"Eugenia and her indiscreet tongue," Edmund stated.

Isabella gave a guilty nod.

"I have reason to believe it is Wethersby," Ruskington said gently. Walking over to her, he knelt down before her and took her hands. "Mother will neither confirm nor deny it, but she wept so freely as to make me believe it is true."

"Wethersby?" Isabella whispered with a mixture of disgust and disbelief.

"I think perhaps he knew, Isabella." Edmund tried to console her. "I think that is why he tried to win you that night. It explains much."

Isabella stared at the wall, as still as a statue. She neither wept nor screamed; she did not make a single sound of distress.

"Oh, how I hate them all!" she finally declared. "And doubtless they will kill each other tomorrow!"

"It has been a long time coming," Ruskington said.

"Why did no one ever tell me the truth? I have been naught but a pawn in their childish games!"

"You have been very ill-used," Edmund agreed.

"Now, my real father will probably be killed tomorrow and yet I will be of age." She looked at Edmund. "I release you from the betrothal. You must be glad to escape!"

"No! I would never be glad to lose you. I still wish to marry you."

"You could hardly remain in the church when married to such a scandal. It is even worse than I thought. I am a bastard."

"Do not say that word. Frompton still recognized you and cannot take that away from you," Alex insisted.

"He is right, Isabella. Once we are married, your part in this hideous affair will not be of any importance. People will remember Frompton and Wethersby."

"I do not know what I should do."

"Then we will wait. We will see what happens tomorrow and you may feel differently afterwards. I would never force you to marry me, but my feelings will not change."

She looked as though her heart was breaking, if such a thing were possible to see. Edmund could understand that, for everything she had believed her entire life had suddenly changed.

If anyone ever deserved to be loved, that person was Isabella, and he would continue to show her, in word and deed, for as long as he lived. He desperately wanted to be married to her, but now was not the time to pursue his suit. They had managed to keep her safe, despite all the forces working against him, and after tomorrow she would no longer be at the duke's mercy. If Wethersby truly was her father, then the threat had been moot after all. If only there had been honesty, so much of this could have been prevented!

Edmund forced his way to his feet and walked clumsily to her side.

"We have time now, there is no need to rush into any decision. I shall be here and ready to lead you up the aisle, should that be your wish when you are ready."

Her face was wrinkled with pain. As Edmund took her into his arms, Ruskington discreetly left the room.

ISABELLA DID NOT know what to feel. She tossed and turned all night and awoke before dawn on what she had thought would be her wedding day. Now, she was going to watch her fathers kill each other, because of stupid, insufferable pride! She was prey to conflicting emotions. Had any of her parents ever truly loved her? Edmund had argued that Frompton had not known the truth until the card game, and perhaps, on reflection, that was true. Yet why had Wethersby wagered for her? It was hard not to hate them both.

Pained by this realization, she turned her thoughts instead to her mother. Being in love herself, Isabella could now understand, if her mother truly loved Wethersby, how she might have given in to the weakness and betrayed her husband. Isabella found the whole tangle deeply confusing; the web of deceit and dishonor pulled at her emotions dreadfully.

*Poor Edmund has suffered so much.* She did not wish to hurt him, but she could not subject him to this marriage until everything else was resolved. Even though she believed their love was true, she had to make certain the storm of unavoidable scandal could be weathered first.

The gentlemen concerned had argued against her attending the duel, of course, but she had made it clear she would be present with or without their sanction or assistance. They had relented. Isabella had therefore borrowed one of the duchess's mourning gowns, feeling the need to dress in black. It suited her mood and the occasion.

A sleepy maid having fastened the tiny buttons and dressed her hair, she pulled on a plain black bonnet and fastened her pelisse before making her way downstairs. The gentlemen were waiting in the study, all four dressed as somberly as the mood which heavily cloaked the room.

They settled into the duke's town carriage, a bit of a squeeze with four large men and herself, but Isabella nestled between Edmund and her brother and found comfort in the closeness. They drove in silence, yet every sound seemed muffled and distant to her senses. They set out to Hampstead Heath in the darkness to be present for the dawn meeting.

The northern road was crowded with traffic, and Isabella felt sick at the knowledge that her fathers' duel was a source of entertainment for the *ton*. Much though she hated them both for the hurt they had caused, she did not wish for their deaths.

Edmund must have sensed her anxiety, for he took her hand in his. She watched their entwined fingers for the remainder of the journey, afraid to see the pity in anyone else's face.

When the carriage finally stopped, Isabella had to force herself to leave the safety of the equipage. Staying inside would not stop the inevitable, however. She stepped onto the dewy grass with the help of her brother and looked up into his eyes.

"Are you sure you wish to watch?" he asked. "It is not the done thing, you know."

"No," she answered honestly, "but I need to be here."

A large crowd had already gathered on the barren heath, the sun beginning to creep over the horizon as mist rose from the earth. At their arrival, the mass of people turned to stare and then slowly parted to allow the ducal party to pass. As the five of them walked forward, two gentlemen on either side of her, Isabella clung to Edmund for mutual support. He did his best not to limp, but she could sense his struggle. When the onlookers saw Edmund alive, they began to whisper in scandalized tones. The mutterings quickly grew to a hum of speculative interest and Isabella lifted her chin.

Doubtless those gathered had also realized who the female in the group was, she reflected, with Ruskington being on her other side.

They walked to the edge of the viewing throng who surrounded Wethersby and Frompton and their seconds. A doctor stood off to the side, his black bag on the ground beside him, but Isabella hardly noticed anything but the two participants.

She looked at Wethersby in a different light. Had he truly tried to save her at the auction that night? She did not think she looked much like him, which was no doubt how the deception had been perpetrated for so long. While she had inherited her mother's eyes and dark hair, perhaps her chin and nose belonged to Wethersby. She swallowed hard, grief thick in her throat. Would she ever have the chance to know her real father? Was that what the wager had been about? Had Wethersby wished to claim her and Frompton had refused? Perhaps she was being too generous, but it hurt to think neither father had had honorable intentions towards her.

Wethersby noticed her then and stared as though he had been struck. He had seen her that night at the auction in all of her womanly glory, but had not seen her face. He began walking towards her; simultaneously, Edmund and Alex drew in a breath.

Wethersby stopped before her and bowed as he reached for her hand. Some unknown force compelled her to give it to him. He kissed it and looked up at her while still bent forward.

"Isabella."

She could find no words with which to reply.

"I wish circumstances had been different," he said quietly. "Forgive me." He straightened and turned back towards the dueling field, where Frompton watched with fury. Isabella did not meet his eyes, instead allowing hers to drift beyond him to where her mother was standing with a handkerchief over her mouth. Isabella quickly averted her gaze.

Soon, the scene unfolded before her as though she were watching a play. It could not be real.

"Stand back!" One of the seconds directed the spectators to withdraw. Amidst much grumbling and objecting, the main body of fashionable curious reluctantly removed a short distance.

This achieved, the seconds approached each other in the center of the field and spoke too quietly for the crowd to hear, although they strained forward nevertheless.

Isabella could only watch with horror. She did not want either man to die. Though she was disgusted with Frompton, she had always thought of him as her father. Of Wethersby, on the other hand, she knew not what to think. Perhaps everything about him was not as she had previously thought. Whatever the truth, she was not yet ready to embrace him.

The seconds approached the opponents and presented swords as the weapon. Isabella watched with surprise. She had thought duels were fought with pistols and concluded quickly.

She knew little about swordplay or fencing, except it required extraordinary agility and wit. To her untutored eye, the gentlemen did not appear as equals. Wethersby looked to be the better conditioned of the two, although they must be of an age to have vied for the hand of her mother. Frompton, meanwhile, looked old and unfit; however, she knew he had been a superb fencer in his younger days.

Both men stripped off their outer garments and having passed these to two waiting lackeys, stood in their shirt sleeves and buckskins, testing their weapons with a few passes through the air. The seconds stood back and called the gentlemen en guard. Swords drawn, the principals offered a begrudging salute and one of the seconds dropped a white handkerchief. Immediately, Frompton went on the attack. Isabella wondered if he considered a short fight his only hope of winning.

The crowd was surprisingly silent, the only sounds coming from the clash of steel and the heavy breaths of both duelists. Back and forth across the field they went as they parried and thrust, their feet moving faster than any dance Isabella had ever learned. Wethersby looked graceful and almost as if he were toying with the duke. Frompton's face was soon red and he more resembled a charging bull than an exponent of the fine art of sword-defense. This was no friendly *duello*, despite their claims to fight for honor.

Frompton lunged and tried to disarm Wethersby, but he easily countered it. Then Frompton lost his footing; Wethersby saw his opportunity and drove forward with a thrust. The crowd gasped. He could have ended it there and then, but Wethersby merely sliced the top of the duke's sleeve. This drew a few jeers from the spectators, who had probably wagered heavily on the outcome. Instead of being grateful for the reprieve, Frompton appeared angered by the fact and charged forward, his attack aimed straight for the heart.

Wethersby blocked the sword and they locked blades, each pushing one against the other. Perspiration poured down both gentlemen's brows, and Isabella could see their arms shaking and their chests heaving, neither willing to concede. They remained thus for some few minutes, but the duke was unequal to the task. At length, his sword was thrust aside and it spun out of his hand in a graceful arc to the ground. Lungs heaving, he was left, standing, at Wethersby's mercy.

Isabella lurched forward but an arm held her back.

"Let them finish," Alex whispered in her ear.

Wethersby stepped forward, the tip of his sword held horizontally just beneath Frompton's chin. Instead of conceding the victory, the duke sneered.

"You prefer death to apologies?" Wethersby raised his brows, but his blade did not waver.

"I am not the cheat."

"Henry, no!" the duchess called.

"Hush, woman!" the duke spat without taking his eyes from his adversary.

A look of tenderness flashed through Wethersby's eyes, and for a moment Isabella was worried the duke might take advantage.

"Go ahead, coward," Frompton taunted.

"You are not worth the blot on my conscience," Wethersby responded. Drawing back slightly, he pinked Frompton in the shoulder and turned to walk away.

"How dare you!" the duke raged and started forward, hands raised towards Wethersby as though he intended to strangle his lordship.

Wethersby turned back again at the same moment the duke lunged, but his sword was still in his hand, and the duke impaled himself upon the blade. A mutual look of horror crossed both of their faces as blood soaked His Grace's shirt. The crowd gasped in consternation—or ghoulish pleasure. Frompton collapsed heavily to his side, clutching the hilt.

Ruskington hastened on to the duelling ground and was already on his knees beside Frompton when the doctor came running to tend to him.

"Edmund, keep her with you!" Knighton ordered, beckoning to Heath and striding to join Isabella's brother. They stood directly in her line of vision, shielding her from what was going forward.

From that moment, everything happened in a whirl around her. Vaguely she was aware of her mother rushing to Wethersby's side and the crowd slowly dispersing now the excitement was at an end, but she clung to Edmund and turned her face into his coat. She did not feel she had the right to go to either man and offer comfort. Edmund's hand rubbed her upper arm in a soothing motion, although he did not speak.

It would not be seemly, in such a public place, for him to hold her within his embrace, even though it was her dearest wish. About them, she heard loud discussions of the event, and stakeholders arguing with those who had staked their blunt, as Alex would term it. She felt quite ill.

"Take me home, Edmund," she whispered. His chest lifted in a slow sigh.

"I fear that will not be possible as yet, my love. You should perhaps prepare yourself, for I think my services might soon be required."

She swung her gaze from contemplation of his burnished brass buttons to search his face.

"Do you mean...?"

He patted her gloved hand, his expression grave. "He ran himself through. Such a wound..."

Isabella bit her lip. Edmund did not need to finish the sentence. While she had worried about such an eventuality, there was an added oppression in hearing the words. She wanted to scream and rail against the futility of a masculine pride which had allowed death to end her fathers' bitter rivalry, yet that, too, was unseemly. Instead, she clenched her jaw and strode the few yards to the little group in the centre of the field. Uttering a low protest, Edmund limped after her.

The doctor rose at her approach and gave a slight shake of his head. Frompton was lying on the ground and her parents were standing together, her mother clutching Wethersby's arm. Someone had placed a rolled-up coat beneath the duke's head and his breathing was weak and rough.

"Father…" She could not say any more. He tilted his head on the impromptu pillow and looked at her. His eyes were clouded with pain.

"Isabella…" Feebly, he raised one hand towards her and inhaled as though preparing to say more. A wet, crackling sound issued from his mouth instead and his hand flopped on the grass. "Forgive—"

He said no more. His head fell sideways, accompanied by a gurgling noise that would haunt her dreams. Easing her to one side, Edmund bent over the duke and swiftly murmured words of strength and encouragement as Frompton passed into the next life.

Isabella stared at the body on the ground. The gentleman she had always believed to be her father was dead and she felt… nothing. Her face set, she turned and walked back to the waiting carriage.

# CHAPTER TWENTY

E DMUND WISHED HE could do more to support Isabella, but she needed time to reflect and come to terms with what had happened. She had returned to Frompton House with her brother and mother after the wretched duel, and he was trying to give her that time to decide upon her future. He had always considered himself a patient man, but he was about to run mad. He had resigned his living at Saint Michael's, and was staying at Knighton House while recovering. He grew stronger physically every day, but knew he would never be whole again without Isabella.

"You really have to do something, Edmund," Eugenia said, coming in to the study where Edmund had taken up residence. Surely it had nothing to do with the fact that his chair sat in front of the window that overlooked the square opposite Frompton House?

"You cannot watch for her every moment, hoping for a glimpse of her," she scolded.

"I do not know what to do," he confessed quietly. "Funny, is it not, that I have spent the last few years advising others, yet I cannot see my own path?"

"You are too close to it," Eugenia said, sliding down onto the sofa nearest to him.

"And you are here to offer wise counsel?" he retorted.

She gave him a look of disdain. "Sarcasm does not become you,

Edmund. You may choose to abandon your courtship of Isabella, if you are an idiot, but do not let it change you into a bitter person."

He let his head fall back a little and stared at the ceiling. He closed his eyes. "Forgive me. I am afraid that she will no longer have me."

Eugenia snorted. "I imagine she is sitting, in a similar fashion, in her room across the square, thinking much the same thing. Consider her situation. Very likely, she thinks she is unworthy of you now."

"She is in mourning for a father who was not really her father," Edmund replied. "I want to give her time to consider her feelings."

"But you must not let her forget yours. She needs your reassurance now more than ever."

"You are right. But how? I have sent flowers."

"Along with every other member of the *ton*. You must woo her subtly," she advised.

Edmund opened his eyes and turned to stare at her. "I am beset by utter astonishment. I did not know you knew that word."

She threw one of the sofa pillows at him, causing one of the first smiles he'd had in days.

"Are you able to walk across the square?" she asked.

"I believe so."

"Then it is time for some fresh air. Meet me here in half an hour." Her tone brooked no argument.

She walked over to help him up from the couch and they walked arm in arm together up the stairs to the bedchambers. Rowley's valet helped Edmund to dress, and he felt more light of heart and eager at the prospect of seeing Isabella. He could only imagine her suffering as she tried to assimilate losing one father and gaining another... coming to terms with her illegitimacy. Eugenia was right—he let out a little laugh—that this was not the time to abandon Isabella, leaving her to mistake his absence as a change of mind and heart. He had not thought of it as such, but he, of all people, should know better. Grief was an all-consuming emotion that changed like the wind.

"Are you ready?" Eugenia asked, coming up behind him in the entrance hall. She was dressed somberly in a lavender gown, but still managed not to look somber. He shook his head. Eugenia was her own woman, and of that he was glad.

"I asked Quincy to purchase some flowers," she said, dimpling as she took them from the table and handed them to Edmund. It was a lovely bouquet of primroses making him think of the cottage that day back at the Grange. They held double meaning for him and Isabella: the flowers themselves meant *I cannot live without you.*

Had Eugenia known their meaning?

"Thank you, Eugenia. I see you are back to being your singular self."

"I will take that as a compliment."

They set off slowly across the square, and Edmund began to feel a nervous quiver inside.

"What if they are not receiving?" he asked.

"They will see us," she said, over-confident as was her habit.

There was crepe over the knocker, but the butler opened the door as they approached.

"Good day, my lord, my lady." He welcomed them with a bow.

"Is the family receiving?"

"His Grace asked that you be shown into the drawing room."

The butler escorted them across the stately entrance hall to the large receiving room decorated in ivory and gold, with large gilt-framed portraits and landscapes adorning the walls. It felt overly bright for a house in mourning.

"Is there anything I may get you while you wait?" he asked.

"No, thank you," Edmund answered. The butler bowed and closed the door.

"It is strange to think of Lord Ruskington as Frompton now when his father made such a name for himself," Eugenia said, staring at the large portrait of the recently deceased duke, which hung over the fireplace.

"It is, but he is strong enough to make name of it too, and a better one, if he so chooses."

The door opened and the new duke walked in, looking as though he were carrying the weight of the world on his shoulders. Edmund felt for him. He bowed and Eugenia curtsied.

"Thank God you are here," Alex said.

"Has something happened? We have kept away to give you the opportunity to grieve in private," Edmund said, feeling anxious for Isabella.

"I do not think Isabella knows who or what to grieve for. Wethersby has called every day, but she refuses to see him. She scarcely leaves her rooms. Will you go to her?"

"Of course." He looked at Eugenia, who inclined her head, indicating for him to go. "I will be quite comfortable here," she said to both men. "You go to her."

Edmund followed Alex slowly up the stairs, wishing his body was more cooperative. He wanted to run.

Alex stopped before a chamber and held out a hand. "I will leave you to what may be a thankless task. I shall not deny I am praying you can work a miracle."

Edmund took a deep breath and then rapped his knuckles on the door. There was no answer. He frowned and turned to look for Alex, but he had disappeared. It was bad enough to be alone in an unwed female's chamber, but to enter without permission was unthinkable.

Alex did not seem to have any concerns about it, so he gently lifted the latch.

She was sitting curled up in a chair, looking like a shell of herself in a wrinkled gown and her hair disheveled. That shell was still a feast to his deprived eyes for all that, he mused wryly. He walked in and closed the door, yet she still did not move.

"Isabella?" he called before walking towards her. He went down on his knees in front of her.

"Edmund?" she asked, sounding almost as frail and disoriented as she had been at the little hut in the woods.

"Yes, my love, I am here." Oh, how he wished he were whole, that he might take her into his arms. But it was enough to be with her, so he put his arms around her. She clung to him as though he were a lifeline that she might die without. He was probably clinging as desperately to her.

"I thought you did not want me," she confessed, burying her head in his shoulder.

"How could you think that? Nothing could keep me from wanting you." He showered kisses on her disheveled locks.

"I did not want to live without you. I am a coward," she whispered.

"I was trying to give you time; I did not want to rush you into marriage if it was not your wish now you are free," he said, pulling her as close as he could and stroking her back.

"I do not want any more time. If I spend any more of it in reflection, I shall end in Bedlam!" There was a wisp of her old vigor in her tone.

"You shall have whatever is in my power to give you."

"Then let us marry now, at once."

"Now? What of your mourning?" Edmund asked in concern. The Lord knew, he did not want to wait, but her name had already been much bandied about the town.

"I hardly think my reputation could be more tarnished," she countered.

"Then I will speak to the bishop. We have the special license."

Her face brightened into a smile, and she responded with a simple kiss. A light, innocent touch, it nevertheless warmed Edmund inside.

"Would you come down and inform your brother with me?"

"Yes, I should like to do that." She stood up and catching sight of her reflection in the glass, squeaked with surprise as though she had not noticed herself at all for days. "I look a fright! Why did you not say something?"

"You will always be the most beautiful woman in the world to me, Isabella," he said. Hoisting himself from the chair with difficulty, he walked over to stand behind her. She picked up her brush and worked through a few tangles. Edmund tied her curls back with a simple riband and they walked from the room together to share the news with her brother and his sister.

When they entered the drawing room, Alex smiled warmly at the sight of them together and looked visibly relieved.

Eugenia leaped to her feet and walked towards Isabella. Without a word, she took Isabella into her arms and hugged her. It was the first time they had seen each other since the duel, and Isabella seemed to welcome the familiarity and comfort. Perhaps it was another sign of acceptance to one with raw insecurities.

Edmund saw Eugenia whisper something to Isabella. She pulled back and looked at her brother.

"We would like to be married tomorrow," she announced.

"So soon?" Alex asked.

"Yes," was Isabella's simple reply.

Blessedly, he did not argue.

"It is somewhat unconventional, but I have no objections. I would only ask that you tell Mother. She feels as though she is only now free to fully know you, and I am sure this will be hard for her to deal with at such a time. Please do not think I am disagreeing with your decision. Frankly, I think it will do a great deal to restore your reputation."

"I understand," she said. As she spoke, the butler could be heard admitting someone into the house. Edmund sensed Isabella's unease, so he walked to her side as the door opened and the butler announced Lord Wethersby.

It took a great deal of brass to call at the house of the person you had killed, even though the death had been unintentional.

Wethersby was standing just behind the butler, and Edmund could sense the bearing of a desolate man. Would Isabella able to forgive him?

⫸⫷

ISABELLA CLUNG TO Edmund. She was not ready to face Wethersby yet. Somehow she knew she must face him one day but not now, and not for some considerable time. How could he think to call here, and worse, why was he being admitted?

"I think I will take a turn about the garden," Eugenia muttered before sliding surreptitiously from the room.

"Why are you here?" Isabella asked, unable to hide her disbelief.

"I wanted a chance to explain, and I was afraid you would leave Town. I do not expect acceptance overnight, but perhaps, one day, you might come to tolerate me."

Isabella did not want to deal with this yet, but she could sense the sincerity in his voice... his face.

"I did not mean for things to happen this way, you must believe that."

Something began to brew within Isabella and her words burst forth before she could consider.

"I cannot tell what you intended; I know the provocation was great, but how could there ever be a good outcome?" She dropped her face into her hands.

"I could make a thousand excuses, and God knows, I have done little right in my life, but I will never call you a mistake. I hope that, one day, you will be able to forgive me. I know I am intruding, but I was afraid I would forever lose my chance to speak with you."

"I do not know," she whispered, responding as honestly as she was

221

able.

"That is better than an outright 'no.' I am willing to accept whatever crumbs you will toss my way."

He bowed and turned to leave.

"Wait!" she called.

He turned back; she could easily discern the glimmer of hope in his eyes.

"Edmund and I are to be married tomorrow. I would be pleased if you would be there."

She was not ready to accept his arm to walk down the aisle, but somehow she knew inside that one day she would regret it were he not there.

He walked over and kissed her hands. "Thank you. This means more to me than you will ever know. Well, perhaps you will understand when you have a child." He took his leave, and Alex and Edmund both looked at her with some surprise.

"I believe Edmund is having a good influence on me," she said, trying to force a smile. Nothing was going to dim her happiness about her marriage.

"For what it is worth," Alex said, "I think you have made the best decision in the circumstances. Whatever the rights and wrongs, it would seem he is your father. You would not wish to be estranged from a second sire. I think you should speak with Mother now."

Isabella agreed. Taking Edmund's hand, she led him upstairs to the duchess's apartments. Yes, if *she* had been miserable, then she thought her mother must be doubly so.

A maid answered their knock, and showed them into the sitting room. Her mother was seated at her escritoire, writing letters. She looked up and smiled at Isabella's entrance.

"Isabella," she said, as though the name brought her pleasure.

"You are looking well, Mother," Isabella said, perhaps a little too formally. She was uncertain how to behave towards her after the events and disclosures of recent weeks. "Are you acquainted with Lord Edmund Knight?"

"We have some small acquaintance, yes," she answered. "How do you do, Lord Edmund?"

He bowed gracefully despite his injuries. "May I express my condolences on your loss?"

Isabella noticed her avert her eyes. It was a difficult matter, the duke's death, and they would have to face the consequences sooner or later. She inclined her head instead of speaking.

"Edmund and I are to be married tomorrow, Mama," Isabella said.

"So suddenly? If it is your reputation you are worried about, we will weather the storm."

"Absolutely not! Edmund and I were betrothed before the feud became a matter of public speculation. We truly wish to marry—for love. Surely you can understand this?" She could see from the flash of hurt in her mother's eyes that she did. Isabella had not meant to cause her mother pain, but was not about to make the same mistake.

"Of course; then you have my blessing," she answered, her manner more reserved than in her previous objections.

"I spoke with Lord Wethersby a few moments ago," Isabella remarked. She thought it was best to forewarn her mother.

"Yes, I suppose you know the whole by now." She leaned back in her chair, looking defeated. "He has been desperate to tell you for some time."

"I have invited him to the wedding. It will be small, of course."

She did not miss the look of shock on the duchess's face. Isabella herself was surprised she had done such a thing.

"Of course. You must do what you think is best," she said politely. "You are now of age and free to make your own decisions."

Despite the practiced responses, Isabella could tell it pained her mother to say them. Dutifully she curtsied, Edmund bowed, and they left her mother to her letters and returned downstairs. They took a detour to the garden for a few minutes alone.

Seeing them approaching, Eugenia waved and tactfully turned in another direction.

"It seems I cannot make everyone happy," Isabella said as Edmund handed her into a wooden bench. It stood in the middle of a circular portion of the garden, surrounded by trellises of bright pink roses. "Did you see the look of distress on my mother's face when I told her I had invited him?"

"I cannot deny it," Edmund answered. He took her hands in his, rubbing lazy circles with his thumb on the back of one of them. "There are a great many wounds to be healed, and it will take a long time. I think this is the first step, and you were right to take it."

"I hope so," she whispered. "I do not know why I did it."

"You deserve to know your father—in time," he said, emphasizing the last word with a devilish grin. "First, you will be mine."

➤➤➤❈◀◀◀

THE NEXT MORNING came quickly. It was not the simplest of tasks to arrange a wedding in less than a day, but it was a welcome distraction from the last, painful week, with the duel and the funeral. Everyone was present except for Lord Felix, who had shipped back to the Peninsula with his regiment. Edmund and Isabella chose to wed at Saint Michael's, far away from the watchful eyes of the *ton*, and in the place that had been Edmund's first parish.

Mrs. Lowe had outdone herself—with the help of Emma, more than likely—to have flowers placed around the small church. Mother had bestirred herself sufficiently to ensure that Isabella had a beautiful lavender gown of embossed silk, with an embroidered overdress remade from one of her own for the occasion, and the use of her dresser to style her hair. This was done in a befitting cascade of curls, cleverly arranged to fall down over her shoulders from a knot high on the crown of her head. As Isabella admired her reflection, thinking herself to look like a princess, her mother entered, carrying a velvet box.

She smiled gently. "I know we are in mourning, and I know you have been very hurt by my actions and those of your father – both of your fathers, for they were equally to blame. Frompton loved you in his own way, even after he discovered the truth. I do hope that one day you will be able to forgive what he did. He was so very hurt. It does not excuse his actions, yet..." Her voice trailed off and she turned away to compose herself. "He always intended these for you for your come out." She opened the box to reveal a parure with a tiara, necklace and earrings of amethysts and diamonds.

Isabella fingered them delicately. She had never owned anything like it. "I do not know what to say."

"You need not say anything. He would want you to wear them today."

Isabella nodded and her mother placed the necklace around her neck and fastened the clasp. Then she slid the tiara on to her head around her coiffure.

Alex was waiting to escort them both to Saint Michael's. It was some considerable distance from Mayfair to Shoreditch, but Isabella was happy to leave the house. Both her mother and brother were somber, and Isabella felt guilty for she was fair to bursting with happiness.

When the carriage pulled up in front of the grey stone church, Alex stepped out and helped their mother to alight. He escorted her inside, then returned for Isabella.

"Are you ready?" he asked.

"Oh, yes." She could not contain her smile as she stepped down from the carriage.

"I am pleased your story is to have a happy conclusion. No one deserves happiness more than you."

"Thank you, Alex. I hope you will find it again," she said, and she stood on tiptoe to kiss his cheek.

"Shall we?" He held out his arm and led her through the doors to where a surprising number of people were already seated in the pews. Isabella did not see many people she knew, and thought perhaps these were Edmund's parishioners. It surprised her not at all to know he was well loved.

"I would hardly call this a small, private ceremony," Alex teased.

"It is by *ton* standards, and that, my dear brother, makes it quite perfect!"

They began to walk down the aisle, and Isabella saw her mother and her father in one of the forward pews. She almost forgot to walk. Even though she had known they would be there, it was disconcerting, to say the least, to see them side-by-side.

"Keep going and look at Edmund," Alex advised, as if he knew what she was thinking. It was excellent advice, for when she looked forward, her sole attention was at once distracted by Edmund. He was strikingly handsome, looking lean yet vigorous with his easy smile. He was wearing an elegant black coat and breeches with a pomona green silk waistcoat, instead of vestments, and it struck her that he was sacrificing a great deal. They would make their way together. And when he smiled at her, she knew everything would be well.

Alex gave her to Edmund, and the bishop began the ceremony. It was short and simple – just as it ought to be. She was proud to have remembered when to repeat her vows, and once Edmund placed a ring on her finger, her overruling emotion was relief. They signed the register and partook of Holy Communion, and then were pronounced man and wife. Did every woman feel such a poignant change when they received a new name? She doubted it. At last she felt as though the name was real—her own. No longer would she have a name that did not truly belong to her.

Edmund led her down the nave, and they stood to greet people as he would after a service. Was he sad to leave this post? Hopefully, he would find another parish or some other occupation to fulfill his need for altruism. She vowed to make it so.

"I am ready for the peace and quiet of the country for a while," she said softly while they accepted well wishes and farewells from his parishioners.

"We have been on a merry dance," he agreed.

Isabella laughed. "Not the words I would choose—more like a badly written penny Gothic novel."

"Then let us start a new chapter—no, a new book entirely," he suggested.

"I like that very much. We could call it *From Darkness to Light,* or such."

"*Night and Day,*" he offered with a dramatic flair.

"Call it whatever you like as long as we are together," she said, beaming at him with a smile that rose like the sun from within.

# EPILOGUE

EDMUND WAS WALKING through the gardens at Primrose House, deep into his morning meditations and prayers when he heard hoof beats. He looked up to see his brother and smiled and gave a little wave. Rowley dismounted and tied the horse to a post.

"Good morning," he greeted.

"Good morning. I was beginning to wonder if anyone else was on the estate," Edmund returned jovially.

"We were attempting to give you privacy for your newly wedded state," Rowley retorted with a wry smile. "I take it all was well?"

"Could not be better," Edmund agreed. Being wed to Isabella was as close to Heaven on earth as Edmund could imagine.

"I do not suppose you would consider taking a wedding trip?"

"I had not considered," Edmund replied. "Being here seems like a holiday unto itself." However, Rowley had a look in his eyes that made Edmund suspicious. "What is it?"

"There are some documents that need to be delivered to Felix in Spain. He had asked Heath to do it before he left, but with Cecelia being in a delicate condition, Heath does not want to leave her right now."

"So you would like me to do it?"

"I can ask Tinsley or Petersham if you think it is too dangerous."

"Where and how exactly would we take the papers?"

"You would take the yacht to the port of Bilbao then arrange for a meeting with Felix."

"Why not send the papers on one of the supply packets? They go back and forth frequently."

"Because the documents are of too delicate a nature to be trusted with anyone else. To the outside world, Felix will be simply receiving a visit from his newly wedded brother and wife, if you even speak with him at all. He will arrange the meeting once we send word you are there." Rowley spoke quietly, his eyes constantly scanning to ensure no one was around.

Edmund leaned close. "Is Felix in danger?"

Rowley answered with a quick flick of his eyes.

"Then Isabella and I would be delighted to perform this task and enjoy a trip to Spain in the process."

Rowley smiled. "Felix will be delighted to see you in person. I will make the arrangements while you inform your bride."

"When shall we be prepared to leave?"

"With the evening tide."

"So soon. Very well."

Edmund watched as his brother mounted and rode away. He gave a little shake of his head and then walked back to the house. He found Isabella inside going over menus with their new cook, Martha.

She looked up and smiled when he came into the room. That would never get old.

"May I have a few moments of your time? I have some news and it might affect your menus for the next little while."

"Of course," Isabella answered while a little wrinkle of concern appeared between her brows.

Martha excused herself and curtsied.

"What is it?"

Edmund took the seat next to her on the green and cream striped sofa and gathered her hands into his. "What do you think of a trip to

Spain?"

"Spain? Are they not in the midst of a war?"

"Indeed they are. Something needs to be delivered to Felix, and Rowley has asked me to do it. He thought we might enjoy it as a wedding trip. If you fear for your safety, you may of course stay here."

"But you must go either way?"

"Yes. We should not be in danger going together as a newly married couple. We will appear harmless."

"Then I should like to go with you."

He smiled then indulged in the sweet taste of his new wife for a few minutes. "I suggest we start packing. We leave this evening with the tide."

The next few hours were a whirl of packing. Rowley's crew was efficient and he saw to the food supplies. This time, they would sail from the West Coast of Devon and they stood on the dock to wave their goodbyes and watch as the beautiful craggy cliffs went by.

"This is the most beautiful place I have ever been," Isabella remarked as Edmund put his arms around his wife from behind and placed his chin on her shoulder. Feeling her in his arms and smelling that unique mixture of lavender, vanilla, and warm female was pure bliss.

"I am glad that we will soon be away from the coast. I do not know if I can compete," he muttered while lavishing kisses on her cheek and neck.

"Edmund, someone might see!" Isabella giggled.

"Who would see besides one of the crew? They will likely cheer us on!" he teased. "This is our wedding trip," he reminded her. As they sailed farther from the coast, he began to lead her down to their cabin.

"We are quite safe from any curious eyes in here," he remarked with a mischievous grin as he bolted the cabin shut.

He took her into his arms and kissed her so thoroughly that she would not be thinking of anything but him.

Sometime later, they lay contentedly in each other's arms, the boat swaying as it culled through the sea. "I remember the last time we were lying on this bed," Isabella remarked.

"Much has happened since then."

"Yes," she answered softly.

"I regret that you had to go through so much for us to be together. Would that I could have prevented that."

She shook her head. "I refuse to dwell on what we cannot change. Perhaps in time, some of it will not hurt so much."

She initiated the next round of intimacies and it was some time before they spoke again. Most of their voyage was spent in the cabin in each other's arms, which was just where they should be as they learned each other as man and wife.

The day the captain informed them they were set to arrive at Bilbao, Edmund hated for the magic to end. Too soon they docked, and Rowley's messenger took one of the rowing boats into the town to leave a message for Felix at the appointed place.

"How long will it take for him to come?"

"I have no idea. For now we wait."

"I suppose you have ideas for how to occupy our time," she added wryly.

"Indeed I do."

It was two more days before they received word. The messenger returned with a meeting location and time where Felix would be found. They dressed for town and took the small rowing boat to the appointed location. Rowley had thought it best to take Isabella so anyone keeping watch would be less suspicious. The town was unlike anything Edmund had ever seen. He'd heard tell of the south's warm clime and sun, but experiencing it was unlike anything he had expected. They climbed from the boat, docked amongst fishermen bringing in their morning haul and preparing them for selling them on the shore, to Isabella's disgust.

Edmund laughed, and hoped they looked like a young couple in love. They were.

"I'd never known the sun could shine so brightly!" Isabella exclaimed, shielding her eyes as they walked on into the town. "Even the wind feels hot."

"Indeed I was just thinking the same. It is beautiful though. Even the briny air smells stronger."

Bright red and purple flowers poured from windowsills and seemed to crawl up every wall in the coastal town. They walked arm in arm up the steep narrow pathways and streets, winding through the white stone terrace houses that were small but tidy.

"It does not look like a place of war," she remarked quietly.

"There is rarely a place that does. Pray it stays away from the towns where the women and children are."

Isabella remained quiet.

They arrived at their destination, a small cafe with a patio overlooking the sea. It was enchanting. Only one other person was there, and Edmund ordered some coffee with xuxo an coca, local delicacies.

"One could easily forget why we are here," Isabella sighed.

"Yes," Edmund agreed.

The other patron let out a cough that caused both Edmund and Isabella to look up.

"The poor man. He sounds consumptive," Isabella said full of concern.

Edmund took a harder look then almost laughed. Felix was sitting there disguised with a full beard in commoners clothing, peasant's hat pulled low. Edmund began to rise, but Felix signaled for him to stay put. It took a great deal of strength for Edmund not to go to his brother and embrace him. The situation must be more dire than he knew.

"I believe our consumptive is merely trying to gain our attention."

Isabella took another look. "That is he?" she asked, her voice full of admiration.

"Quite clever, is it not?"

After they sipped their coffee and consumed their pastries, Edmund removed the packet from Rowley and slipped it carefully beneath the napkin on the table as they rose to leave. It took a great deal of strength not to look back and go to his younger brother, for he strongly suspected Felix was a spy.

# The End

# About the Author

Like many writers, Elizabeth Johns was first an avid reader, though she was a reluctant convert. It was Jane Austen's clever wit and unique turn of phrase that hooked Johns when she was "forced" to read Pride and Prejudice for a school assignment. She began writing when she ran out of her favorite author's books and decided to try her hand at crafting a Regency romance novel. Her journey into publishing began with the release of Surrender the Past, book one of the Loring-Abbott Series. Johns makes no pretensions to Austen's wit but hopes readers will perhaps laugh and find some enjoyment in her writing.

Johns attributes much of her inspiration to her mother, a former English teacher. During their last summer together, Johns would sit on the porch swing and read her stories to her mother, who encouraged her to continue writing. Busy with multiple careers, including a professional job in the medical field, author and mother of two children, Johns squeezes in time for reading whenever possible.

Made in the USA
Las Vegas, NV
05 September 2022

54739985R00133